America's Soul

D1506381

WHERE
HIP HOP
LITERATURE
BEGINS...

AUGUSTUS
PUBLISHING

© 2012 Augustus Publishing, Inc.
ISBN: 978-09825415-4-8

Novel by Erick S Gray
Edited by Anthony Whyte
Creative Direction & Design by Jason Claiborne
Photography By Sanyi Gomez

Augustus Publishing paperback November 2012
www.augustuspublishing.com

Acknowledgements

First of all I'd like to thank the Lord, my personal savior, for what He has done for me. I know that without Him I am nothing and I give all glory to Him.

I endured the trials and tribulations that made me bend, but not break, that made me bruised, but not broken, that made me frown, but with faith, I always come around.

I have to thank all my readers, fans, family, and my fellow authors who supported me all these years. Personal thanks goes out to Charlene Braithwaite-Lovett for showing me support and love when things got crazy. You are the best. Lorraine Anthony, for loving me and being there for me in my time of need. Linda Williams, who's been there for me since day one in this game, Deborah Cardona, aka Sexy, for staying on her grind and being a sister to me, Locksie Locks, for her continuing love and support in this crazy book game, Latasha Gaudy, a very beautiful and talented woman with so much potential. Mesha Bennett, keep your head up and continue writing. Natasha Herman, I can never forget you, when sometimes you think I do, but much love to you. Tenesha Walters, who keeps me smiling and laughing, Jada Curtis, Divine Harris, K'wan, Terry Wroten, Chris B, holding down Brooklyn with the books, Akieon Charles, aka Tokes, for showing me love and support, and making it happen in downtown Brookyln, J.M Benjamin, Anthony Whyte, Jason Claiborne, all my brothers from another mother, and this entire literary genre... It's our time to shine. It's our world. Our time... sSo let's stay on this grind and do it right.
It doesn't get easier, we only get stronger.

R.I.P
Aaron M. McMillon
Conway Rice
William Edward Burroughs aka Billie
R.I.P Mary Lee Miller
Gone but never forgotten...

Foreword

I read that from January 1 to October 14th of this year, there had been 41 murders in the South East Queens neighborhood alone, that's an average of four murders a month. It's a horrifying number that our children are dying in these streets at a staggering rate. I was born and raised in Jamaica, Queens and I'm no stranger to the violence myself, suffering the lost of a best friend, a few friends and a young cousin through gun violence.

There are too many black mothers visiting their children in prison and burying their kids—and dying over a broken heart. I've witnessed it too many times and been to too many funerals, one as recently in August, where I watched a mother grieve over her murdered young son lying in a casket. I once wrote in a poem, "Mothers tremble from the grief that grabs them tight like a cold winter night. You can't cover that shit with no coat; cuz is seeps within, runs thick through their veins as they watch their child to lay... Deceased to the gunplay or some other wicked way."

For so many of us, the violence had hit home and torn families apart. The sudden lost of anyone to violence is a feeling that aches with an intense chill, sometimes tears never dry and an absence fills the air. I've witnessed the grief, the healing and the struggle within my own family a few times and it never gets easier. The streets are snatching up our youth with guns, drugs and gangs. The war on terrorism is not just aboard, but it is within our own communities as well, for our unity as a village is folding within itself because of so many afflictions that plague black communities today—lack of education, gangs, drugs, diseases and the absence of morality.

I once was caught up in that struggle of anger and fear, picked up a gun for revenge once, but thank God I stopped myself seconds away from taking my action any further. I wrote in my poem, "got the gun cocked and feeling such an anger presiding over me...feeling this cold freezing me in such an atrocious way, sayin' fuck this book shit, I'm ready to just kill shit...cuz common sense and humanity done been left me."

I'm living proof of how strong parenting can affect and change someone; I always had a praying and loving mother, a strong father and family support. I went through many trials and tribulation, where I wrote, "the way my timeline went, man I knew one day my mother was goin' to bury me, went to my first strip club at thirteen, and got stabbed at fourteen, almost got caught with that .45 at fifteen."

Bettering our children starts with parenting, it starts at home and continues with a village, and unfortunately, some of our kids have a lack of a good home and strong parenting. They lack the process of promoting and supporting the physical, emotional, social, and intellectual development of a child from infancy to adulthood. So they look to other means for support and comfort.

I wrote America's Soul, not just as a form of entertainment, but to tell a story about the inner city violence, and the effect it has within the community, the mothers and individuals. I wanted to open the eyes to those who are unaware what is going on within our streets, with our kids and with our morality. The story is fictional, but some of the characters I've created and the scenes I've written are real to some of my readers. The book tells a story of one young man coming to age through a series of events and finally finding his true identity. Where my poem ends, "I'm changing and growing, becoming more educated and more knowing. I try to read a verse before I spit a curse. I love all y'all and say keep God close. I learned to be quick to forgive and use hard times to develop a better stepping stone in you—hard times should produce better results in you."

But I want to acknowledge the mothers that have lost sons and daughters over the years, Ms. Louise McMillon, Agnes Saxon, Jean Gray, Gevondis

Anne Whittingtondo Gray (RIP), Alinda Gray, Stephanie Anne Butler and Mildred Butler, and Hannah Gray Greer.

Prologue
In The Streets...

The salty breeze lifted off Jamaica Bay and drifted in the air, past the towering high rises of Rochdale Village, the twenty building housing complex. It continued over the rooftops of the one family houses in Jamaica, Queens. The air over the Jamaica housing projects, AKA The 40 projects, was deadly calm. Dusk was settling over the notorious neighborhood known for its drug kingpins and crime ridden streets since the early eighties. In was the second month of spring, the weather was warm.

A dark blue Tahoe, with chrome wheels shiny like mirrors was traveling north on Guy R. Brewer Blvd. The tinted windows veiled three gun-toting Jamaican men with murderous intentions sitting inside of the luxurious vehicle. Heavy weed smoke lingered from them puffing some potent kush. A fully loaded Uzi and two sawed off shotguns, cocked and ready to spread terror were on the seats.

To keep the boys in blue off their radar, the driver maintained a moderate speed. Lounging behind the wheel, he waited for his turn to take a few pulls from the raw. They had orders to search out and kill anyone of Omega's men on sight. They were hit men sent by Demetrious, a Jamaican born gangsta from the Shower Posse.

Over the past eighteen months, war between Omega and Demetrius brewed out of control. Jamaica, Queens and the Prospect Park area of Brooklyn were now battlefields. Deadly shootouts filled the neighborhoods with terror and despair. Warfare still raged despite heavy casualties on both sides.

Local authorities appeared powerless to stop the violence. Gangs warred for the control of territories. Omega had control of the crystal meth sweeping through New York City like an epidemic. Some made their riches from drug sales. Others felt the pain and suffering of the addicts to this dangerous illicit drug. The media dubbed this the new crack. With a ninety percent relapse rate, the drug resulted in many deaths.

Crime in the city increased nearly twenty percent over the same time. Murders, burglaries and violent crimes were noticeably on the increase. The mayor announced a zero tolerance policy for drug users and dealers who continued to operate meth labs. The labs spread through the boroughs like bodegas in the Bronx. This resulted in increased havoc in the communities.

Meth lab explosions became common place. Often the damage would be the death of children and families living above those labs. In one month three such explosions occurred. The police, agents, lawyers and drug counselors had their hands full with the rising drug epidemic developing in the city. Court cases were piled up to the ceilings and detoxification sounded like something from yesteryear.

Omega and Biscuit became the new Supreme and Fat Cat of the neighborhoods. They flaunted their riches and flexed their power like the city streets were fashion runways. The Jamaicans were illegal immigrants from Kingston who lived for the violence and were used to bodies piled up on the streets like trash.

Nearing the projects, the Tahoe made a slow left onto 110th Ave. The driver took a long pull from the burning weed. His eyes were bloodshot red from smoking and sipping on Jamaican rum.

"Wi gwan fuck dem real good. Yuh hear mi, bredren? Yankee boi fuck wid mi blood-claat money like dat… Feel mi machete pon dem throat!" the passenger said with his teeth clenched. "Pass dat bombo-claat Uzi!"

The third passenger in the backseat removed all three guns and put one in each man's hand. The passenger took the Uzi sub-machine gun and checked it.

It was a warm, spring evening and dusk enveloped the bustling Queens neighborhood. Children played across the street in front of the project buildings. Local hustlers loitered across the street near the school yard. Teens gathered in a tight circle. Bobbing their heads to an imaginary beat as one of the teens held their attention. He flowed like Biggie. The others enjoyed the rhymes of the young, slim teen.

His moniker was *North Star* and he was known for spitting lyrics. A rapper on the come-up, North Star was signed to Omega's Rising Music record label. He was causing a buzz for himself throughout Queens and the rest of the city. Featured on the latest mix tapes in the streets, he was making noise in the music industry. The 40 projects had been his home for nineteen years. It was all he knew.

"Oh shit, yo North Star, kick that shit again, my nigga!" His boy E-Mann shouted excitedly.

North Star smiled, gave E-Mann dap, and continued rapping.

> *They call me North Star shining brighter*
> *Hittin' ya harder hot shells wit' da Rockwell,*
> *Creep like spring creek, stand tall my 9 mill*
> *Stretch my deadly reach fuck wit' me beware*
> *Ya mind get leery, ya body get weary…*

The six teens were hyped. They knew their home-boy could be the next 50 Cent. So engrossed were they in the rhyming skills of North Star, that no one paid attention to the dark blue Tahoe. The vehicle slowly crept on them and the windows were coming down.

King was in the passenger seat. With a twisted grin, he took deadly aim with the Uzi at the teens standing in the cipher.

"Lay dem all fuckin' down!" He said with a wicked smirk.

The Tahoe had already closed in on the teens when E-Mann noticed. Something wasn't right. The lights flashed and sparks flew from the window of the Tahoe. E-Mann heard the threatening staccato sound of automatic fire. Then the sawed-off shotgun exploded on the block. Before he could react, there was a big boom.

Bullets sent one of the young teens in the circle flying back against the chain link fence of the schoolyard. There was a basketball-size hole in his chest. A barrage from the Uzi caused the entire corner to panic. King opened fire on everyone like he was in a shooting gallery. He had a bead on North Star and hit him up with multiple shots. North Star collapsed to the pavement, while his friends scattered for cover.

E-Mann reached for the .45 concealed in his waistband, but he couldn't remove it in time. He staggered, and King fired with accuracy hitting E-Mann several times in the abdomen.

Mothers were screaming, racing for their kids, and seeking concealment anywhere. Loud gunfire terrified everyone, sending innocent bystanders scrambling for cover. The sound of death left many of the onlookers curling into fetal positions and cringing as they hide.

"Bomba-claat, mi rain down terror on those dat defy Shotta!" King taunted.

The Tahoe screeched off, leaving three dead, and two seriously injured. Dazed and confused, residents across the street from the shoot out, slowly emerged. Terrified, they gazed around trying to comprehend what had taken place.

The bodies of several young men were sprawled across the street near the public school. Women were screaming, shocked they rushed to the aid of the young teens that had fallen. Sirens were soon heard blaring in the distance.

Later dozens of uniformed police officers, homicide detectives, and EMS workers were on the scene—of the five men shot, three were DOA, and the other two were in critical condition. They were rushed to Jamaica hospital. NYPD had their hands full. Yellow and black crime scene tape was looped around the area. Then came the many questions, but witnesses could only give police the truck's description.

Word of the shooting traveled fast in the hood. Soon it reached one of the mothers of the victim. A forty-five-year old woman in a brown housedress and bare feet came sprinting down the sidewalk beside the long chain link fence. Closely behind her was family, mostly sisters and aunts. She came running to her son in an undignified haste. Her expression grew ghastly when she saw the bodies of three young men sprawled out on the hard chipped concrete. She instantly knew that one of the dead teens was her son, Jerome AKA North Star.

The distraught woman ran to her son with a great sense of urgency. A uniformed officer stopped her from proceeding.

"I'm sorry m'am, but you can't pass," the cop informed the traumatized mother.

"That's my son! That's my baby! That's my baby!!" she cried in a bloodcurdling scream.

She pounded her fist against the officer's chest and tried to fight her way past the officer. The officer hugged the grieving mother in his arms. His face registered her pain. Tears streamed down the mother's face, and her cries were heard blocks away. The oldest daughter slowly pulled away her hysterical mother from the officer's arm. Both women fell to the ground.

One of the six teens observed the scene from a short distance. Shaking his head in disbelief, he said, "Yo them fuckin' Jamaicans! Man, they fuckin' shit up. They fucking killed North Star!"

1

Omar vs. Soul

Three days left until my release. I had spent eighteen months in a damn hell hole. It was a place that I could never call home. It would be the last time I'd ever see a prison cell again. My life had changed drastically. I was tired of my old life and wanted to make many changes.

When I came back to prison, I was angry and bitter. The first week in Franklin Correctional Facility, I got in a fight and put another inmate in ICU. I spent ninety days in the hole. My thoughts were the only thing I had in a dark, barren, cold room, that was made to break a man. After that, my man, Rahmel brought me light. He spoke to me about letting go of my aggression and rage. He encouraged me to think of my newborn son.

I had to become a better, wiser man for my son. I could no longer let my rage control me. It had cost me my freedom, my wife, and seeing my son being born.

America came to see me twice. Both times the visits seemed short-lived and distant. She provided me with updates on my son, Khalil. America told me that he was a healthy boy. Although there was small talk, it was clear that things had definitely changed between us. No longer were the visits about us holding hands for the entire duration. Back then I'd look in her eyes and knew that she would always love me. They were soft, brown and spoke volumes to me.

She was in a new relationship now, and her music career had taken off. I heard it through the grapevine that she'd put out an album and it was doing really well. I didn't like the place I was in with her, but I respected it.

Pictures of Kahlil were plastered on the walls of my cell, along with pictures of America and me during happier times. The poems she had written for me while we were still together were also proudly displayed. I missed my family so much. Even though we weren't a family physically, in my heart I felt them like the blood running through my veins. Seventy-two hours until freedom. Finally I could be liberated from my old ways.

I started getting more into the bible. Reading from Genesis to Revelations while renewing my mind, I was becoming a righteous man. It was as if the world around me was crumbling. My only chance of not coming back to prison was restoring my faith. I was determined to go back out into the world a completely different man.

Inside the prison day room, I sat minding my business and watching *Judge Judy* on the mounted TV. The hard face judge implementing her version of justice in small claim cases was fun to watch. Every evening at four I'd watched that bitch meter out her pious verdicts and just laugh.

It was quiet in the day room, only a handful of inmates. I sat in the front row thinking about my freedom. The civil case on TV had me thinking. What were my options once I stepped out these gates? I had kept in contact with Mr. Jenkins at the community center. He assured me that he would rehire me once I was released. I was encouraged by that, and looked forward to the opportunity to work with the kids at the center.

At the entrance of the dayroom, I saw Lil' Goon walking in. I knew him from the neighborhood. Lil' Goon was young, and still trapped in his ways. Having shot a kid in the back over a kilo, he was doing fifteen years for drugs and attempted murder. Rahmel tried to guide Lil' Goon and helped school the young hustler the way he did me, but Lil' Goon wasn't hearing it.

Lil' Goon spotted me and nodded. He then walked over to me and sat next to me with his growing dreads and hardened image. I knew that he had some bad news to pass on by the look he gave me. We exchanged dap and Lil' Goon shook his head.

"Yo Soul, I just got word, son... They bodied North Star the other night."

"What...?"

"Word, some Jamaicans shot up the corner, slaughtered them niggas. He was just on da corner, rhyming with some other kids... Mu'fuckin' Jamaicans, they's some ruthless muthafuckas!" Lil' Goon said through clenched teeth.

"Damn," I uttered.

I knew North Star since he was wearing diapers. He was cool a lil' nigga who look up to me and admired me like an older brother. Jerome was a skilled rapper, one of the best around the way. I knew he was definitely making noise for himself. His family was going through a lot of pain. His mom used to have cookouts in the park, and feed us like we were her own kids. She was one of the best cooks in the projects. I used to fuck with his older sister, Monica, back in the days. She was really close to her brother. He had a beautiful family, and beautiful sisters. It was news that I hated hearing, especially so close to my release.

"When is the funeral?" I asked.

"I heard this Thursday," he answered.

I was being released Monday. Maybe I'll go by and pay my respects.

"It's ugly out there, Soul," Lil' Goon added. "That's four dead that I know of this month alone. But don't worry, Soul. They wanna get ugly out there, we gonna get ugly wid it in here."

Staring at Lil' Goon, I wanted clarification and asked, "What ya mean, man?"

"We gonna hit them yardie muthafuckas in here, fo' real! Fuck they whole shit up," Lil' Goon said. "You down, right Soul...? You and North Star were real tight. I know you wanna taste some revenge."

I felt his anger, but I had come too far. Spiritually, I had risen too much and just couldn't even think of letting go. There was no falling back into that darkened pit of revenge, murder and hate. Those were the things I didn't want to do. My heart went out for North Star and his family, but I had a son to think about.

Lil' Goon stared at me, waiting for the answer. He reached into the linen of his DOC jumpsuit and pulled out a long makeshift shank with a sharpened steel edge.

"Soul, you down?" he asked again.

"Yo, it ain't gotta go down like that," I said, hoping to put sense in this hothead.

"Fuck that! North Star was my nigga. For every one of my niggas da yardies drop out there, we killing more up in here! And we startin' wid da nigga Pepper Seed. He real tight wid 'em muthafuckas!"

He wasn't just spitting venom. Lil' Goon had already marked a victim for death to kickoff this round of violence. There was bound to be retaliation. I couldn't see myself being involved in this type of war. There was a hollow feeling in my stomach when Lil' Goon continued.

"Yeah, I forgot, ya gettin' released from this bitch soon. And ya found ya way huh…? But a nigga like me, I'm doin' a long bid, Soul."

His cold stare went through, x-raying me. Then Lil' Goon casually walked away ready to put his murderous plot into action. I sat back and sighed, listening to my thoughts. This bullshit you don't need right now. Three more days, Soul, three more days…

The sun was fresh in the sky the next morning. Sleep was still in my eyes as I counted down the hours before my release. I sat calmly reading the Bible. Glancing at the walls of my cell, one of America's poems and a picture of Khalil caught my attention. I still pour over her old letters looking for inspiration. Even though I didn't have a future with her, my thoughts were constantly on her.

Tick, my cellmate, and I talked for a moment while we got ready for the morning count. We formed a queue on the tier, remained quiet, and the C.O. visually checked that we were all present. Tick and I were cool types, just wanted to chill, do our time in peace then get the fuck up outta dodge. He had a year left on a five-year robbery bid, Tick just wanted to make it home to his wife. He was from Brownsville, Brooklyn and was good with numbers and history. He schooled me on a few books to read and we connected like brothers.

After headcount, I went to the showers and prepared for the day—chow, work detail, and the other bullshit in between. Walking in line down the long corridor with other inmates on my way to chow, I saw Rahmel approaching with a look of urgency. He pulled me to the side. The C.O leading us didn't intervene, Rahmel was an OG he had a way with people and the system. They didn't fuck with him, and he didn't fuck with them. He always held his head high and walked around the facility with respect from every corner. He did seventeen years, and was up for a parole hearing soon.

"Rahmel, what's good?" I asked.

"You keeping good, right?" he asked, staring at me like father to a son.

"Yeah, I'm good indeed. How you...?"

"I'm concern... I know Lil' Goon came to talk to you yesterday. I know what he's up too. I heard about North Star, Soul. You was close with him, Soul. But you only have two days left in this hell hole, my brother. Do not fuck it up!"

"Lil' Goon already know that I ain't down."

"Good, because it's going to be real ugly... I tried talkin' to the young brother, but the look he had in his eyes made me know I wasn't reaching him. He's on the same bitterness... The same rage that once had you, Soul."

"True indeed, but I'm good, Rahmel. Foremost on my mind is my son. When I get out, I just wanna start a new life, and put all this bullshit behind me."

"Good, my brother. Soul, stay away from Lil' Goon."

"Indeed, my brother," I said nodding.

As he walked away in the opposite direction, Rahmel glanced at me once more. His eyes spoke volumes. I hung around him so much that I knew what he was thinking. Rahmel was once a man of violence back in the days, now he was a man of wisdom, and peace.

I caught up with the line to chow. The prison cafeteria was bustling with inmates, staff and officers. Some inmates liked it, but it was always an uncomfortable situation for me. The inmates in the cafeteria outnumbered the armed officers five to one. Even though the CO's also had batons, fierce looks and pepper spray. There was something always going down, business transactions, and contract killings. The reaction time for the CO's to lock down the place was never fast enough.

I noticed Lil' Goon standing across the room. He was with his cronies, and above the food, I smelled trouble. He glanced at me, nodded, and smirked. He discreetly motioned toward the front of the line. I scanned the room. Pepper Seed was nearby, with another dreadlocked inmate.

It was going down. Only a couple CO's were posted nearby, and they were too loose. I could snitch, inform one of the CO's of the plot and maybe stop the murder. I was never a rat. Since I had prior knowledge of the hit, if Lil' Goon killed Pepper Seed, his blood could be on my hands too. North Star's death made me fall-back. Maybe I wanted revenge for my friend in some indirect way.

Lil' Goon kept his eyes on Pepper Seed. Then he slowly crept to the target. Moving ahead of the line in an unhurried walk, Lil' Goon got closer. Pepper Seed stood only a few feet from me. Lil' Goon turned and nodded at two of the CO's in the cafeteria. Both turned their backs and walked away for a moment, ignoring the trouble that was brewing. It was definitely an orchestrated hit, money had to be exchanged and the prison guards were down.

Slowly, the shank emerged from the inside of Lil' Goon's discreet location in his jumpsuit. I seemed to be the only one who saw. His eyes narrowed, and his face was twisted in a hardened scowl. Lil' Goon stood one man behind Pepper Seed. I looked at Lil' Goon. He was a lion stalking an unsuspecting prey in a jungle called life. Lil' Goon in one rapid motion rushed Pepper Seed, thrusting the sharpened shank into the side of the man's neck.

"Dis for my nigga North Star! Muthafucka!"

The shank was deep in Pepper Seed's neck. The injured inmate jerked like he was being electrocuted. Lil' Goon violently struck him several times in the back of the neck. Another inmate rushed up behind the dread and thrust an ice-pick into the friend's spine with fierce intensity. Collapsing to the floor, Pepper Seed squirmed in his own pool of blood, clutching his wounds. His death was gruesome. His dread friend was still on the cold tiled floor, lifeless with the ice-pick protruding from his back.

Chaos broke out. The alarm sounded and there was instant lock down. Knowing the drill, I hugged the floor with tremendous urgency and watched

Pepper Seed's death dance. He stopped moving and was on the floor like a twisted display of death, near his friend's sickening corpse. I prayed that it would be the last time I saw a man murdered.

The S.W.A.T. team rushed into the room. Wearing bulky riot gear and protective armor, shields and menacing batons, they moved in on the inmates like a swarm of bees. Goons with authority, their mission was to maintain control and restrain the perpetrators. They had Lil' Goon stretched out on his stomach not too far from me his hands were covered in Pepper Seed's blood. Lil' Goon smiled at me, there was no remorse. I was frozen to the floor and watched the CO's over us. Then I closed my eyes and thought of going home.

"Two more days…" I said to myself. Forty-eight hours.

2
America

The bright lights shining on me made it difficult, but I looked down from the stage at the crowd of young fans. They were gathered for my performance at St. Johns University in Queens. I felt both anxiety and excitement. It was my tenth show for the month and surprisingly, they were all sold out. The lights in the huge hall were dimmed softly, and the vibe I was getting from the crowd was overwhelming.

My fan base was growing and I had a major buzz going on through the city. The new CD was doing well, and the radio rotation from major stations was helping tremendously. I wasn't a pop star yet, but was well on my way to join the ranks of Beyonce and A. Keys. The networking, marketing, shows, and touring were paying dividends.

Kendal was the major reason for my success. Not only was he a genius in the studio, he was also an excellent manager. With his networking skills, Kendal was now getting to be like Diddy, well known in the industry. On the other hand he was a run of the mill type, medicore at best.

His insecurities cost him points, and at times Kendal was way too possessive. In our personal relationship, I saw good days and bad days— mostly bad. Kendal could be the most jealous, overbearing jerk. Sometimes he actually thought that every male artist, producer or promoter I worked with, wanted to fuck me. Or that I wanted to fuck them.

For over a year now, Kendal and I been together and I knew he loved me. I loved him too, but not the way I did Omar. A part of me really missed him.

There was so much chemistry and we have a son. Omar been locked up over a year now. I saw him three months ago. We were divorced, and I thought I had moved on. There are nights I wished that Omar was on stage with me, collaborating on a song.

In my performances in the studio and onstage, I'd sing these heartfelt songs. Even though I tried to lie, I knew who I was really reaching out to. I couldn't let Kendal know the truth. He was jealous of Omar and hated when I brought up my ex-husband's name. He wanted to me to forget Omar and focus on my career. Omar and I had a son together, and I knew that Omar will be home soon. I just didn't know the exact date.

Kendal loved Kahlil like his own flesh and blood, and lately he started telling everyone Kahlil was his. He was in need of a family and was waiting to marry me. He wanted babies too, and even though I told him no, it didn't end his ambitions. I had just gotten a divorce, wasn't ready to remarry, and I certainly wasn't ready to get pregnant again. My career was bubbling, I was a rising star so unbeknownst to Kendal I took my birth control pills regularly.

He refused to wear condoms, and when we had sex, I would still ask him to pull-out. There were many times when he would let off inside me, grinning. There was no humor in it. He knew that I wasn't ready to have anymore children. My son was already staying with my aunt while I was doing shows. I didn't want to be the *Brady Bunch*.

Even though the man was locked away miles up north, Kendal felt that Omar was a threat to him. Kendal was very competitive he was aware of my love for Omar, and yearned that I give him the same. Showering me with gifts and praises, he took care of me and was wonderful for my career. I was grateful, but always felt there was something missing.

Kendal didn't have the edge Omar had. Kendal was trying to buy my love. I hated to admit it to myself, but I'd compare the two. Most of the times, I wished it was Omar handling my career. He and I would be standing onstage in front of hundreds of people, displaying his skillful talent to the world.

Clad in a sparkling bolero top with sequin detail, tight fitting denim jeans, and a pair of black five-inch studded zipper back heels. My long hair was down to my shoulders, and my radiant smile was seen by everyone.

I gripped the microphone like it was a part of me and stood center-stage. My heart raced like a thoroughbred. Exhaling deeply, trying to keep my composure, my thoughts held me grounded. The fans were cheering so wildly, it brought a rush. I was in a zone.

In the background through the applause, I could hear Kendal's beat revving. It was a song I'd written. *I know somebody's gonna love me 2nite.* It was a funky, laid-back R&B joint with Mary J style. I let the beat ride, influencing the crowd. They got out of their seats, clapped and nodded their heads smiling. Some started singing the lyrics to the song. I embraced their gratitude and belted the joint with confidence.

> *I love it when you start feelin' on me…*
> *The way you start to hold and tease me…*
> *I think it's time we start this mission…*
> *Love the way you carry my attention…*
> *I know it's gonna be a problem…*
> *Oooh shorti, cuz the look you show,*
> *The things you do…*
> *You love the air I breathe…*
> *You ready to snatch off my jeans…*
> *It's crazy what we do…*
> *Cuz the look you show says to me…*
> *Somebody's gonna love me 2nite,*
> *Somebody's gonna hug me right…*
> *Ooh shorti, cuz you got my body on fire,*
> *Put my flames out and quench my desire…*

The crowd was into it. Few of the ladies down front started dancing and singing along. It was one of my favorite songs to perform and I was enjoying every minute of it. To the right of the stage, Kendal stood unseen. With his Yankee's fitted tilted to the side, Kendal was nodding to the beat and smiling. Looking sexy in his jeans, and button-up, he gave me two thumbs-up. Kendal was bejeweled with a Bentley watch and diamond chain. When he was doing his gig, Kendal was flashy.

I performed three other songs, *I keep holdin' on, A damn thang,* and *I remember the time.* The fans loved me. Judging from the roaring applause that I received, I knew I'd rocked the show. When I went backstage there were handshakes and hugs waiting to greet me. The life of a superstar, but I always remembered this line, 'Industry rule number four-thousand and eighty— record company people are shady...' Q-Tip said it and I carried it offstage. Kendal was there to meet me with a huge kiss.

"You did good, baby. You really tore up that shit tonight!" he gushed.

Smiling and sweating, I wanted to go home and take a cool shower. Kendal handed me a towel and bottled water. It was busy backstage with people moving about. A rap group, *Time Served* was next. They were a duo, Jay Stacks and Nino, straight out of Brownsville. They were two talented cuties that had a sound like *Brand Nubian's*.

Smiling, they stopped by to say hi. Nino was the finer of the duo. His long stylish braids and chiseled body defined him as a heartthrob. His demeanor was definitely street cut and reminded me a lot of Omar. We locked eyes. He gave me a hug and said, "I'm just lovin' it! America you did your thing-thang. We need to do a track together soon."

"I'm definitely down," I smiled.

"Nino, you know all you need to do is holla at me, man. I'll see what America's schedule's looking like," Kendal said, interrupting us.

The he grabbed my arm and slowly pulled me away from Nino. I was fuming while being dragged away by my jealous, insecure boyfriend.

"What's up with you?" I lashed out.

"Nothing," he abruptly replied.

"So why'd you do that?" I asked angrily.

"Do what?"

"I was talkin' to Nino, and you just came up and embarrassed me in front of him. What's the matter with you, Kendal?"

"You really don't need to be talking to him, America. He ain't even on your level, a'ight? Besides, I know what he's trying to get from you. You feelin' me? And it's more than just doin' a track with him!"

"Kendal, please stop it. You know I don't get down like that. I'm with you, so you don't have any reason to be so fuckin' jealous all the time!"

"I'm sorry, baby... It's just that I know these industry niggas and I be

trippin'."

"Don't!"

"I understand, but you know how I get. I just care about you a lot. I love you, baby."

There was passion in his tone, but I didn't respond. I was too upset. He acted as if I was his child, pulling me away from Nino like that. Kendal got jealous all because I was smiling at someone while having a conversation.

"Look Kendal, I'll be in the car. Alright...?" I said, walking away.

So what I found Nino attractive? I wasn't about to fuck him. Nino had a reputation with the ladies. I wasn't trying to become another notch on a rapper's belt.

Kendal followed behind, offering apologies.

"America, please forgive me. I'm sorry. It won't happen again, but it's just that..."

I wasn't trying to hear him. This routine was becoming tiresome. He was the type that had to feel that his dick was the biggest. He wanted to know if he fucked better than Omar. My ex was the only man I'd been with, besides Kendal. It felt like he wanted to outperform Omar in all aspects of my life. This behavior had me contemplating giving him his walking papers. I didn't like how Kendal was purposely trying to get me pregnant so he could lock me down. Omar and I had a son together. Now with no thoughts about my career, Kendal wanted his own child by me.

I got into the backseat of the black Escalade, pouting. Tonight's show was a real good one. Then Kendal had to fuck up my mood with his bullshit jealousy. Couple minutes later, he jumped in. Kendal was on the phone talking business. He looked at me and smiled. I ignored his overtures.

"Where's the damn driver?" I asked, getting irritated.

"Take it easy, honey. He's on his way."

Kendal liked living large and doing things lavishly as if we were huge celebrity figures. Although we were making money, we were not yet platinum. Two homes in different states or private planes flying us around were not our forte. Neither was spending money like it was water. Shit, I wasn't a rich bitch yet. I was still on a budget, and was definitely against hiring a private driver. Kendal convinced me that at two grand a month, we should try it for one month. His selling point was that having a driver was good for our image. I was competent enough to drive.

Clutching a hotdog and Pepsi, the driver ran over to the truck. He rushed inside and apologized for the delay. I was cool with it. Kendal chose him over the others. He was a nice dude. They'd known each other since college and Kendal knew he needed a job, so he gave him one. Kendal always had a good heart.

I rode without saying anything. Cellphone glued to his ear, Kendal was talking business as usual. My mind roamed while I stared out the window. It was after eleven, and the hectic activities of my day had worn me out. I needed to be home, soaking in my bathtub, and coming up with new songs. We were half way home before Kendal curtailed his cellphone call. He smiled at me like he had won the lotto.

"You should love me because I'm the fuckin' man, baby."

"What happened?" I quietly asked.

"You're lookin' at the man who's going to get you the opening act for Beyonce's next concert. I just got off the phone with the right peeps who are about to make that happen."

"Are you serious?"

"Serious, like how I love you so much."

"Oh my God !"

My whole attitude changed. I went from being upset with him, to hugging and kissing Kendal. The proud smile on his face, told me he was enjoying the groupie-like affection I was exhibiting.

"Who's the man?" he gushed.

"You are, baby," I smiled affectionately.

"America, I love you."

"I love you too, Kendal."

A short while later we made it home to our quiet three-bedroom home in Rockville Centre, Long Island. Kendal had wanted to be as far away from Brooklyn and Queens as we could possibly get without falling into the water. The area of Rockville Centre was nice, and it was almost affordable. We put a sizable down payment on the home, due to a tidy advance I'd received from the record label. Then we moved in together right away. I wasn't even gold

or platinum yet for that matter, but we were on point with the bills.

I was signed to an indie label, and they were marketing me the way I needed to be plugged into the music scene. This helped pushed the CD onto the local charts. AMG records had been around for a couple of years. It was formed by two upcoming musician and brothers. Like me, they had a deep-rooted passion for music. A few years ago, they had come into serious money, and knew the power of investing and business. Both were from Washington Heights and had success in many entrepreneurial ventures. They also owned a bodega, a restaurant, and signed a dual-release agreement with a major label.

Being the label's prime star was very exhausting. It took quality time away from raising my son, but I loved everything about it and wouldn't trade it. Kendal and I were getting so much done in such a short time.

Inside my sprawling stylish home, the porcelain floors shone brightly. The house was quiet. There were granite countertops, crown molding, and custom banisters. Our oversized backyard with a heated pool sat below the master suite with a breathtaking view of the lake across the street. It was tastefully expensive, and I felt at home. This was a better place to raise my son than Jamaica, Queens. On the surface it appeared as if we were rich. I was really working hard to maintain everything, and possibly gain more.

It was close to midnight, I exhaled heading to the bedroom in dire need of sleep. Kendal was right behind me. I started to undress and looked at myself in the mirror. I was a beautiful woman. Three weeks after giving birth, I went back to the gym and worked on my figure. I didn't gain too much weight during my pregnancy, and lost the baby-fat in record time. I stood in front of the large silver framed wall mirror. It was a birthday gift from Kendal. Stripping down to my Victoria Secret, I was admiring myself.

"Baby, you're gorgeous," Kendal complimented.

Shirtless, he approached me from behind. I glanced at him in the mirror. Kendal passionately wrapped his arms around me, kissing my neck. Staring at our image in the mirror he said, "We look so good together, baby."

Kendal's arms were around me and he continued kissing me slowly. He ran his tongue along my neck. His lips and tongue were saturating my neck while he rubbed my breasts. His hard on speared me. He had once admitted that watching my performance caused him to be aroused. I just wanted to go to sleep, but Kendal wanted to be passionate.

The kisses went from melting my spine, and causing my earlobes to tingle. His hands cupped my breasts then slid down to my panties. His touch was achingly nice, awakening my senses and inviting me to ecstasy. I allowed him to move his hand between my thighs. He delicately fondled my shaven pussy. I closed my eyes.

"Ooh…" I moaned when he thrust two of his fingers inside my inviting gap.

"I love you so much, baby," he whispered in my ear, playing with my clit.

His hot breath in my ear and chills traveled up my spine. I loved the way Kendal held me like he wanted me. He made me feel like a woman and he was always passionate, loving me like I was his gem. With one hand, Kendal played with my pussy. He was cupping my breast with the other hand. Kendal continued kissing my neck. His warm kisses were teasing me into bliss. It felt like I was about to melt in his arms. Quickly, I went from being tired and sleepy, to wanting him to fuck me real good.

"Hmm… Your skin's so smooth, America."

I felt his heart racing like it was ready to burst out of his chest. He craved me and I wanted him. Scooping me up, Kendal carried me over to the king size bed. He pulled my panties off and tossed them to the floor. Sinking his tongue in my pussy juice, Kendal was between the depths of my thighs instantly fervently eating me out. Spreading my legs like wings, I moaned as Kendal licked and sucked on every inch of my dripping pussy.

"Oh yes, God! Ooh yeah, yeah…" I moaned.

Gripping the white silk sheets, I closed my eyes. A few tears escaped as Kendal ravaged my pussy. His licking and sucking on my clit and pussy never stopped until I exploded in multiple orgasms.

"Damn, I love the way you taste, America," he smiled, swallowing me.

Kendal's tongue action was good and I got carried off into bliss. I clamped my legs around his head and my loud cries, echoed off the bedroom walls, traveling through the corridors like a soft breeze. Kendal gripped my thighs, and made his tongue stick and move against my sensitive clit like it

was a sparring match.

"A-a-ah-h-h-h shit! Baby, don't stop! Oh shit!"

My body was still shaking with my third orgasm when Kendal came out his jeans. He wedged himself between my thighs and thrust his thick eight inch dick deep inside my hot throbbing pussy. He tore my ass up like a tornado going through a small town. I sucked on his neck, pulling him deep inside my moistness. I wanted him to give it to me deeper, and harder. After this session I would be able to sleep like a baby. My legs straddled his waist, his erection opening me up like a gateway.

"Oh yes, Kendal. Oh yes!" I moaned, dragging my nails down his back.

He fucked me like he was a porn-star. His dick probed my stomach like an x-ray. Gripping my thighs, Kendal tried to fill me. He sucked on my breasts while my body wiggled in a pleasure dance of love.

"Oh, you feel so good, baby. You feel real good. Yeah, so fuckin' good... I'm about..." he chanted.

Kendal started fucking me like he was a beast. Pinning me against him and the bed, frog-style, he busted a nut while aggressively stroking me.

"Take it out! Ah... Yes! No Kendal, pull it out... Please, oh yes!"

"Oh baby yes. Take this dick!"

"No!"

Even with my plea, he came deep inside me anyway. It was purposely done. Shivering and jerking for a moment, Kendal rolled off me. He wore nothing but a huge smile of complete satisfaction.

"Damn, you felt soo good, baby, I just couldn't pull-out," he said, huffing.

I remained lying on my stomach, praying that the birth control was working one hundred percent. Kendal was close by my side for a moment. Then he got out of bed and went to the bathroom. Shutting the door to our intimacy, he left me lying there trying to collect myself. He didn't want to lose me and Kendal knew I enjoyed being fucked well. Once when we were only platonic friends, Kendal overheard me raving about Omar bedroom skills.

Left alone for ten minutes, I could smell the after-sex aroma lingering in our bedroom. The sheets were sweaty and wrinkled. A short while later, Kendal came out the bathroom clad in his bathrobe. He smiled, coming closer. I was still butt-ass naked. He had this look in his eyes. It was a mischievous gleam that had me a little nervous.

"What's wrong with you?"

"I'm just happy, that's all. You mean a lot to me."

He reached into his robe and surprised me by pulling out a small black velvet ring box. It was a hint of what was to come next. Kendal got down on one knee, opened up the ring box, revealing an awesome eight karat diamond engagement ring.

"America, I love you so much, baby. I want us to become the Bonnie and Clyde of the music industry. Will you marry me?"

I was speechless. Kendal was aware of my position regarding that, but the man was persistent. He stared at me with eyes that waited for a positive reply. Trying to get over the shock, I stared dumbfounded. I couldn't tell him yes. Accepting his proposal was out of the question. My heart was constantly reminding of the fact that it wasn't really over with my ex-husband. I still loved Omar and yearned for him. There still wasn't any closure between us. Kendal loved me, but marriage wasn't happening.

3
Omega

It was one in the morning and Omega sat in the leather swivel chair behind the huge mixer, a king seated on a throne. The dark studio came alive with pieces of beats and rhymes being coordinated like a puzzle. He watched his signed rapper, Kemistry, record a track in the soundproof booth. Flanked by an armed bodyguard, Rocky, Omega nodded to the beat. His turf war had forced Omega to hire the six-three, trigger man who came armed with a holstered Desert Eagle.

Omega sat next to Mike One, a famed producer from Harlem, known for his catchy and multi-selling beats. The two were discussing business and music. Kemistry's album had caused a buzz on the streets, but it wasn't commercial. Wanting his label to shine, Omega pushed for his rappers and artists to go commercial. He wanted the cream of the crop and had invested hundreds of thousands of dollars into Kemistry. Omega wanted to recoup his investment in full.

Kemistry was signed to an air tight contract which benefited the label and Omega mostly—some may have called it highway robbery. Omega was a gangsta like Suge Knight, and not too many people challenged his shady business ways. He had a gang of killers at his beckon call. Omega's street rep preceded him. Rich and successful, he was about his cream. Omega was able to get things done in days that took months for many others. He had influence and reach in every aspect of the business.

Omega formed an artist management company and signed prominent rappers and singers. He even secured a distribution deal with a major label. Omega was on the rise with his music label, but the street war with Demetrius was troubling and deadly. When he heard of the murder of North Star, Omega was so enraged he threw a chair through a glass window.

"Fuck me!"

Omega had invested thousands in the teen's career—studio time, photo shoots, appearances, wardrobe and jewelry. North Star was to be his next big project—his rising star. Now all he had invested was down the drain. Demetrius and his Jamaican hit squad were slowly putting an end to his dreams.

When they killed North Star, Omega immediately hollered at Biscuit. He wanted the heads of every Jamaican crew involved. Biscuit was operating as Omega's right hand man, and did as ordered. Omega had the music industry by the balls, but still kept his clutch on the streets.

Biscuit traveled with a pack of wolves. Hungry and vicious, they were ready to devour anything that they came across. Biscuit and his wild crew of hoodlums were as deadly and ruthless as the Jamaicans. Because of his violent activities, Biscuit quickly became the number one target on Demetrius hit list. The word on the streets was that there was a hundred-thousand dollar contract on Biscuit's head. Difficult to reach and hard to kill, Biscuit was skillful in street warfare. He was always armed and stayed aware of his surroundings.

Omega was business savvy. With his violent and deadly past, eyes were always on him—especially the feds. Pretending to be about his music label, Omega kept a clean image for his investors and the authorities. Behind this facade, he was responsible for murders, violence, extortions, racketeering, and hundreds of thousands of kilos of meth and cocaine transported into the city. His Mexican connect were still good and business with them was thriving.

Omega cooked his books for the IRS, and his artists. Three different accounting records for his business existed. There was one for the government, another for cheated royalties, and one for the streets. His money was long enough to pay a savvy business accountant who was just about as corrupt as he was. Omega felt untouchable.

Sitting behind the mixer, Omega seemed content with the beat. The studio was alive with excitement and everything was normal. Mike One and Omega were laughing and sharing a bottle of Grey Goose Vodka while Kemistry was spitting lyrics to a new song. *They call me sir.*

> *They call me sir, cuz niggas respect what's mine,*
> *Cross that line, I clap you wit' my nine,*
> *Have ya soul shake from ya skin,*
> *Mixin' like you in a Doo Wop blend.*
> *Death is a trend, fuck that bickery within,*
> *That mockery you hear, fuck da life you live*
> *Why ya warring wit' sin come up against my Berlin,*
> *My wall don't crumble, the life I live ain't humble,*
> *Forty Cal with the silencer, my gun hears my pain*
> *It roars like thunder, crash against ya brain*
> *I'm a tumor, muthafucka, love you like a brother*
> *Ill thinker, they hatin on me like no other,*
> *Fuck wit' my riches, you better ante up fo' war,*
> *All over ya like dawn across ya suburban lawns*
> *I'm that nigga built for war why they call me sir,*
> *Survived it all, five star general being born...*

Omega heard the hot lyrics coming from Kemistry rhymes and was getting hyped. Nodding his head hard to the bounce of the beat, he was shouting.

"Yeah my nigga, you killing that shit. Dats twenty-five to life, my dude! This shit's muthafuckin' platinum, my nigga!"

Mike One slapped fived, glad handing with Omega. His neck jerked in approval. The beat was a classic. Rhymes from Kemistry were appealing to Omega, and he took a quick swig of Grey Goose. With North Star dead, he now would have to put his budget and time behind Kemistry.

While the studio was producing track after track the cellphone on the hip of a laid-back looking Rocky vibrated. It was Biscuit. Omega didn't want direct contact with Biscuit through phones. They only talked to each other in person. Rocky was the middle man. He answered Biscuit's call in his usual deep baritone voice.

"Yeah, what up…?"

"I need to link up…"

"I'll let him know…"

Rocky hung up and walked over to Omega who was still engaged on the mixer. Omega turned around, feeling the presence of the hulky man behind him.

"What up?"

Rocky leaned in closer to his boss and whispered, "Biscuit said he wanted to link up."

"Tell him to meet me in an hour, third floor of the parking garage, he knows where."

Rocky nodded and called Biscuit. Omega immediately went back to work. Kemistry continued spitting rhymes and Omega forgot the streets for now. He was in his element at the studio. He felt peaceful.

Forty minutes later, a black Escalade slowly made its way toward the third upper deck of a remote parking garage in Long Island. The cool night was descending on the area and the parking lot was sparse. Rocky was behind the wheel. The truck pulled up close to a gray Lexus LX. Biscuit sat patiently in the driver's seat. One of his goons was seated in the passenger seat. When the Escalade parked, Biscuit and his boy stepped out the Lexus and greeted Omega with an impish smile.

"Mega, what's poppin' my dude," Biscuit greeted, giving Omega dap.

"You got sumthin' for me…?" Omega asked, getting straight to business.

"You know I got you, my nigga. I'm on it fo' real! They hit us– we hittin' em fuckin' harder. Just like the old days, you feel me?" Biscuit smiled.

He walked to the back of the Lexus and popped the trunk. Omega walked over and looked inside. A wicked smile crossed his mug when he saw Node. King's little brother was duct-taped and gagged in the fetal position in the

trunk. The twenty-two year old kid was butt naked and had been beaten. He squirmed when he looked up and saw Omega. In his predicament it was like seeing the face of death.

"You like that, my nigga?" Biscuit asked with a confident smile.

"Love it," Omega replied, nodding.

Omega neared closer to the bonded Node. He smiled at the helpless Jamaican, knowing how close he was to his older brother, King. Omega's demeanor changed. Instantaneously he started physically attacking Node. He punched the young man in the face repeatedly, all the time shouting, "You take from me, muthafucka? Huh, you take from me? You know how much I had invested in that nigga, huh?"

Node received a beat-down as payback for the killing of North Star and Omega's dreams. Omega punched the confined man repeatedly and only stopped when he saw blood on his fist. He looked down at the man and spat.

"Fuckin' yardie! Somebody give me sump'n to wipe this muthafuckin' blood from my hand."

Rocky passed him some tissue. Omega wiped his hand, looked over at Biscuit and said, "Take care of this muthafucka. Send out that message, Biscuit. I want a good one."

"I got you, fo' real, boss," Biscuit said, smiling and shaking his head.

It wasn't King or Demetrius in the trunk of the car, but Omega felt a little satisfaction. The younger brother of King would do for the entrée. His murder would send a message to the Jamaicans that they were on the menu. King was the most heartless and ruthless of them. A fierce street soldier, King had spilled lots of blood during the past six months. His name was ringing. Straight out of Jones Town, Jamaica, King was one of Demetrius' most deadly enforcer. Publicly flaunting his brand of mayhem and destruction, the thirty-one year old immigrant was deadly and dangerous.

Omega made King a high priority. King was the main course in this street war. Omega knew that if he killed one Jamaican, Demetrius would fly in two more to take his place. There was always going to be war. Omega knew he would have to take the war onto the soil of their own homeland— Kingston.

Biscuit would handle the murder of Node in a tidy, but gruesome way. Omega got back into the truck and Rocky reversed out of the parking spot. Omega locked eyes with Biscuit's, and nodded like a proud father to his son. He had watched Biscuit grow from a young reckless killer, to a seasoned killer. The eighteen year old was as deadly as any of the Jamaicans Demetrius brought in.

Biscuit watched the Escalade drive away. Looking down at Node with a sinister grin, he said, "I'm a have some fun wit' ya bitch ass. Fo' real!"

He slammed the trunk shut and jumped behind the wheel.

Omega and Rocky were tired. They crossed the Brooklyn Bridge after a long, busy day. Omega lived about an hour from the city in a reclusive New Jersey neighborhood. He wanted to go home and relax in the sprawling and stylish five bedroom home he owned. The revered suburban locale was made up of doctors, lawyers, entertainers and entrepreneurs in Cedar Grove. It was his fourth home in two years. Knowing he had blood thirsty enemies, Omega didn't feel comfortable living in one place for too long. He made it a part of his business to move his family around.

The midnight colored Escalade drove up a steep hill leading to his three-car garage. Elaborate state-of-the-art wiring for lighting, security, and sound, premium finishes were some of its features. The five-bedroom home had impeccable styling and spacious rooms with hardwood floors. There was a pool, a built-in barbecue, spa, terrace and meticulously manicured lawns. Omega lived in a home fit for a king. His security system was high-end. He kept all the best guns in his home.

He stepped out of the Escalade and secured the 9mm in his waistband. Rocky asked, "You gonna be okay, boss?"

"I'm good. Come get me tomorrow morning at nine. We have a lot to do."

Rocky nodded and made sure Omega was inside before pulling off.

Omega strutted through the foyer.

"Jazmin..." he called out.

"I'm in the bedroom," she shouted.

Omega made his way to the master suite. The rooms were dimmed and quiet. They had only lived in their new home for three months, but it was one of his better ones. It was further away from the city, and a heavily armed security team constantly patrolled the area. He had a panic button to press just in case there was trouble and he needed them. It was a last option that was designed for Jazmin to utilize in case of an emergency and he wasn't there. Omega was a gangsta and felt his guns were his best security.

He walked into the master suite to find Jazmin lying on their king size bed. She was with their sixteen months old son who was asleep. Six months pregnant with their second child, Jazmin smiled when Omega walked inside.

"Hey baby," Jazmin greeted, extending her arms for a hug.

Omega pulled his pregnant woman into his arms, giving her a loving hug, and kissing her deeply.

"I see lil' man is knocked out," he said.

"Yeah, he's been sleep like that for an hour. I know he's gonna wake up and I'm not gonna get any sleep tonight."

"That's my lil' soldier right there," Omega said with a proud smile.

"Well your lil' soldier's been acting up all day."

"How was your day baby?

"Busy," Omega replied.

Omega was short with her, not wanting to discuss his business. He wanted to come home and forget about the streets and music. He wanted to fuck his pregnant girl and play with his son. His son was asleep so Omega eyed his girl lustfully. Jazmin was clad in a pair of sweats and a T-shirt.

"Why you lookin' at me like that?" Jazmin asked.

"Cuz you know why."

"Baby, I'm tired."

Picking up his sleeping son, Omega kissed him gently, and took him into the baby's room. He carefully put Anthony down on his stomach in the small bed that was decorated with *Sponge Bob Square Pants* sheets and pillows.

Omega walked back into the master bedroom where Jazmin was fiddling with the remote, channel surfing on their sixty-three inch Sony flat screen. Omega removed the 9mm from his waistband and rested it on the mahogany nightstand.

"Why do you still carry that? I thought you were done with that street nonsense," Jazmin sighed.

"I got enemies, baby."

"You're a business man now. I thought you were legit."

"You know I got an ugly past. And the war wit' the Jamaicans, ain't gettin' any better."

Jazmin rubbed her belly. Omega was hardly around to help raise the first one that they had. Now she was worried about their second child. She lived good and had everything she needed for the kids and herself, but it was getting lonely with Omega constantly on the go. After making a house into a home, Jazmin hated to be suddenly uprooted, starting over, and refurnishing. She would argue with Omega about his lifestyle and the constant moving around. Omega was adamant about not settling into any home for more than six months. He didn't want to make it easier for his foes to track him down.

"Omega please put that away. I hate seeing it here," Jazmin said, pointing at the gun.

"Da safety is on. You ain't gotta worry 'bout it. I'd rather have it close. Beside, you know what the fuck I'm about, Jazmin… Stop acting brand new. You living good, right? Your hair's always done. You got jewelry, money, clothes cars, spas and shit. What da fuck you complaining 'bout? You know how many bitches would love to be in your position right now?"

"Then let 'em, cuz baby I'm tired! I'm due to drop in three months! You expect me to keep moving around like this with two kids. I just want some stability with you," Jazmin complained.

"Stability…? You got stability, bitch! What da fuck else you want from a nigga?" Omega barked.

"Try staying alive to see your fuckin' kids grow up!" Jazmin exclaimed.

The Lexus LX slowly crept toward the Long Island shore under darkened skies. The gravel path they traveled led to a shaded dead end covered by thick shrubberies, tall weeds and trees. Quiet and secluded, it was the perfect spot for the two men to commit their deadly deed.

When the car came to a stop, Biscuit stepped out. He was closely followed by Narmer, who was a hotheaded seventeen year old. Biscuit took a drag from the cigarette clinging to his lips then he glanced at Narmer.

"You ready to do this?" Biscuit asked.

Without saying a word, Narmer nodded. Biscuit took another pull from the Newport and looked around. Satisfied with the area, he walked to the back of the car, and popped the latch. Node stared up at his kidnappers with worried look in his eyes. He squirmed and fidgeted with the restraining duct-tape binding his limbs. Biscuit looked at the beaten down, immobilized man. He removed the .380 from his waistband.

"You fucked up now, nigga," Biscuit said.

Butt-naked and gagged, Node watched Biscuit cock the .380. Unveiling a sinister grin, Biscuit looked over at Narmer and said, "Take that shit off his mouth. I wanna hear what his punk-ass gotta say."

Narmer snatched the dirty, bloodied duct-tape from Node's swollen lips.

"Mi brother King gawn kill ya blood-claat ass fo' this!" Node quickly exclaimed.

"Fo' real, muthafucka? Well you first!" Biscuit retorted, putting the gun to Node's forehead.

He squeezed the trigger and the resulting explosion caused the back of Node's brains to be blown out. Biscuit fired again and again. Four hot rounds pushed the man's wig way back. The muzzle flash from the .380 lit up the shaded area like firecrackers. Node's face was contorted and burnt. Biscuit glanced at Narmer. He seemed cool.

"Yo, go get that from the backseat," Biscuit instructed.

Narmer walked away and Biscuit stood there, eyeing the body. Wearing the same sinister smile, he walked closer, studying death like it was an art form.

"Bitch ass, muthafucka!" he spat.

Narmer returned clutching a large machete, a surgeon's robe and a container of gasoline. Biscuit put on the surgeon's robe and took the machete from Narmer.

"You wanna do the honor?" Biscuit asked.

"Fuck that! I'll shoot a nigga, but that decapitation shit... I ain't got the stomach for," Narmer returned, taking a step back from the body.

"This is how you fuckin send a message, fo' real, Narmer. King gonna know we ain't fuckin' around."

Biscuit skillfully positioned the body for contact. Then he raised the machete and put tremendous force to Node's neck and slowly began decapitating Node's head from his lifeless body. A gruesome sight that left Narmer squirming. Biscuit went about the grotesque act like a butcher in the meat market. Node's head dropped to the ground with a few powerful strokes. Picking up the deformed body-part, Biscuit jokingly presented it to Narmer.

"He looks good like this, right," Biscuit joked, clutching the dreads attached to the severed head.

"I wanna throw up!" Narmer said, grabbing his stomach.

"Nigga, stop being a fuckin' pussy... This is how we do! The same fuckin' blood that runs through me runs through you, nigga. We family in this shit, you my brother," Biscuit said. "Just go get me da garbage bag."

Narmer rushed for the black trash bag. The quicker the skull was out of his sight, the better. Biscuit dropped the head into the bag and tossed it into the trunk with the body. Biscuit removed the surgeon's robe and both men quickly cleaned up the area and drove away.

An hour later, Biscuit dowsed the body and the car with gasoline and quickly set everything ablaze. He held onto the garbage bag with Node's head inside. Both men watched the car burst into flames in a dark alley near the Jamaican café on Flatbush Ave in Brooklyn. They then slipped into an idling truck and sped off. There was still one more thing that Biscuit had to do.

The truck came to a halt in front. It was two in the morning and Biscuit wore the same sinister grin when the store glass shattered. He watched Node's head, still in the black trash bag, crashing through the popular Jamaican Café. The place was frequented by King's goons.

"Bomba clot that, muthafucka!" Biscuit shouted, flashing his middle finger at the place.

His act would send King into complete frenzy. Seeing the head of his dead little brother, and the charred body in the car would leave King thinking twice. The bloodthirsty Biscuit was now satiated, and jumped into the truck. Racing away, he laughed knowing that he had brought the war to a whole new, deadlier level.

4
Omar AKA Soul

"You a free man again, my brother. This time, please stay the hell away," Rahmel said.

He quickly followed up with a hug, handshake and a big smile.

"Indeed Rah, I will. I ain't trying to see this place no more. You got my word on that. I'm moving on. I'm building a better a life for me and my son."

"It feels good to hear you thinking that way. I know you seen enough of the joint. Hopefully, in two months, I'll be free also. My parole hearing is coming up, seventeen years and with God watching over me, I know I'm blessed and my time to be free is coming," Rahmel said with conviction.

"That's in the bag, Rahmel. Look at you, talking like Louis Farrakhan and looking like Martin Luther King, they gonna love you on that board," I joked.

"Yessir..." Rahmel chuckled.

"True indeed..."

I hated to leave him and the knowledge he dropped, but was happy to be walking out the front gate in a few. Rahmel didn't boggle me down with any righteous and spiritual talk. I guess he did enough talking to me while I was incarcerated. He knew that I had been listening. Handing me a sealed letter to read when I was on the bus, Rahmel wished me the best. We hugged again and I departed from him.

"Soul, don't look back on me when we depart. You just keep your head forward and walk out them damn gates a renewed man. But don't look back on me, just leave. I'm gonna be okay," Rahmel instructed.

"Indeed…"

I nodded, walking down the shifty, dirty prison corridor one last time. Without once glancing back, wearing a deadpan gaze, I was slowly escorted to my freedom by CO's. I had all my property in one hand. The good book was in the other. This time I was certainly ready.

"How long, huh…?" I heard one of the CO's asked.

Ignoring the uncertainty written on the prison cadres' faces, I kept it moving. I was getting older and knew my chances were becoming slimmer. I felt in my heart that this was it— now or never. I prayed to God.

This had to be the brightest Monday morning. I exited out of Franklin correctional facility a breathing, free man. The sun was shining brightly and the weather was warm and for a minute I just relished the moment. It was a sign. I wasn't the only one being let out. There was a half dozen more men that came out behind me.

I looked around and sighed heavily. America wasn't here waiting with hugs and kisses. I miss not having a ride back with my woman ready to love me, and help me adjust to society. Holding my things, I pulled my collar tight, and waited on the next Greyhound to New York.

Reminiscing about the last time I was set free, I remembered the smile on America's face. I yearned to have America here this morning. Instead I had the hardened look of six ex-cons glaring at me. It was a pretty fucked up feeling.

The shuttle arrived shortly, and one by one we all piled on. On the way to the town of Malone, the bus was in an uncomfortable silence. Like everyone else, I was peering out the window without a sound, thinking and enjoying the view of the countryside. A few miles from town, I opened Rahmel's letter. I thought it would be a long winded speech he had written. It was one sentence.

No matter what a man's past may have been his future is spotless. John R. Rice.

Reading it over, I pondered the statement for a few minutes. It was one of the most profound statements that I had ever heard. The driver announced that we had arrived in town. This was the exchange connection for the Greyhound to New York City. Getting off the bus, I could feel my heartbeat increasing.

The hour ride to Manhattan was lonely and tiresome. It wasn't the crowd on the bus, it just wasn't a car. I had to adjust. I was divorced, practically homeless, and wasted so many years of my life behind bars. A good friend was waiting for my arrival in New York. With God by my side, I was off to a great start.

The sun was almost settling for dusk and the bus pulled into the Port Authority bus station. I was excited to be home. The concrete jungle was just like how I'd left it—bustling and alive with diversity. I only had my carryon, so I stepped off the bus and looked around me, people were coming and going. I allowed the rush of the bustling city to envelop me.

Following the crowd, heading to the exit, brought me back alive. Anticipation was building, I was home. It was almost eight at night and walking into the grand lobby, I looked around for my friend. He already knew my bus schedule, I hoped he didn't forget. I needed a shower, some good food, and a peaceful night's sleep. The crowd quickly dispersed into the busy city streets. I looked around and there he was wheelchair bound. Even though he couldn't walk anymore, Vincent Grey looked happy. He smiled when he saw me approaching. His woman was by his side and she was a beauty.

Standing behind his wheelchair in her skirt and white top, she helped guide Vincent through the crowd.

"What up, Vincent?"

"It's good to see you home, Soul," Vincent replied with a warm smile.

I leaned forward and gave him a hug. We had been locked up together upstate. He was released a year ago. Multiple gunshot wounds he suffered while he was in the drug game left Vincent paralyzed from the waist down. He was a rock and didn't let his condition stop him. Vincent came home a changed man. He was now helping to build up his community rather than destroying it.

While running in the streets, we had come up together under the same crew. He was a few years older than me, and always looked out. The day I got locked up, Vincent had warned me, but I refused to listen. Vincent was a friend who wrote me on the regular, and kept his word. The irony about our friendship was my best friend, Omega, had his best friend, Tyriq killed a few years back. There was a lot of bad blood behind Tyriq's murder and was an ugly situation. Through it all, Vincent and I remained cool.

Seeing Vincent's condition made me feel very fortunate. We were both alive and free, but I was still able to walk. The game took away his ability to walk. I was counting my blessings.

"Yo, you look good, Soul," Vincent complimented. "Hey, this is my lady, Shae."

"Hi Shae," I greeted.

"Nice to meet you," Shae said, smiling and shaking my hand.

Shae reminded me of America. They had the same rich qualities. She was with a man that was handicapped. It took a strong woman to love, and take care of a man confined to a wheelchair for the rest of his life.

"Yo, let me take that for you," Vincent offered, reaching for my bag.

"Nah, I'm good, Vince," I said.

"Yo Soul, stop acting like that, my legs may not work, but my arms do, give it here, man," he replied.

I shook my head with a smile and passed him my bag. He placed it on his lap.

"See, I got you."

"C'mon baby, let's roll," Vincent joked.

I laughed. It was good to be home. It wasn't America picking me up, showing me the affection that I loved, but it was still nice to have someone there looking out. I followed Vincent and his girl to the parking garage. We chatted about unimportant things and I absorbed the sights of the city once again. It had been only eighteen months, but it was a long five hundred and forty-six days away from home.

Vincent and Shae moved around the city in a minivan. The van doors were remotely operated. A small ramp unfolded from inside allowing Vincent easy access. After a few minutes we were settled. Shae did the driving. Vincent and I sat in the backseat.

We were about to go across the Queensboro Bridge I asked, "So, what's goin' on in the hood?"

Vincent shook his head and looked at me with furrowed brows. The conversation took on a serious tone when he spoke.

"It's getting uglier every day, Soul. That meth shit is hittin' hard out there. There's a war between Omega and the Jamaicans. They killing too many of our young brothers, they're dropping like flies. I'm counseling kids at the center, give 'em some hope, something to believe in. But the majority of them are too caught up."

"True indeed, I hear you," I nodded, listening intently. Vincent became impassioned as he continued.

"They ain't trying to hear what I gotta say. Omega got these young kids brainwashed. He got them believing that they're soldiers out there, fighting for damn poison. He recruiting teens, got them fighting for him like he Uncle Sam."

"It's serious, huh?"

"I mean, look at me, Soul. You would think that I'm evidence enough to make 'em stray from the game, scare them to do right. But nah! They in it deeper and harder than we ever were— murdering each other on the streets like some type a game."

"Damn!" I replied, shaking my head. "It's that bad, huh?"

"Yeah, damn bad. But we talk to them at the center some of these kids are listening, but they're not listening hard enough. That shit with North Star, it got these kids wildin' and gunning for revenge."

"Whoa…"

"The other night they found a headless torched body in a Brooklyn alley, and they threw the head through a store window. Word is that it was King's little brother."

"King…?"

"He's a crazy-ass Jamaican, straight off the banana boat. He's supposed to be Demetrius' top enforcer. People 'round the way calling him the boogie man. Word going round that he's the one who gunned down North Star and the other teens on the corner. I mean to spray people down like that in broad daylight…? A man has to be evil to commit such a heinous act. I don't know Soul the world is losing its damn mind."

"It's the same way upstate," I said.

"But you're home now, Soul, and you don't need to stress yourself with these streets. No parole, no probation, no papers only freedom," Vincent said with a smile.

"Yeah, I'm free."

The ride to Queens made me feel like a tourist. Taking in the scenery, reminiscing, I was chilling. The hood hadn't changed much, except for the extreme violence. Vincent and Shae had a three bedroom house out in Rosedale, Queens. I was impressed.

The van pulled into the driveway and I helped Vincent maneuver his wheelchair to the front porch and unto the wheelchair ramp. I walked inside and their furnishing was up to par—flat screen television, plush couches, family portraits displayed on the walls and a high end stereo system.

"Nice," I said.

"Yeah, we make it do," Vincent said.

"It looks like you do more than make it do," I joked.

Vincent chuckled.

"You'll be sleeping in the guest bedroom. We already got it set up. It's really comfortable," Vincent said.

"That's cool."

"Are you hungry…? Something to drink, maybe…?" Shae asked me.

"I'll take something to drink," I said.

Shae went into the kitchen leaving me and Vincent in the living room to talk. Vincent wheeled himself over to the home entertainment center and began fiddling with the CD's. He put a CD in the drive, and R&B music played. Shae came out the kitchen holding two glasses of juice. She handed one to me with a smile then kissed Vincent goodnight, handing him the other.

"Goodnight, Soul," she said.

Kissing Vincent again, she left. The affection they had reminded me of what I had with America back in the days.

"You got sumthin' special there," I said.

"You think I don't know that, man? The problems I put her through back in the days, sometimes I ask myself, 'Why did she ever come back?' Look at me," he said, pointing to his wheelchair. "She's a strong woman."

"True indeed..."

"It's funny, Soul. Back in the days, when I was hustling for Tyriq, I had all the money, bitches, cars... I thought I was happy. But this here, my family, my wife, my son, and not having to watch my back in the streets, this is pure joy and happiness. I can't walk, but I acquired the meaning of what life should really be about."

"I definitely hear you, Vincent."

"Man, put that juice down and let me pour you a real drink," Vincent said.

He rolled over to the mini bar and began pouring me a shot of Vodka and cranberry. He made two glasses and passed me one.

"A toast my brother. To us, becoming men and surviving these streets, and having a sense of awareness. Now let's pass this knowledge on to our lost brothers and bring them out of the fire, as we are living proof that there is life after death," Vincent said, raising his glass above his head.

Our glasses clinked and we downed our drinks. Vincent and I continued talking and drinking for an hour. Then Vincent went to bed. I went upstairs and got settled in the guest bedroom. I had nowhere else to go and felt blessed they took me in. My life felt like an uphill climb.

I walked into the small room and dropped my bag to the floor. Then I sat at the edge of the bed, looking around and thinking. Shades closed, the quiet room with no television was imprisoning. Seeing Vincent and Shae together reminded me of America and me.

"I fucked that up."

The envy for what Vincent had, left me sighing. It was the American dream. He had a fine wife, a loving home, steady income and a place to call his own. I got undressed, said a prayer and went to bed. Tonight would be my first night in a comfortable bed. Tomorrow was a new day, and my journey would fully begin.

5
America

Kendal wanted a quickie before we went to the studio to record a few tracks with the rapper, Alimony. I gave him some. His hard-on slid in and out of me like a thick stick churning butter. Straddling my legs around him, he sturdily grinded between my thighs. Cupping my tits, I moaned and we kissed. It was routine. I wanted it to be over. He was only trying hard to get me pregnant. I felt that I should have been honest with him, but the man was a big baby.

We fucked for twenty minutes in our bedroom while the driver waited outside. Kendal was like a horny-toad. Sometimes I thought it was more of his insecurities surfacing. It seemed like every time I had to record a track with another handsome male rapper or singer, the man wanted to fuck me before we leave. If we didn't fuck before arriving to the studio, then he would try and tap the ass right after coming from the studio. It was the same routine when I was doing a show. I was getting bored with this habit of his. Then he would always surprise me with gifts. Sweet talking me into staying with him and managing me—like the chance of me opening up for Beyonce.

Kendal grunted and thrust himself deeper into me. I moaned, running my nails down his sweaty back.

"I'm gonna cum," he shouted.

I felt him swelling inside me. A few more deep thrust then he was grunting and coming in me. His body went limp and Kendal rolled off of me, blowing out his mouth. He was sprawled out on his sweaty back, panting, and looking up at the ceiling.

"Oh shit, that was good, baby. You're the best," he said.

It wasn't his best performance because he didn't do it because he loved me. He fucked me out of sheer jealousy. I got up and went inside the bathroom. I wiped myself down and locked the door. I didn't want Kendal to catch me taking my birth control pills, he would throw a tantrum. I was cleaning up myself when I heard Kendal knocking on the bathroom door.

"Baby, hurry up. We gotta be at the studio in an hour. You know this studio time doesn't come cheap."

After tapping my pussy he wanted to rush me. I needed a complete shower. I didn't want to leave smelling like sex. Quickly, I washed and got dressed. We were running late, but I knew that it wasn't a big deal. I slipped into a pair of denim boot cut jeans with a pair of open-toe sandals. Throwing on a cotton top with side slits, I rushed into the truck with Kendal. The driver drove off, heading to the city.

The driver hit the Long Island Expressway with Kendal on his cellphone. My own thoughts were entertaining me. The three songs I wanted to record when I hit the studio. The one with Alimony, I had the lyrics down, but I wasn't sure about the title. When Kendal finally got off the phone, I looked at him and said, "I want to go to his funeral."

"Whose funeral?" he asked.

"North Star…"

The way he looked at me, told me that he wasn't too happy with what I said.

"What, for what? You don't need to be there," Kendal said.

"I knew him and his family from around the way. And I want to show my respect," I said.

"America, that funeral is gonna be a damn circus. And it's way too dangerous. We gonna need extra security that's gonna cost—"

"I'm going, Kendal," I said with conviction.

"Baby, c'mon now, just think rational. You're better than that. You can pay your respect by sending the family flowers, or a card. Shit, write them a fuckin' check with your condolences, but to attend that boys' funeral, we can't do that," Kendal said in his arrogant tone.

"I'm going, Kendal!"

Kendal let out a frustrated sigh and shook his head.

"I'm just trying to keep you from making mistakes, baby. I know what's best for your career. I got you this far, right baby? I just need for you to keep making the right choices. With me by your side, I'm gonna have you on top in no time. But you don't need to be at that gangster's funeral."

Kendal was trying my last nerves, always playing the career card. He did help spark my career, but I don't need him constantly reminding me.

"Baby, look," Kendal began, softening his tone and looking at me caringly. "I just don't wanna see you get hurt out there, cuz it's a dangerous place."

"Kendal, I've lived with a gangsta for ten years of my life. I've seen it all baby. I know how to take care of myself. I don't need you to hold my hand constantly like I'm a two year old. Omar taught me how to handle myself on these streets. I'm good, my man."

Kendal didn't like hearing Omar's name. He didn't want to be reminded about the past I had with him. Kendal was just too jealous of my ex.

"America, I'm your future. Besides, that thug is locked up. He fucked up his chance with you. I'm not trying to do that," Kendal acidly said.

I smiled, thinking, if he only knew that his whining and insecurities were gradually pushing me away. I'm glad we weren't married.

The truck moved down the LIE toward the Midtown Tunnel. Kendal was back on the cellphone discussing business. I sat there quietly, singing lyrics to myself and going over songs. We drove into the heart of the city. The studio was just a few blocks from the Empire State building. Pulling up front, I was escorted out the truck still upset.

"You mad at me, baby?" he asked when I brushed by him.

I didn't answer him. I waited at the elevator to arrive at the lobby floor. When the doors opened, I rushed inside and pushed for the fourth floor. Kendal stood by close. He had hung up with his call and now had his attention back on me.

"Whatever I did to you baby, I'm sorry, a'ight?"

"It ain't about always being sorry. But you know what... Just forget it."

"America, I don't wanna fight wit' you."

"Who's fighting? I'm cool."

We got off on the fourth floor, and walked three doors down the hallway to the studio. The beat was playing as we approached. Kendal walked a few steps behind me, sulking. I turned, glanced at him, sucking my teeth. Then I rang the buzzer and identified myself. Quickly, I was into the studio.

The place was electrified with activities. Producer Mike One was there and he was already working on the track. It sounded hot, my head was already bobbing.

"America, my girl," Mike One greeted me with a smile and a hug.

Sporting a very icy link chain with the diamond mixer pendant down to his stomach, Mike One was built like Timberland. He made beats like Swizzie and Dallas Austin combined. Full of laughs and talent, Mike One was a great person to work with. He pulled his fitted Yankee to the brim. I felt blessed to be working with him. He was expensive, but was worth it.

"You ready…?" Mike One asked.

"I'm amped," I shouted.

Kendal walked into the room and greeted Mike One. The two also worked well together. Mike One was married with children and Kendal took an immediate liking to him.

The studio was dimmed. Nothing but the fluorescent lights shone from the custom keyboard workstation desk. Made of polished maple finish hardwood floors, it stood out against the top quality soundproof booths and bass racks. Whenever I was here, I'd fall in love with the place and hated to leave. Alimony, the rapper was running late. So after some chitchat, Mike One dropped a couple of his new beats for us. While listening to the tracks, I made up lyrics in my head.

"I like," I said, nodding and smiling.

"Yeah, I worked on these four all night," Mike One said.

"They're tight and I'm feeling them," Kendal said.

Kendal and Mike One were both phenomenal when it came to producing beats. They would share ideas and talk almost all night. I sat on the leather couch and pulled out my pad filled with lyrics and song titles.

Alimony and his crew from Bed-Stuy arrived an hour late. Bejeweled in ice and swag off the radar, he stood only five-nine. His confidence and rhyming skills were enticing. Smiling behind his butter-soft leather jacket, black Timberlands, fitted jeans and a Yankees fitted, Alimony greeted me with a warm hug.

"Ya lookin' fine America. I can't wait to get on this track wit you."

"Alimony, I'm ready. Let's do this."

"Time is money, Alimony. We sat here for an hour waiting," Kendal said, intervening.

He was upset with Alimony for being an hour late. Alimony looked displeased with Kendal's statement.

"Who cares, nigga. What, you on PMS or sumthin? I'm here now right," he joked.

I chuckled.

Alimony was a cutie and thug. I could tell that Kendal was uncomfortable with me recording and being around him. Alimony had rhyming skills and I wanted to work with him ever since I heard him rhyme on DJ Clue mix tape.

Quickly, we got situated, and I stepped into the booth with Alimony. Once the door was shut, Alimony whispered, "Yo America, why you fuck wit' that nigga anyway? Look at him, he corny. He be up in ya ass tighter than a fart."

I laughed out loud.

"You know I feel you, right? Let me take you out to dinner some time."

"I'm a one man type of woman, Alimony. The offer is tempting, but yeah, Kendal do have his ways, but he's been good to me," I smiled.

"I can do better," Alimony said, sucking his teeth.

"I bet you can," I smiled.

I looked up and saw Kendal staring at me. He didn't like the way Alimony was all over me. I wasn't doing any better, smiling, and laughing. Alimony had his arm around my waist, holding me tight. If looks could kill—Kendal would have gone up for murder one. We looked at each other for a moment. Kendal had a mean face on.

Alimony looked over and also saw Kendal's negative expression. With a devilish grin, Alimony said,"Look at him, hating on a nigga, I should fuck wit' his head."

"Nah, don't do that. I don't need the drama," I said.

"America, you're too beautiful to be having that tight-ass nigga sweating ya like that. C'mon, you in the industry, niggas gonna definitely holla at you and wanna work wit' you. That corny ass nigga, he gonna fuck things up for you if he keep actin' like that," Alimony whispered in my ear.

It was bad enough that the collaboration was titled, *You and I*. Alimony was fine and openly taunted Kendal by vicariously flirting with me. He showed no respect for my jealous boyfriend who was also my manager.

"A'ight, ya ready to do this?" Mike One asked, working on the mixing board.

"Money, I been ready," Alimony cockily replied.

Mike One played an upbeat, jazzy rhythm with electric guitar instrumental. It was different and I liked it. Mike One came correct. Clutching my headphones, I nodded my head ready to go in with Alimony by my side.

Alimony was to rhyme first and I was to follow in with the song. He nodded along with me and smiled. And then on cue, he began to spit out his first verse. He was fierce on the microphone.

> *"Yo, ma, heard you broke up wit' ya man,*
> *Sorry to hear that boo.*
> *I'm lyin', ya know he cheated on you,*
> *Lie to you, his action wasn't shit to prove.*
> *Remember the day we met,*
> *Could never take my eyes off ya*
> *Kept my mind on ya,*
> *I desire you like the air in me*
> *I wanted you but you shoot da breeze.*
> *I guess it was the way ya walk,*
> *the way ya talk, the way ya move,*
> *made me just wanna groove with ya,*
> *do things with ya, get curious with ya,*
>
> *run it up all in ya.*

Don't mean to be rude,
I had to ask if it be cool
me an ya together and do a little sumthin,
ya know let a nigga ease ya pain,
let me sex ya up,
Unbutton that dress let ya body do the talkin',
I been wantin' to do some serious hittin'.
Do me that flavor, come ta my crib stay all day.
So we can cum out da clothes,
Touchin' skins doin' each other favors,
Sexin' up that bitty and play wit' ya titties,
Turn your frown to moanin',
Have ya smilin' bigger than the city,
Ya sittin' back, relaxin' and enjoyin' this,
Like that Big nigga from Brooklyn said,
'I'M FUCKING U TONIGHT,'"

I went in, singing confidently. The music was crispy clear in my headphones. It was easy for me to let my vocals ride the beat. I relaxed and belted.

Oooh, ya know it, and I love it…
The way you come up on me
Like a rude boy ready to expose it.
I just wanna rock wit' ya,
Feel ya close to my hips
Have ya ready to scratch this itch,
Baby can you feel it?
Oooh can you feel it, sure you can…
Cuz it's you and I…
Comin' together like the blue in sky,
cuz it's you and I tighter
Mike and the Jackson Five…
Let 'em talk about us,
cuz I don't care,

let 'em hate on us,
cuz we don't hear…

Like Whitney Houston's, my vocals traveled lively, almost shattering the microphone. I caught a glimpse of Mike One bobbing his head. Alimony was feeling the groove that we were creating. The collaboration was great. Alimony and I had a lot of chemistry performing in the booth. I never took my eyes off him during the time I was singing. He never looked away from me.

Our bodies drifted closer and I felt his heartbeat against mines as our bodies ride the track. Alimony wrapped his arms around me playfully and whispered, "Why you teasing?"

"Who said that I was teasing," I flirted back, feeling his hot breath against my ear.

Mike One wanted us to record again. Of course, I was down. I smiled when I saw Kendal fuming. His eyes were narrowed. Kendal had a keen eye on us like a parent on chaperone duties.

Alimony looked over at Kendal and smirked.

"Damn, it's hot in this booth. I gotta get more comfortable," he said.

Alimony pulled off his shirt, exposing tattoos and defined muscles rippling through his wife beater. Liking what I saw, I smiled flirtatiously. Alimony caught me in the moment. He moved closer, and I gently placed my hand against his six-pack. His chiseled stomach felt like rock hard waves. Alimony had a tight body and when he stood close to me. I felt his confidence and energy pass through me. I was definitely getting turned on. He smiled at me. I was aware of what he was doing. Honestly, I wanted him to keep doing more of it.

Mike One was ready to record again and Alimony went on to spit another verse. His second verse was more passionate than the first one. This time Alimony pulled me near and slid his hand down my backside, and felt on my booty. He turned and smirked at Kendal who was eyeing our every movement like a hawk. It happened too fast. All of a sudden the door to the booth flew open and Kendal rushed in.

"Get ya fuckin' hands off my woman!" he shouted.

Kendal pushed me away from Alimony, and the two men were toe-to-toe arguing.

"Nigga fuck you! You got more bitch in you than a fuckin' brothel!" Alimony shouted.

"Nigga, what…?"

"Kendal, stop it!" I screamed on top of my lungs.

"Nah, he ain't got no fuckin' right touching you like that. I ain't having that shit!"

"Nigga, you just mad cuz ya bitch wanna fuck me," Alimony spat.

Kendal didn't like the statement, and hit Alimony. After striking the rapper in his face, a fight ensued in the booth. Mike One was shouting at them to chill. Alimony was getting the best of Kendal and I felt embarrassed. Alimony's crew came rushing into the studio. It quickly became a madhouse. Mike One ran into the fray and tried to break up the scuffle. Kendal got in a good punch or two, but Alimony whipped his ass.

Embarrassed, I hurried out the booth and immediately left the studio. Kendal's bullshit had ruined my studio session with Alimony and Mike One. I just wanted to go home. Livid, I entered the elevator before security came running.

I rode it down alone to the lobby and walked out. I made it outside and the craziness made me want to pick up a cigarette. I tried to collect myself, looking around for the truck, but I didn't see it.

"I swear, this man is gonna get me locked up," I said to myself.

It was a warm spring night and I knew that if I went back into that studio, everyone was going to experience the bitch in me. So I stayed outside. I noticed a black Escalade with tinted windows coming to a stop. I wasn't familiar with the truck. It had been ten minutes since I had been standing outside.

The driver got out first. He was tall, husky, black and intimidating. He was dressed in all black and I knew an ex-con when I saw one. I already knew that the driver had to be security. The passenger stepped out next, and when I saw who it was, I almost went into shock. He was dressed like he was about to attend the Vibe awards, dapper down in ice and brand name clothing, from his blue Yankee fitted, to his designer jeans, dark shades and white uptowns. He spotted me and turned on a mischievous smile.

"Oh shit, look who we got here. Damn, it's been a long time," Omega said.

I remained quiet, instantly catching an attitude.

"What, no love from America? I thought we were mad cool," Omega continued.

"Why are you here?" I asked with attitude.

"Same as you, luv... On my platinum grind, but I see your career is taking off. I'm definitely hearing 'bout you a lot. But you know, ya ride wit' me and I can do things for you that you ain't never expected."

"I'm good."

"You sure...? Cuz my label is doing it. We be international in a few months. Any amount of money I invest in you will be recouped in no time," Omega smiled.

"You can't do anything for me that I haven't been doing myself," I fired back.

"You were always so fuckin' stubborn and naïve, America. Even when you had Soul around...Where your man at, or shall I say your baby daddy at now? He ain't here for you anymore, but ya doin' a'ight for yourself, but you know, soon, we gonna run into each other. I'm taking control of this industry, and I smell money when I see it. And with you, you reek of talent and success. And hopefully I can get a bite out of you sometime soon," Omega said.

"Go fuck yourself, Omega. I don't want any dealings with you now or never. I'd rather starve then deal with your devil ass," I barked.

"You know I woulda smack the shit out of a bitch fo' coming at me so disrespectful. But you boo, you get a free pass. Here's my card, holla sometime, America," he said, passing me his card. "You know, despite our differences, America, I always respected you. You're a feisty, bitter bitch, but I love that. You put feeling into your fuckin' music and it shows. Do me a favor and holla at Soul for me when you see that nigga."

Omega and his goon walked into the building and I quickly tossed his card to the curb. I thought that I was going to have a good night, but it went sour quickly. I needed time alone.

I'll take the subway I thought walking away. Kendal came running out the lobby, looking for me. I sighed. He came running behind me and tried stopping me.

"Baby, where you going?" he questioned, grabbing my arm.

"Home!" I exclaimed, jerking my arm free.

"America, look, I'm sorry, a'ight? I know I overreacted, but that nigga had no right putting his hands on you like that."

"And you needed to come in and play my hero, right. You embarrassed me! I'm so sick of you, Kendal," I said, walking away.

"America, be serious. We're in the city, miles away from home. How're you gonna get back, huh?"

"I'll find a way. I'm a grown woman, a fact that you keep failing to realize."

"America, I'm sorry, a'ight? I'm sorry. I'll change. I promise."

"I'm so tired of hearing that same record. I'm gone."

With a little more pep in my step, I kept it moving. Kendal stopped following me. He became very frustrated, kicked over a trashcan and walked back to the studio. I hailed a cab and jumped inside. I didn't want to go straight home, so I told the cabbie to take me to Brooklyn. I needed to see my friend, Joanna. I knew she would be happy to see me. I needed to talk and I needed a break. Kendal was fuckin' up and slowly pushing me away. He started out good for my career and personal life. He somewhat provided the cure I needed to get over Omar. Now he had changed into an overbearing asshole. Kendal was damaging my sanity and well-being. If I didn't walk away, I'd have strangled him my damn self.

6
Omega

Sounds of ecstasy traveled from a motel room in a remote town in New Jersey. The room reeked of sex. A woman, her face buried in the pillow, and her legs spread was getting some. Clothing was strewn all over the room, including a gun-belt, shield and a police radio. The radio squelched urgently, but Officer Judith Wagner paid it no mind. She was busy handling a stiff case of dick up her butt and this situation required more urgent attention.

"Ah… Ugh! Oh yes…!" Judy whimpered as Omega thrust his dick deep inside her protruding, sweaty asshole.

Officer Judith Wagner met with Omega on a regular for two reasons. Good dick was top on the list. The next was for her dosage of methamphetamine. She kept her addiction a secret from her family and co-workers. It helped her perform on the job she felt that she had her drug usage under control. She crushed the meth into a fine powder then sharply inhaled it with a rolled up banknote before getting into her nasty, sexual encounter with Omega. High off the drug, she instantly transformed to a freak. Omega relished her dual roles, his secret jump-off, and police informant.

Omega squeezed Judy's round ass cheeks and slapped her backside while he continued to fuck her. Both were butt-naked, twisting and turning on the white soiled bed sheets.

"Ugh, hell yeah I'm coming!" he grunted.

The rhythm of his strokes increased. Omega gripped Judy's sweaty thin hips. He felt the urgency of an explosion getting ready to happen. He thrust a few more times and like water rushing from a garden hose Judy's ass was hosed down. Squeezing her plump cheeks tightly, Omega bit down on her shoulder. The sudden sensation of coming drained him and he pulled out, falling flat on his back. Judy sat upright, took a deep breath, exhaled and took another hit of meth on the nightstand.

"You better take it easy wit' that shit," he warned.

"I'm good, baby," she smiled crookedly while taking another hit.

Judy's head rocked back slowly. Reeling in the high, she fell back into Omega's arm. Judy rested her head against Omega's chest and felt the soreness in her rectum from the constant friction. They were quiet for a moment and tried to collect themselves. For this hour and a half, Omega felt secured. Rocky was waiting in the truck for him outside.

Judy was tweaking a bit, but Omega was used to her addiction. Soon, they were getting dressed. Omega never stayed too long in one place and he had business to handle. It was late in the evening, and he had to link up with Biscuit.

Judy donned her NYPD shirt, with the sleeves now displaying sergeant stripes. She was slowly moving up in ranks and Omega loved having this sergeant on his payroll. Omega passed Judy a lumpy brown envelope, containing ten thousand dollars cash. Judy received the paper for providing valuable information to Biscuit and his crew. Judy put surveillance on the Jamaican born man. At the right time she made the call. Twenty-four hours later, Node's murder had made the evening news.

Fastening her gun belt, Judy said, "It's becoming more difficult out there. Omega, the murders have to stop. This war is out of control. I heard that they're setting up an anti gang task force in Brooklyn and southeast Queens. They're not playing, boo. I can only do so much to help you. They're starting to watch us cops closer."

"You just keep doin' what ya doin' and don't fuckin' worry 'bout me. I take care of you, right?"

"Yeah, you do, boo."

"A'ight you gettin' paid. Then just keep ya damn mouth shut, and do ya job!"

Snatching up her payment and the drugs, Judy hurried to to the exit. Before walking out, she looked back at Omega and asked, "How's your wife?"

"That's none of your damn business."

Still feeling like one of New York's finest, Judy smiled and left. Omega waited for a moment before he walked out the motel room. He peered out the window and watched Judy driving out the parking lot in a dark blue unmarked car. Collecting his things, Omega concealed his weapon, and walked out to the SUV. Rocky did what he was told and never questioned his boss. Omega got in, adjusted his weapon and sat back.

"Where to boss…?" Rocky asked.

"I need to meet up with, Biscuit. Let's go to Long Island. Drive slow."

Rocky nodded, started the car and slowly made the exit from the motel parking lot. The traffic was light and easy. Omega looked relax and Rocky merged onto the nearest interstate, heading to the Holland Tunnel.

Lollipop by Lil' Wayne blared from the elaborate, expensive sound system in Biscuit's sleek, black Benz. He whipped it east on the Long Island Expressway. Narmer was in the passenger seat, rapping along with Lil' Wayne's lyrics. They were on their way to Hicksville for a drug pickup from the Mexicans. It was that time of the month, and the Mexicans had a complex operation setup for their drug distribution.

Ever since Greasy's unfortunate demise nearly two years ago, Biscuit became the head honcho in charge. Narmer was by his side, they had built up trust with the Mexicans. Omega and Biscuit had a good relationship with the Mexican cartels and business was good. Both sides were making money hand-over-fist. But the war with the Jamaicans had the Mexicans concerned.

Biscuit whipped his Benz toward the exit. He navigated through the quiet streets and headed to the closed shopping mall not far from the highway.

It was the arrangement set up by the Mexicans. All the money for the drugs and the processing material was paid beforehand by Omega. A week later the product arrived in a standard U-Haul van — gift-wrapped and closely watched by Mexican thugs.

A U-Haul van was used because it was large enough to hold everything needed. It was common to see one in the streets, it brought on less suspicion from residents and cops. Biscuit remembered the address and followed the directions coming from his GPS. He slowly turned on the street. Narmer looked around for the location, and spotted the truck parked near a gas station. There were other U-haul vehicles parked there also. Biscuit stopped his ride and zeroed in on a few plate numbers until he recognized the one that match.

"Bingo. We on it fo' sure," Biscuit said.

Biscuit jumped out the Benz and walked over to the truck. The keys were already in the ignition. He looked in the back compartment and it contained everything they needed. Biscuit then looked around and noticed a dark Impala parked across the street with two passengers. They had to be Mexican muscles. He got in the U-Haul truck and saw a cellphone lying in the passenger seat. As soon as Biscuit picked up the cellphone it started to ring.

"Hello…"

The voice on the other end was low and demanding.

"When you drive off, make a right. Then turn another right on W. John Street, drive five lights down the road. You'll see that 7-Eleven on the left. Pull in there. We need to talk."

Biscuit was baffled, but did as instructed. A short while later he made it to the 7-Eleven. Narmer followed closely behind Biscuit in the Benz. Biscuit parked and abruptly a man jumped into the passenger's side. Biscuit clutched his 9mm, ready to shoot.

"Relax, there's no need for that," the man in the dark suit said.

Biscuit glared at him. He wasn't muscle and never gave his name. The man eyed Biscuit.

"Inform your employer that his feud with the Jamaicans is costly. Your organization is stirring up too much trouble with law enforcement and my employers are becoming considerably worried. My employer wants to arrange a meeting with your employer soon."

"I'll let him know," Biscuit said.

"Your employer needs to reach my employer at this number within forty-eight hours. It's to his well-being if he wants to continue with our business," the man said, passing a phone number to Biscuit.

Biscuit took the number and the man got out the van and walked away into the shadow.

"Fuckin' weirdo."

A half-hour later, the U-haul van pulled into the driveway of a Hempstead home. A block from the house there was a group of young thugs hanging-out. Some of them were lookouts for the stash-house. Biscuit drove the van into the garage and closed the gate. He exited the vehicle and met with a small group of men who were waiting to unload.

"We good?" one of the men asked.

Biscuit nodded. Opening the backdoor to the van, he revealed four hundred pounds of meth along with the reagents to produce the drug—large quantities of pseudoephedrine, anti freeze bottles, iodine crystals, and Coleman fuel. The men began offloading. They were prepared to work all night, processing the drug for street distribution.

Narmer walked up to Biscuit and asked, "Yo, what the fuck was that shit about back at the spot?"

"Business yo," Biscuit said.

The house was one of Omega's main stash and processing spots. He made sure that security was tight and low-key. Traffic was kept to a minimum. There were guns prevalent throughout the place.

It was eleven at night and the men were geared up, hard at work. On the streets a quarter of a gram went for twenty-five dollars and an eight-ball went for three hundred dollars. It was easy money for everyone. Biscuit supervised production and made sure that everything was handled correctly. His cellphone rang, it was Omega.

"What's good?" Biscuit answered.

"I'm parked outside, come holla at me," Omega said.

"A'ight."

"I'll be right back," Biscuit said to Narmer.

Biscuit walked outside to the parked Escalade. Glancing around, he strutted over to the vehicle. Rocky stepped out the truck, giving the men some privacy to talk. Biscuit got into the backseat and gave Omega dap.

"Everything's okay inside?" Omega asked.

"Yeah, the pickup went good. But there's was this one thing," Biscuit added.

"What's that?"

"It seems that the Mexicans are starting to worry about our war wit' the Jamaicans. They sayin' that if the war keeps going down fo' sure it be costly to us," Biscuit said.

"Fuck they care who I beef wit? They's gettin' their money on the regular. Fuck's wrong wit' Falco...?"

"They want ya to call 'em, gave me a number for you to reach them by," Biscuit said, passing the number to Omega.

"What ya gonna do?" Biscuit asked.

"Handle this," Omega answered, staring at the number.

Biscuit nodded and gave Omega dap. He exited the truck and walked by Rocky, who nodded. Biscuit acknowledge him, and kept walking into the house. Immediately he smelled the fumes from the chemical reactions.

"We good...?" Biscuit asked.

"Yeah, we good," Narmer answered.

"A'ight, give me a minute. I'm goin' upstairs to take care of sumthin," Biscuit said.

Biscuit went upstairs and closed the door to one of the bedrooms. Reaching into his jean pocket, he pulled out a small cellophane bag containing some meth. He spread the drug on a square table and snorted it through a rolled up banknote. Biscuit kept this habit a secret. He was satisfied with the high, but was most interested in trying a new drug common in West Africa, called brown-brown.

7
Omar vs Soul

Two days of freedom and I was feeling great. This time there was a breath of fresh air passing over me. Vincent and I became closer, and his wife was a good friend. I got my old job back at the youth center and had a decent talk with Mr. Jenkins. He was happy to see me and we spoke for an hour inside his office. Mr. Jenkins offered me the position of youth counselor like Vincent. He told me the youth could learn a lot from me. I didn't see myself as an inspiration to anybody— let alone a group of street kids who idolized my past life. I was reluctant, but Mr. Jenkins gave me a piece of advice.

"It doesn't get any easier. We can only become stronger, and our kids need to know that."

I understood what he was saying and it meant a lot. My first priority was to see my son. I wanted to hold him and kiss him. Finally I could see him without the restraints of a prison wall and the CO watching me. I would love him and be there like a good father.

America was a busy woman. She was living the good life in her new home in Long Island. Her new man must be doing for her what I never got the chance to do— take her out the hood and be a happy family. He had my woman, was raising my son, and living my dream. I couldn't dwell on the past, but look to the future. Becoming a better man for my son, Kahlil was my main responsibility.

On my third day of freedom, I joined Vincent in one of his counseling sessions with ten teens, boys and girls. Vincent was familiar with their faces, but I didn't know any of these teens. I was there to observe Vincent teaching the kids.

Rolling his wheelchair to the center of the classroom, Vincent took charge immediately. The teens were seated in a circle and he was there to help them find their way. I stood near the doorway and remained quiet. Some of the teens in the room had the attitude of wanting to be the next big-time dope dealer. Getting an education and learning a trade were not even options.

"Y'all know me right?" Vincent exclaimed, looking into the faces of every teen sitting in the room.

"Yeah…"

"What y'all know about me?" Vincent asked.

"That ya can't walk," one smartass kid joked.

Vincent whipped his chair into the direction of the comment, quickly confronting the young man.

"What you say?" Vincent asked.

"Man, I ain't say nothing," the teen answered.

He was slouched in his chair, his pants sagging off his ass. He wore a NY Yankee fitted and sported a thick, gold chain around his neck.

"You find my condition funny, huh?"

"Nah, I don't find shit funny."

"I hope not. You laugh now and cry later. What's your name? You're new in this group?" Vincent asked.

"They call me Grudge," the teen reluctantly said.

Vincent moved closer to Grudge and said, "This could be your future if you wanna keep messing around in the damn streets. You ain't immune to the consequences. Y'all have a choice. Make it the right one. I survived the game and I'm a changed man now. I have a family that loves me and a son that knows me. Some of you in this room, y'all might not have that second chance. Some of you if y'all wanna continue to gangbang and sling your drugs, you'll find yourself locked up or dead."

Vincent glanced around the room, studying the faces of the teens. My throat went dry when he stated his son knows him. Having been incarcerated for the past two years, my seed had no idea of who I was.

"I know y'all done already heard about what happened to that rapper, North Star. How many in this room knew him personally?"

Two boys raised their hands. One said, "He was my dude, yo. I was down the block when that shit went down. Fuck them niggas... Word, shit ain't had to go down like that."

"It did. I know how it feels to lose a friend to that kind of violence," Vincent said, reaching out to the teen. "But that's the harsh reality. You're all dying out there in great numbers, casualties of war. It's not the war you think, killing each other over drugs, gangs and nonsense. Nah, the war I'm talking about, is the one you don't know exist. The war y'all chose to ignore, and y'all are on the front line. Lack of education in the poor neighborhoods, drug addiction, poor medical services, unemployment, STD's, incarceration, ignorance, these are the things killing our young men and women. I constantly ask myself, when we gonna wake up and do better for ourselves...?"

There was laughter, but Vincent didn't budge from bringing his message to them.

"I look around and you know what I see...? I see that by you all just sitting here in this room with me, says that y'all do want something better for y'all selves. Because for most of you, being in this classroom is a choice that you chose to make, and that right there is already a step in the right direction," he continued.

The group discussion went on for about forty-five minutes and then everyone was dismissed. I could see that they were a hard group to reach. After the last teen exited the classroom, Vincent looked at me and asked, "You think you can handle it?"

"You did good but me...? I don't know if I got the patience you have. These young-ass-wannabes probably make me wanna revert to my old self. You know...? Show 'em what a gangsta is really about."

"Some are just playing tough. They're just being influenced by the wrong source. When I started out a year ago, I didn't know what to do or say to these kids. I was lost. Knowing how I messed up, and the shit I done seen, it just clicked— it will come to you, Soul."

We left the classroom, and I stayed around for a few hours at the center, trying to get the feel of things again. It was busier than ever. There were staff and kids of all ages in the Community Center. About quarter to ten, the place started to empty. I stayed around waiting while Vincent conducted a meeting with his staff in a small conference room. I was standing near the gym area where the sound of a bouncing basketball caught my attention.

Inside the gym was a teen shooting hoops. From the doorway, I could clearly see him. He was about seventeen with a wicked jump-shot and nice ball handling skills. Shirtless, his chest, arms and back was tattooed, some gang affiliated. I watched him for a couple minutes. He saw me looking, grounded the ball, and threw up his arms.

"What the fuck you lookin' at, man?"

"I was just watching you shoot. You got skills."

"Yeah, a'ight... You a scout?"

"Nah... I—"

"Then what the fuck you care?"

I chuckled at his brash bullshit.

"And what the fuck is so funny?"

"You man."

"What nigga?" he asked, coming closer.

"How old are you man?" I asked, not intimidated.

"Fuck you all in my business for...? You da police or something, nigga?"

"Nah, I just came home. I don't care 'bout your business."

He sucked his teeth and wasn't trying to hear me out.

"Fuck you, nigga! It's safer for you to go out that way," he said, pointing to the gym exit. "You don't know who ya dealin' wit'."

The look on his face, told me that he was for real. He wasn't one of the wannabes gang bangers Vincent spoke of earlier. His athletic frame and height, six-one, along with a few war scars showing across his skin screamed hooligan. The dark teardrop under his right eye indicated that he either caught a body or did some devious shit in the streets.

"I don't want any beef wit' you man. I was just talking."

"I know there ain't gonna be no beef!"

For a moment we locked eyes, and I saw a younger version of myself glaring back at me. The same angry, fearless and really hood swagger were there. I didn't know the man, and it was obvious that he didn't want to know me.

Vincent came rolling in as I was about to exit. His meeting was finished and the staff was leaving. He glanced at the teen I just had the harsh exchange with and said, "Narmer, you know the gym is closed. What you doing here?"

"I'm just waiting for my girl, Vincent," he nonchalantly answered.

"She's on her way out. But you know the rules, you can't be in here unless there's supervision," Vincent said.

"Yeah, I know man... C'mon, why ya keep riding me for? Shit, I was just shooting around."

"Don't let it happen again," Vincent warned.

Narmer kicked the basketball and stormed out of the gym. He sneered at us before he left.

"There goes your valedictorian right there," I joked.

Vincent and I both laughed as we continued to stare at the angry young man.

"He's sticking around here because of his girl. She's a good girl who volunteers a lot, but him... He runs with Omega's crew. He ain't a wannabe and ain't afraid. I know he's putting in work on the streets."

"I see that."

When Vincent and I left the gym we spotted Narmer with his girlfriend. She was a beautiful, pregnant young woman. Narmer smirked, placed his arm around his woman, and strutted out the center.

"Damn young'n," I joked.

It was a busy Thursday evening, Vincent and I arrived at North Star's funeral. The Greater Allen A.M.E cathedral on Merrick Blvd was transformed into a madhouse. Nearly five thousand people came to show their respect. There was a heavy police presence outside with plenty patrol cars in the area. Fear of further gang conflict sparked the police into shutting down the area. There was gridlock alert because of the cars and crowd. We had to park several blocks away and navigate our way through hordes of people milling on the sidewalks. Dressed in a pair of black slacks and gray shirt, I strolled behind Vincent. He was in something similar, but had on a charcoal shirt with his black wingtips.

There were familiar faces, some were surprised I was home again. After greeting several peeps, I guided Vincent to the massive building where Floyd Flake did his ministering. I remembered the many run-ins I had with Reverend Flake back when I was a full-fledged-hustler. He was trying to keep the peace in the streets, organizing events for trouble kids.

North Star was well known and well liked. I heard him on a few mix tapes. He was in the unsigned hype section of the Source and a few months ago there was an article about the up and coming rapper in Vibe magazine. It was a tragedy his life was short-circuited.

With so many folks standing around, the foot traffic was a nightmare. Guiding Vincent's wheelchair through the crowd turned into a headache. It took us a moment to get through the doorway, but finally we made it inside the building. There was a massive sea of people. A lot of young teens clad in black T-shirts with a picture of North Star posed throwing up gang signs.

His life was celebrated with pictures, stories and I even overheard some kids talking about how they retaliated for their homie. Shaking my head, I kept it moving. When we stepped into the cathedral, the pianist was playing *Amazing Grace*, but you could still hear the loud cries, shouts and screams of his loved ones and grieving family up front.

My heart fell. He died violently like my young cousin, Greasy. I couldn't attend Greasy's funeral because of my incarceration. In an awkward way it was good to be out in time so I could represent the new me at North Star's funeral.

I slowly pushed Vincent near the casket, which was a silver exterior casket with white crepe interior. Flowers, cards and photos of North Star were everywhere. It looked like a garden near his casket. North Star was resting in peace in a pinstripe two button suit with a white shirt and blue tie. The funeral home did a nice job with the body.

I stood there with Vincent, and I stared at him and felt this great sadness enveloped me. It was as if I'd fallen into a dark pit. I heard that it was the fourth funeral in five weeks. The violence was getting bad and people were dying, innocent people were being affected. The war Omega was fighting with the Jamaicans had to end.

"This ain't right man. He ain't supposed to be dead," I said, shaking my head.

"I know how you feel, Soul," Vincent said.

How many before we finally wake up and realize we're fucking up? I thought looking at the body. My stomach started churning and my body felt faint. I used to be a heavy part of this violent equation. Now my spirit was renewed. I had faith in a higher being.

I glanced at his family and saw his mother. Mama Jones is what some of us used to call her. Dressed in all black, her eyes were red with tears and her face saturated with grief. To her left were her two daughters, Monica and Janet. Monica was still beautiful with her smooth, caramel complexion and soft black hair. Monica's eyes were tearing, but she was clutching her mother, trying to console her.

A heavy sigh escaped me as I walked over to where they were and offered my condolences. Vincent and I needed to say something. Monica saw me coming and just stared at me. She knew who I used to be. It had been years since we had seen each other.

My face was saddened, but I still tried to find courage. I said, "Mama Jones, I'm so sorry for your loss. Jerome was like a brother to me."

Vincent reached out and held her hand, giving his respects. Mama Jones barely managed a smile. She took my hand, held it tightly and said to me, "Omar, thank you. Jerome always talked about you. Even when you were doing wrong, I knew one day you'd change."

It was a surprise. She still remembered my name. I was eight and used to escape to her house when things were going badly. Vincent said a few words to her and I looked at Monica. We locked eyes and she stood up and hugged me tightly.

"They took him from us, Soul. They took my baby brother from me," Monica cried, clutching me.

While in her vice-like grip, her tears fell on my shoulder. Embracing her gently, I said, "You gonna be okay, Monica. I'm here now. I'm here for y'all. Anything you need, just come to me, a'ight?"

She didn't respond, but continued to hug me tightly. A moment later, she released me, dried her tears, and said, "Thank you. I'm glad you came, Soul."

"I'm here now," I repeated.

Vincent and I moved to the back of the church. It was standing room only and as the piano played, the crowd hummed the lyrics to *Amazing Grace*.

Amazing Grace how sweet the sound, that saved a wretch like me…

The service continued. I wanted to leave, but something propelled me to stay. The home-going service was heartbreaking. Several times it was interrupted by loud, painful cries of love ones. I read his obituary written on a pamphlet I was given. The home-going poem in the back, titled *Home*.

Home is the place your heart resides.
Home is the place that you decide.
Home is the womb that holds the soul.
Home is the place where one is whole.
Home is the glow you hold in your eye.
Home is the emotion that makes you cry.
Home is safe and a place of peace.
Home is where all striving cease.
Home is all these wonderful things.
Home is the place you develop wings.
Home is the place that you'll find one day.
Home is the place where your heart will stay.

Beautifully written by Aisha Patterson, the poem drove my mind right back to the place I grew up. Looking around the church, I noticed that every eye was teary as North Star's five year old daughter read a poem for her slain dad. I had to dry a few of my own tears. My heart sank even further, thinking about my own son. I couldn't take the sadness.

"Yo Vincent, I'm a be outside for a moment."

He nodded, and I hurried out the church. Thanking God for my chance at life, I took a breath of air. Funerals were always hard for me. Outside on the steps and in the streets there were just as many folks in the church. I stood around and chilled for a moment. Then I saw Narmer standing with his girlfriend. Smoking a cigarette, he was wearing a black T-Shirt with North Star's picture front and center on it. Narmer looked at me and continued focusing on his expecting girlfriend and the cigarette.

The crowd on the steps was overwhelming. I walked to the corner and stood there for a moment. I started talking to a few people who were glad to see me home. While kicking it to an old friend, I turned to my right and I thought my eyes were playing tricks. I was astounded. It had to be fate. My gaze held onto her like a kid looking at porno for the first time. It was America strutting toward the building and she was with a female friend.

I had not seen or heard from her in months. In tight black jeans, accentuating her curvy hips, a sand linen tie jacket, sporting a pair of long black heels and dark shades, America was more beautiful than ever.

"Yo, I'll be right back," I said to my friend.

I quickly walked to where America was. She didn't even know I was home. My arrival had been on the hush-hush. I was glad to finally see her. Walking up behind her, I called out her name.

"America…"

She turned slowly, probably thinking that I was a fan getting ready to ask her for an autograph. She stopped near the foot of the church stairs and glanced at me. When she realized it was me, a sudden look of surprise covered her face. Removing her shades, America had a quizzical look.

"Omar…?"

I smiled, nodding.

"Ohmygod! When did you get home?" she asked excitedly.

Throwing her arms around me, she hugged me tightly. It was good to be in her warmth again. In her warm embrace I sighed regretting the choices I had made. The divorce was eating me up on the inside.

"I got out Monday morning."

"You never contacted me…?"

"I wanted to, but I heard you moved from Queens and was now enjoying the finer things in life. I'm glad to see you doing your thang, America."

"It doesn't matter you could get word to me."

"Things are going great for you, huh?"

"I'm trying."

"You're doing more than trying. You're doing it… Blowing up, I heard."

Her smile came natural and easy. America was so beautiful. She opened her mouth, but nothing came.

"It's good to see you again," I smiled.

"You look great, Omar."

"Jail makes you stay fit. Either reading or working out. I was doing a lot of both," I smiled. "But how's my son?"

"He's fine. He's at my aunt in Brooklyn. I been so busy, she's been helping me a lot with him," she explained.

"I would like to see him soon, America."

"Yeah, you gotta see him soon as possible," America smiled.

"I miss him."

I wanted to scream, letting her know how much I missed her. Instead, I kept my composure. America had been my woman for twelve years. She was my heart, now she had someone new in her life and I didn't know how to react. I was jealous of her new relationship, but swallowed my pride and kept it cool.

America and I locked eyes. An uncomfortable silence crowded us for a moment. Then she asked, "Did you go inside yet?"

"Yeah, but I had to leave… Needed some air."

My mind was whirling in her splendor. I hated to meet her like we were just friends. I wanted more. Her lips were moving, but I was trying to read her heart.

"North Star… Damn! I liked him and wanted to work with him in the studio. What is going on out here, Omar? What's happening?"

"Shit is bad out here..."

"It's your friend, Omega. He's doing this to our neighborhood. Ever since he brought in meth and got these young kids working for him, it became twisted and ugly out here in these streets. That's why I couldn't live here anymore. I needed to leave, too many sad memories."

"I feel you. You know I'm back at the youth center. I might get a job there as a counselor," I said, changing the subject.

"Really, Omar...? I'm so happy for you. Congratulations," she said, hugging me tightly.

My body relaxed with her touch, I yearned for her. America had to feel what my heart was saying because it was pumping loud enough.

"Yeah, I'm taking it one day at a time."

"You need too. But where are you staying?"

"Oh, I'm at Vincent's and his wife."

"It's so good to see you again. Kahlil will be so excited seeing his daddy on the regular."

"You think he's gonna remember me?"

"You're his father. Why not? You haven't been out of his life for that long."

"But it's been long enough, America."

"You'll be okay, Soul. Here's my number to reach me, and I'll text you the address to my aunt. Just let her know that you're home and you want to see your son."

America passed me her cellphone number. The sound of her voice came off as casual to me. There was no hint that she missed me. I wanted to ask her if there was a chance for us getting back together, but changed my mind.

"Let me go inside and show my respect to the family. We'll talk Omar. I wish you would have told me that you were getting out."

"I didn't want it to be a big deal."

"It is to me," she smiled.

America hugged me again. Then she walked away with her friend. I stood there, thinking about our past and aching for a future with her. Hating that she was with Kendal, he came off the sidelines and took what I once had. I still loved America. I sighed and knew I couldn't hang around any longer.

America's Soul

My heart was in pain after being at a close friend's funeral and seeing my ex. I stood outside for five minutes then I went back inside the church, looking for Vincent.

Fifteen minutes later, we walked out. I didn't want to attend the burial, I just wanted to leave this hectic scene and get my head right. I told Vincent about America. He asked if I was alright. I explained that I was. I didn't tell him I wanted to drink my sorrows away.

8
Omega

Sitting in the passenger seat of the Escalade with a deadpan stare, Omega stared at the hordes of folks gathered outside the church. Rocky sat behind the wheel. Biscuit was in the backseat toying with a .9mm. The three men were parked a block down from the church. Knowing that the Jamaicans had a rep for the spontaneity of their violence, Omega had his soldiers spread throughout the area. Node's gruesome death had been broadcasted on every news channel and Omega knew that the inevitable was soon to happen—the Jamaicans wanted revenge. Omega wanted North Star to have a peaceful funeral. The rapper had been one of the best on the label. The NYPD made their presence discreetly known, Omega's crew was doing the same.

"You not goin' in boss?" Rocky asked.

"Nah…"

Omega's abject response was a telling story. He had sent the family flowers and fifty thousand dollars through a messenger. It was his way of showing respect. He couldn't risk attending the funeral. There were too many eyes, too many people, too many police. Omega wanted to remain inconspicuous. He couldn't afford an incident. There were enemies and some of them were ruthless enough to shoot him in plain view.

Observing from the safety of his truck, Omega kept his security close, including one of his most skilled killers, Biscuit.

The trio sat parked near the church. It was quiet inside, each man entertained by his own thought. Omega looked around and someone quickly caught his attention. He rose up in his seat and zeroed in on the person. He smiled.

"Oh shit, that nigga Soul's home," Omega said.

"Who boss?" Rocky asked.

Omega continued watching Soul conversing with an old friend from around the way.

"Da nigga looks good," Omega said.

He watched Soul's every move for a moment and wished that it was a different outcome with his former best friend. Omega still wished that it was Soul by his side running the streets and his business. Omega had gotten word from the inside that Soul had changed. It was official. The once best friends were going down two separate paths. They had two different objectives. One was righteous and the other was corrupt.

"Ain't that ya boy, Mega?" Biscuit asked, staring at Soul.

"Yeah…"

"Bitch-ass home now, huh," Biscuit joked.

Omega ignored the rude statement. He sighed, looked over at Rocky and said, "Get me the fuck outta here."

Rocky nodded and started the ignition. He then turned off onto the street and trio departed. Omega sat quietly in the seat and thought about his meeting with Falco later.

That same evening, Omega was on his way to meet with Falco at a confidential location. Omega was with Rocky and loathed the meeting he was forced to attend. It was business and it wasn't going to be about anything nice.

Rocky pushed the Escalade down the Southern State Parkway where they were only a few miles from their destination. Omega rode silently. The traffic was light and the ride felt tense. Omega didn't fear the Mexicans, but was always cautious when it came to a meeting with his drug connect.

"They think I'm gonna snitch or sumthin?" Omega asked aloud.

"Say what, boss?" Rocky asked, looking over at him.

"Just drive, nigga," Omega hissed.

Rocky shrugged and continued focusing on traffic. Soon they got off the Freeport exit and approached the destination a short while later. The Escalade rolled to a stop on a dead end street in an industrial vicinity of Freeport. The warehouses and auto-body shops were closed for the evening and foot traffic was non-existent. It was the perfect place to meet. Rocky was armed with a .50 Cal handgun. There was a very good chance that Falco only wanted to talk.

A pair of bright headlights slowly approached them from behind. The burgundy Yukon parked behind Omega and Rocky. Headlights were quickly turned off. Omega remained alert, his eyes in the mirror. The passenger in the Yukon stepped out under the rapidly graying dark sky which meant rain soon. Quickly, he approached the truck, and walked up to Omega's side.

"You ride with us."

"Where's Falco?" Omega asked.

"He meet, but you ride. Him stay," the man said, gesturing at Rocky.

It was clear that the six-three man in the white and black tracksuit was muscle and the messenger. He looked like he had the I.Q of an ox, but the muscles of a bull. Omega did not want to leave without Rocky, but it was the only way.

Omega stepped out the truck and was quickly patted down by the messenger. Then he escorted Omega to the Yukon.

"I stay with ya bodyguard, you ride with him to location," the passenger said.

The Yukon started and the driver drove off, leaving one from each party behind for security reasons. Omega sat silently while being driven to the unknown location. The ride was a few miles east and twenty minutes later the truck pulled into the parking lot of a Spanish restaurant in Massapequa. The parking lot was empty but the place looked opened. Omega and the driver jumped out and headed to the entrance. Omega walked with a confident stride, keeping his head up and facial expression unreadable. There was no fear as he followed behind the driver into the restaurant.

Inside the restaurant was like the parking lot, empty with only two of Falco's henchmen standing near in dark suits. The walls were lined with refined glass and the décor was simple with round tabletops and metal window back chairs. There was a thirty-two inch flat screen mounted on the wall for the patrons viewing and it was playing Kemistry's video. The floors were lined with basalt tiles. Above was an acoustic ceiling and dimmed lighting made it easy on the eyes. Omega saw Falco seated in the back of the restaurant near the kitchen entrance. Clad in a posh pinstripe gray business suit, he was dining alone.

Falco didn't look up from his meal when one of his men frisked Omega a second time. He was cleared, and the goon looked over at Falco for further instructions. The man was used to being called on for making the final decision. He dabbed at his mouth with the tablecloth and gestured for them to allow Omega through.

Omega walked over to Falco seated behind the table with a large plate of Spanish rice, chicken and red beans in front of him. Shaven head, thick goatee, and medium built, Falco's appearance hadn't changed much. The two locked eyes and Falco tried to ease the mood.

"Nice video, Mr. Omega, music is good… Have a seat please," he said, gesturing.

Omega nodded and took a seat opposite Falco. He waited for the man in charge to begin.

"It's been a long while since we met face to face."

"Yeah, it's been a minute," Omega said.

"Would you care for something to eat, drink?" Falco asked.

"Nah, I'm good," Omega said, waving him off.

Falco patiently took a few more bites from his plate then went back to discussing business with his connect.

"Business is good, huh?" Falco asked.

"C'mon Falco, you know business is good, let's cut the bullshit. We haven't met direct in two years, but now you wanna send for me. What's the true reason for this meeting?"

Falco stopped dining on his meal, sat back in his chair, crossed his legs and paid full attention on Omega.

"Always up front, never patient, your ways worry me sometimes, Omega… But you bring me good business, I agree. You're smart and loyal. I like that. My concern is this war you have with the Jamaicans. It's attracting too much unwanted attention, and too much attention is never good, my friend."

"What you want me to do, Falco? I got enemies in the streets. They fuckin' want me and my men in a box. I'm a do what I gotta do. These Jamaicans ain't no regular street crew. They come at me and I'm a come at them even uglier. This is the game, Falco. Maybe you been on your high horse too long and forgot how it is on the streets."

"Don't tell me about war, my friend... I've been in the ditches since youth. I first killed a man at the age of thirteen and seen more bloodshed than your kind can imagine."

"My kind...?" Omega asked, in a disgruntled tone.

"Don't get sloppy, Omega... Sloppiness comes with too much risk," Falco warned.

"If I ever go down, I go down alone, Falco. You have my word on that. I'm no fuckin' snitch, so don't worry about my business in the streets. I always come correct. And I always do right by y'all. But I'm a finish what I started. You don't need to worry 'bout me."

"I heard that your heart is more into this music business than our business here," Falco said.

"My business is my business... My heart and my mind is still the same. I'm still that nigga in charge. I'm that muthafucka not to fuck wit' on the streets."

"Still, sometimes I worry about a man that ventures out too much... Music is your passion, I understand. But I still like to have insurance, right. It's the American way."

"What you gettin' at?"

"When was the last times you had your hands dirty?"

"I got soldiers for that."

"Soldiers huh? Lots of men by your side... That's nice. When they see a man about to weaken, the men by your side become wolves."

Omega looked at Falco in bewilderment. He didn't understand where Falco was heading. Falco picked up on his confusion.

"You don't understand, huh?"

"I don't follow puzzles."

"I been a kingpin in my country for a long time, my friend. I been tested, challenged, and tried by many men… The hearts of men can become a very dangerous thing, my friend. And soldiers are good, but soldiers are men too. Men who are waiting for opportunity and often that opportunity mean your life. Sometimes you need to demonstrate your power and remind them why they should fear you first."

Omega sat there listening, wondering what Falco was getting at. Falco leaned forward in his chair, locked eyes with Omega, and continued.

"You were a wolf, Omega. When your opportunity came, you devoured it… Sin vacílacion. You think I don't know you set up your former boss, Tyriq, to get in bed with the Jamaicans?"

Omega was surprised by Falco's revelation about his past. It was five years since the execution. Omega sat there stone faced.

"Like you said, Falco, opportunity came knocking," Omega mocked.

"And when does your opportunity stop?" Falco asked.

"When I'm dead… Put a bullet on that!"

"I see you're a man with ambition. But me, I'm a man of prudence…I'm siempre atento," Falco said.

"It is good to be careful," said Omega.

Falco nodded. He took a sip from his cup of hot coffee, savoring the taste. Then he stood up, fondled the lapels of his suit and said to Omega, "Come, walk with me. I have something to show you."

Omega looked hesitant to follow Falco, but he knew that he wasn't in the position to argue with the man. Sighing, he got up and followed behind Falco. He led Omega through the empty kitchen and down a narrow, badly lit hallway. They came to a silver steel security door that was armed with an alarm. Falco punched in the code and with a hiss the door was unlocked. Omega stood behind the man and studied his surroundings. It didn't look good for him, but with his chin up, he scowled, and followed behind Falco down the concrete stairs.

When Omega came to the end of the stairs, he found himself in a large barren concrete room with a chilly feel. There were no fixtures or manufactured goods about, but another odd door ahead. Omega suddenly noticed two other men in the basement room that were suited with a menacing stare and that he was also standing on sprawling plastic.

"Don't worry, mi friend, you in good hands," Falco said.

Falco then gestured for one of his goons to open the door at the end of the room. The thug unlocked the door which led into the refrigeration room and disappeared inside. Omega could feel the cold air from where he stood. He waited with anticipation, curious to see what this was leading to.

Moments later the goon emerged from the room and forced the unknown man into the room. The man was blindfolded, bonded at his wrists, and only wore his underwear. He shivered uncontrollably. He was an aging and shapeless white man, in his early sixties with salt and pepper hair and a gut. He stood frantically lost in his fears. The goon kicked the man in the back, and he fell to his knees.

"Why are you doing this to me? Please, I've done nothing to anyone," the man pleaded.

Falco chuckled. He walked up to the man on his knees and removed the blindfold. The captive stranger looked around wild-eyed. Falco looked at Omega and said, "He's not in such good hands."

Omega stood quietly and knew that an execution was about to take place. Falco struck the man with such a strong blow it toppled the man to his side. He was left whimpering.

"Oh God...please, let me go," the man cried out, his tears streaming down his cold, beaten face.

"Shut up!" Falco shouted.

Falco nodded. A goon reached into his jacket and removed his holstered Glock 17. He handed it to Falco. Falco gripped the gun then handed it to Omega.

"The honor goes to you my friend."

"What?" Omega asked in bewilderment.

"I need insurance, Omega. Remember it's the American way. I kill a man on a regular, whether they deserve it or not, so I won't forget where I come from. I let the wolves know, I'm still in charge. But this one here, my friend," Falco said, pointing down at the shivering man on the cold concrete floor. "He betrayed us. He takes our bribe, our money, but don't deliver what we ask for. He takes from us, and feels because he is a federal judge he's untouchable. I take my business seriously."

"I have a family, children… Grandchildren for God sakes," the man exclaimed, as he remained upright on his knees.

"And they will miss you," Falco uttered.

Omega gripped the gun, but was reluctant. He eyed Falco with intensity and asked, "You tryin' to set me up?"

"You kill him. Our business continues. You don't, well you're a long way from home."

Omega looked around and then stared down at the beaten man. One of Falco's goons displayed a small camcorder and focused it on Omega and the victim. Omega smiled, knowing the situation.

"Y'all some muthafuckas fo' real," he said.

"We wait," Falco said.

Omega had killed men before, but was aware of the dire situation Falco was putting him in. This would be Falco's private insurance in case the feds swarmed down on his crew. They had Omega on film executing a federal judge.

Omega walked up to the judge, looked the man in the eyes and raised the gun to his forehead. The judge continued to whimper, he even peed in his boxer shorts. His eyes widened with terror. Omega cocked back the Glock and aimed. The prominent judge raised his tied hands in self-defense.

"Please! Oh God no don't do it! No! I have…"

Bam!

The single explosion echoed through the room. Sprawled out in death, Omega looked down at the judge and over at Falco with a wicked smirk and asked, "You satisfied?"

"Pretty much my friend… Now our business continues," Falco said.

The second thug walked up to Omega wearing latex gloves and removed the gun from his hands knowing it had his prints on it. Omega left the basement, knowing he was now deeply embedded into the Mexican's cartel.

A black Denali traveled down the backstreets of Queens. Inside three Jamaican men and one terrified young hostage. King sat in the back of the truck clutching a sharp machete to the throat of one of Biscuit's workers. King gripped the young hustler, pressing the tip of the machete deeper into his neck, drawing blood and demanding the whereabouts of his boss. The only info the young teen could give King was the location of a meth lab.

King's eyes swelled in anger over his brother's violent death. The look of pure hell was in his eyes, malice pumped in his heart.

"Bomba-claat dem batty boys, bredren… Mi gwan kill dem all, yuh ear, breden…ras-claat, mon….disrespect mi family…disrespect mi bloot-claat family," King shouted.

The machete pressed into the neck of the teen causing him to cringe and gasp in fear.

"Wi feel yuh, bredren… Him an' di youth, dem dead, mon," the passenger said, his intentions deadly like a cobra.

The truck raced to the disclosed location that the teen gave up. The men were high and crazy. King wanted total bloodshed and the heads of Omega and Biscuit. King shook rapidly like a rabid beast, drooling and losing his sense of rationality for a moment. He was high from snorting powdered cocaine, cut with gun powder. Brown-brown was a popular drug in West Africa, given to child soldiers in West African armed conflicts prior to battle. The drug became very popular with King and his men. It caused them to commit extreme acts of horrific violence, even in public.

King and his men stopped near one of Omega's lucrative meth labs. It was located on a quiet residential street. The meth house appeared to be like any other home on the block.

"Bredren, wi gwan fuck dem up reel good…" the driver intervened.

"Get out!!" King ordered.

He pushed the hostage out the truck, and eyed the hidden lab with an evil agenda in mind.

"How many inside…?" King asked.

"I don't know man," the teen said.

The other two men exited the truck and flanked King. They were heavily armed and ready to kill on King's order. King quickly crouched over the cowardly, frightened man, restraining him by pressing the machete deep into neck. Then he slowly cut his victim throat open, and left him bleeding on the sidewalk. King's goons went into action.

All three men lit, and threw Molotov cocktails through the windows of the meth lab. They ran off and watched the explosion from a short distance. Screaming and panicking were heard. Standing close to the front entrance of the home, King waited with a smile on his face. The front door abruptly flew open and one of the men came running out, trying to escape the spreading blaze. He was quickly gunned down by automatic fire from the weapon in King's hand. Two more men tried to escape the fire and quickly met the same fate.

The house exploded into an enveloping inferno. High intense flames could be seen for miles. By the time the fire department and police arrived, five men would be killed. Wafting through the neighborhood was the smell of burning flesh. The lingering scent was an ugly reminder to the community that the war wasn't over. The Jamaicans left a deadly mess for Omega and his crew to see.

9
America

I sat in the comfort of Joanna's three bedroom apartment in Canarsie Brooklyn nursing a cold beer. It was early evening and we were engaged in girl talk. Like always, Joanna was trying to be all up in my business. Especially now that she knew Omar was out. She was talking, but I was daydreaming. Taken aback by his presence earlier at the funeral, I caught Joanna reading my look. Knowing me for so many years, she quickly picked up on it.

"You're still in love with him, right?" she asked.

"I don't know what I feel right now. Why'd you ask that?"

"Cuz, I see the shit in your eyes, bitch," Joanna joked.

"I was just thinking about something else. Why it's gotta be about him?"

"Um, I could tell that you been thinking of Omar. I bet he got that coochie wet again," she joked.

"Joanna, let me tell you, it was good seeing him again. That's all."

"I bet it was. It's been what, months since you visited him. I know you missed him."

"Things changed between me and Omar."

"Changed? Not that much..." Joanna laughed before continuing. "You think he got that thug shit out of his system?"

"I don't know, but I really don't care. It doesn't matter. I'm involved now, Joanna. I have Kendal in my life. And we came a long way. I just can't throw away everything we worked so hard for."

"Yeah, you and Kendal came a long way, but not long enough."

"What are you implying?"

"America, all I'm sayin' is that I know you're living this fairytale lifestyle right now. You're living your dreams, pursuing your music career, having the nice big house in the suburbs and a nice car. There's a difference between being happy and trying to fabricate it. I see you with Kendal, and I've known you for a long time, America... I know what makes you happy. Better yet, I know who makes you happy."

"You think huh. Omar fucked up, not me. Kendal has been there for me since day one."

"And Omar hasn't...?"

"Joanna, why are you Omar's cheerleader all of a sudden? Sometimes you guys barely talk. Now you're telling me to dump the man I'm with for someone who's broken my heart so many times."

"No, I'm not saying that. All I'm saying America, is be real with yourself, don't force anything that you know will never fit. C'mon girl, we talk all the time. You think I don't know about the problems that you're having with Kendal. The one thing I give Omar is that he wasn't such an insecure asshole."

"Joanna, why are you tripping now, girl?"

"I don't like it, that your man is treating you like you're some type of property. He needs to give you some damn space."

"Damn girl, shit!"

She was my best friend and cared very deeply about me. Joanna had my back since the old school days. We came up through some hard times and happy times. She was my son's Godmother and I was her daughters' Godmother. Joanna was raising her one year old daughter, Genesis. Thinking she was on her way to being Mrs. Huxtable, but like a bad habit her man started acting up.

Joanna once thought that she was engaged to Michael Mathews. He was Mr. Right who came with a prominent future in medicine. She substituted the thugs she once dated for an educated man. Joanna found out the hard way that sometimes men in shiny wingtips and nice suits are just the same as niggas in Timberlands and jeans. Michael was from a well-to-do family and had a lot, but he was also a playboy with a temper. Joanna ended up with a broken heart. Now she was earnestly looking out for me.

"All I'm saying to you, America, is sometimes it's best to stick with the ones that we already know."

"I feel you."

I took a sip from my wine glass as we continued to talk and tried to get my mind off Omar. Joanna was right, I still had strong feelings for Omar and his absence made my heart yearn for him. I couldn't just jump back into Omar's arms like all was forgotten. Omar and I had history.

Eight that night, I left Joanna's place and drove to Bensonhurst, Brooklyn to see my son and my aunt. I missed my little man, and needed to hug and be close with him. With his father being home, things were about to be different.

Driving on the Belt Parkway, I was a few exits from my Aunt's home. Traffic was light. I exhaled, my past with Omar played in heavy rotation on my mind. There were some good times, but those good times were always at a high cost. I was a few miles from Aunt Gene's home when my cellphone rang. Glancing at the caller I.D, I saw that it was Kendal. He wanted to know my whereabouts. I was supposed to be at a studio session recording new tracks. Tonight I wasn't in the mood for studio work. His call rang through to my voicemail. I didn't want to talk to Kendal. I just wanted to be with my son and have a good night.

I arrived at my aunt's home on Bay 10th Street around eight-thirty. Rushing out the Lexus coupe, I quickly rang her bell. Aunt Gene answered the door wearing a blue housecoat, multicolored slippers, and a huge smile. She was a petite woman in her early fifties, and had always been like a mother to me.

"Hey Pecan," she greeted.

Pecan was the nickname she used to call me since I was three years old. Aunt Gene used to call me Pecan because I used to make a mess when she was done baking. My aunt's pies and cooking were the best, especially her traditional sweet custard pie.

"Hey Aunt Gene," I greeted her with a hug and kiss to the cheek.

Inside her neatly furnished home, I was met by relaxing green tone colored walls. Her light blue classic sleeper couch was always inviting. There was a polished grandfather clock stretching nearly seven feet from the gleaming parquet floors. A traditional style television and pictures of generations of family members decorated the walls. Her windows were a formal swag and panel combination. The panels were loosely gathered with tasseled cords. It was home to Aunt Gene and an escape for me.

"Where's my baby boy?"

"I just put him down to bed, Pecan. We both had a tiring day," my aunt said.

"What y'all did?"

"We went to the zoo, had some ice cream. We went for a walk in the park, talked. He even sang for me. He keeps me very active. That boy gonna be something else when he grows up."

"Yeah, he's gonna be talented like his father."

"Well, let's just hope Kahlil don't end up too much like his father."

"Omar's a good man, Aunt Gene."

"Well he wasn't too good of a man to stay out of jail and see his son being born. And see his son's first steps, hear his first words. You know how I feel about fathers being absent from their child's life?"

"I know Aunt Gene. He's home and he's changing now."

"Oh, he is, huh? I hope he has sense enough to stay his behind put, and become a father. And how's it going with that other young man you've been dating? What's his name…?" Aunt Gene said, snapping her fingers trying to remember.

"Kendal…"

"Yes Kendal. He seems to be a fine young man. Has good manners and he seems to be going in the right direction. He's always buying me things though… Pecan, what do I know about a plasma flat screen in my bedroom and a universal remote? When I was growing up, TV had only but a few channels and some good shows. Now, you have all this input, output, program this, menus and I swear the darn thing ain't nothin' but one big computer watching you. One day, the darn thing done scared me half to death, turning on by itself, had me ready to call nine-one-one."

"It's called technology. You need to get used to it," I laughed.

"Pecan, technology better get used to me. I'm too old to be trying to live with Star Wars in my home," she joked. "But anyway Pecan, I thought you'd be here before Kahlil went to sleep," Aunt Gene continued.

"I was trying, but I soo got caught up working."

"Caught up, huh? Pecan, you know Kahlil always comes first. You have the boy, now you raise him. I don't mind watching him, but a child should always have his mother around," Aunt Gene said to me in a motherly tone.

"I know, Aunt Gene."

"Okay, let's not forget, Pecan. Don't ever put career before your family."

"I won't Aunt Gene."

Walking into my aunt's bedroom, I saw Kahlil peacefully sleeping on his stomach in her bed. He was in his pajamas and really looked handsome. The room was dimmed and quiet. Aunt Gene followed behind me into the room and said, "I just fed him. You're not taking him home tonight, are you?"

"No Aunt Gene, I'll let him stay and rest."

"Good, there ain't no need for you to be dragging Kahlil around this late."

My aunt had raised six kids of her own, including me. I sat on the bed next to my gorgeous, sleeping baby boy and kissed him gently. I noticed how much he was looking like his father everyday.

"You know Omar wants to come and see him."

Aunt Gene didn't seem pleased. She sighed. She then said, "I hope he plans on doing more than just visiting his son."

"He will, Aunt Gene... Believe me, he will," I assured her.

Aunt Gene just looked at me. She exited the room, leaving me alone with Kahlil. I lay next to my son and began singing *Hush little baby*.

"Hush, little baby, don't say a word. Mama's gonna buy you a mockingbird. And if that mockingbird won't sing, Mama's gonna buy you a diamond ring..."

I gently stroked his hair and thought about my family. Quietness surrounded the room. The dimmed light, and thick comforter against my back, reminded me of how comfortable Aunt Gene's place made me feel. Soon I could feel myself falling asleep next to my son, the perfect escape.

The next night I was in the midtown studio with Kendal and a producer. It was late evening and I was exhausted, and my heart was weighing heavy. Kendal stood near the producer and was messing with the mixer, while I was in the booth with the headphones on. I was reading the lyrics to a song I'd written a few days ago, getting ready to blow it when my Blackberry vibrated on my hip. Omar was calling. A part of me wanted to smile, but another part of me felt bitter. I let his call ring through to my voicemail. I didn't want to interfere with the mood I was in, and I didn't want any drama with Kendal. Kendal looked up at me and smiled. He then leaned into the intercom and asked, "You ready to do this boo?"

"Yes," I smiled and nodded.

"A'ight, we gonna knock out this track and make it a fast night," Kendal said.

Exhaling, I focused on the song. The beat had me smiling. Studying the rhythm, I let it ride for a few. I pulled the microphone with the pop shield closer to me, ready to get my flow going. Then I began belting out the song with a lot of energy.

> *You belong to me,*
> *cuz I just can't stop lovin' you,*
> *you bring me joy,*
> *cuz you're beautiful and all…*
> *I open my eyes and can't deny the why,*
> *can't deny who we are….*
> *you're my best friend, my life, my all.*
> *You belong to me, baby,*
> *you're my morning and evening star,*
> *you're the best one of them from all…*

It felt good singing that song. I dedicated it to my son and was truly from my heart. Kendal nodded his head in appreciation, probably thinking the song was about him. His ego was misguiding him. I wiped the small tear from my eye and exhaled.

"Your sound is tremendous, baby," Kendal complimented.

My cellphone rang as soon as I stepped out the booth. Omar was calling again. Voicemail collected the call again. Kendal looked at me without asking any questions. He was curious, but I wanted to go home and get some much needed sleep. We had been in the studio for three long hours. By eleven that night, we were on the Southern State parkway on our way home. I dozed while Kendal pushed the SUV east.

A few miles away from home, I just wanted to kick off my shoes, get undressed and sleep until the afternoon. Traffic on the road home was easy going, and listening to A. Keys on the radio had me chilling. Kendal was quiet and I didn't mind. Then three exits from home, Kendal suddenly turned to me and asked, "So, when were you going to tell me that your ex-husband was home?"

I was dumbfounded, swallowed hard, and the question simmered for a couple gut wrenching heartbeats.

"Why do you care?" I finally asked.

"You saw him at the funeral, didn't you?" Kendal inquired.

"Yes I saw Omar at the funeral, and we spoke for a short moment. That was it. So just let it go, please. I'm really exhausted and..."

My voice trailed and he stared at me without saying a word. His eyes definitely showed that he wasn't pleased. Kendal sighed heavily and continued to drive. I closed my eyes, and rested my head against the window.

"I love you, baby. You know that, right?"

"I know."

"I just wanna continue to make you happy and be a family."

There was no response. I felt as if I didn't need to give a response. Kendal was just setting traps. I secretly rolled my eyes and replied, "I understand."

I hurriedly walked through my front door. Then went up to the bedroom and kicked off my heels before stripping out of my clothing. I crawled into the comfort of my oversize bed in panties and bra. I shut my eyes with my mind set on a good night's sleep.

Kendal climbed in bed with me. I was lying on my back and felt him rub up against me, trying to snuggle.

"We're a team, baby," he whispered in my ear.

I didn't respond. My mind was elsewhere. Kendal disappeared beneath the sheets and I quickly felt him stretching my legs.

"Kendal, no…" I pleaded.

I was far away from feeling anything sexual right at this moment. So I tried to keep his head from my pussy. Kendal was persistent.

"I just wanna please you, baby. Let me put you to sleep the right way."

The more I tried to push him from between my thighs, the harder he fought to stay. After a few weak attempts at blocking him, I let out a defeated sigh. His hot mouth was pressed against my pussy. His tongue penetrated me, ready to conquer my kingdom. Squirming, I wanted to resist, but Kendal began eating me out with an intensive, burning passion.

"I love you, baby," he said, before going back down on me.

My head was against the pillow, I closed my eyes, wishing he would hurry. Kendal ravaged me, but my mind was on Omar. Several times, I really wanted to cry out his name. I had to bite my tongue.

"Oh…yes!" I panted, but was feeling confused.

Kendal was bringing me pleasure, but I couldn't hold back the pain his personal issues were bringing me. His jealousy was one such barrier to our relationship.

"Ah… Oh!"

Our venture into the music business was starting to thrive, but my involvement with Omar was starting to interfere.

"Ugh…"

Kendal thrust his tongue further into me, saturating my walls with sweet loving.

"Ooh…yes, yes, yes…"

Breathlessly moaning, I wished it was Omar who was eating me out instead of Kendal. I bit my lips and let my tears flow.

10
Omar vs. Soul

It felt so good holding my son in my arms and it felt even better knowing that he wasn't crying. I looked in Kahlil's eyes and smiled. It was the best feeling in the world to make him laugh. I wanted Khalil to know his daddy and that I'd do anything for him. It was the first time holding him without the restraints of a prison system holding me back. I took the time to admire my offspring. Like his father, he was handsome, and very active, just like his father—a chip off the old block.

Miss Gene was cool and allowed me into her home to spend time with my son. America's aunt had many issues with me, especially with me being incarcerated from my son's life for a lengthy period. I caught an earful from the older woman's point of view. I was in her home and couldn't even argue.

"Boy, you better stay home for good this time, none of this in and out of that jail like some revolving door. God meant for us to stay steady and grounded to Him and family."

"I understand, Miss Gene."

"Your family, your son needs you to be grounded. You get yourself an education, a trade, a job or something and support your family. It's never too late to start."

"Yes ma'am, I understand."

"I know you want something better for yourself. And selling drugs and going to prison is not better."

"Miss Gene, believe me I'm done with that lifestyle. I renewed my thinking and changed my life around. I know that I ain't gonna mess up anymore. I'm home for good."

Miss Gene smiled and gave me a hug.

"You keep God close and you'll be okay."

"I will, Miss Gene. I will."

Seeing my son walk and talk brought tears to my eyes. I was a very fortunate father. I had met fathers that were locked up and not able to be in their children lives because of lengthy sentences. I stayed with my son for a few hours, hoping that America would come by. I still loved that woman to death and definitely wanted to rekindle something with her. She was a no-show. The past was the past, and my son was the future. Being a reformed gangsta was a funny feeling.

Around ten that night, I left Miss Gene's home. I made an agreement with her for picking up my son on weekends. She was cool, advocating for father and son time.

Cabs were my way of getting around town. I was trying to reconnect with a world where I felt like an outsider. My old gig was mine again. Even though it wasn't much, it was still something. I was still at Vincent's but didn't want to overstay my welcome.

It was eleven on a warm, spring night when the cab dropped me off in front of my child hood home. My old block, near South Road in Queens was buzzing with new faces—mostly young. I felt alien to the area at first. There were so many memories, good and bad on this rundown, grungy block with its dirty corners. Since my young teen years it's been my home. I had not seen my mother in a long, long time. She had been sick, probably dying from her disease. I needed to make amends with her in order for me to move on. My mom had been out of my life for such a long time, I had almost forgotten her.

I stood in front of the dilapidated place that I used to call home. The run-down porch, weathered stairs, and the siding coming apart, seemed ancient. My mother still had a home, which was shocking. I thought that the bank tried to seize the property but mom refused to leave.

Slowly, I made my way inside. The door was open, the locks broken. I stepped into the foyer and although the foul smell of urine and filth hit me, I continued inside. There were still lights on, but they were dimmed and the floors were covered with debris and squeaking with every step I took. It was quiet inside. I looked around the first floor then went upstairs.

Every step I took throughout the place, reminded me of days that I went hungry when my moms was out binging on drugs. There were cold nights that I endured because the heat was either off or broken. When I became a young teenager, my uncle's place became my permanent home. I never looked back.

Walking to the main bedroom on the second floor, I heard noise coming from the bedroom. I moved quietly, but the floors were squeaky. Closer to the bedroom, I heard moaning. I didn't know if it was my moms or strangers occupying the place. But I was ready for anything. Slowly, I gazed inside. I was shocked by what I saw.

It shouldn't even have been anything new to me. I had seen it before, but I could never get used to it. I shook my head in disgust witnessing my mother, down on her knees, and giving a blowjob.

She had aged terribly, and looked like a twig. Her hair was thinning out dramatically and her face looked sunken in. The heavy drug use over the years had taken a vigorous toll on her and she looked fucked up. Her skin was covered with bruises and marks. She had on a pair of shapeless sweatpants pulled down to her ankles and her oversized white T-shirt was pulled back over her head, her frail body was exposed for the stranger's pleasure. His back was lined against the wall. Pants around his ankles, my mother's mouth stretched around his dick while he pinched her badly wrinkled nipples.

I wanted to hate her. Twenty odd years later, and my mother was still degrading herself for five minute highs. It truly bothered me to see a nigga treating my mother like a whore. I tore myself from the doorway and toiled in the hallway. Sounds from their activity were loud and swept the hallway.

"Ah shit, damn, shorti! You suck this dick soo fuckin' good!" he moaned.

My face was screwed up and my fists clenched, I couldn't help but shed a few tears. It went on for a few more minutes before he was finished.

The tears I shed, I quickly dried. Impatiently I waited to confront my mother. I still needed to reconcile with her. It was part of the new me. In order to move on I had to stop being bitter about my past.

Moments later, the man walked out the bedroom zipping up his pants wearing a smile. We locked eyes as he went by. Then he had the audacity to speak.

"The fiend bitch gives great head," he said with a smirk.

It took every godly inch of me not to punch him in the face and break his fucking neck. He walked by me with a cocky attitude and went down the stairs. I stared at him until he disappeared from my sight and waited for mom.

A short moment later, she walked out the room pulling down her shirt and fixing her sweatpants. She glanced at me with this look of unfamiliarity and asked, "You want next?"

"You don't know or recognize your own damn son!" I asked, glaring at her.

She stopped walking and stared at me. Her eyes looked glossy, her movement sluggish. She was high. Her mind soon registered who I was.

"Omar...?"

I smirked without saying anything.

"That's you, huh? Hey baby, how you been? I heard you were locked up."

"After all these years, you still ain't changed. You still doin' the same dumb shit from when I was a shortie."

"You came here to judge me...?"

"No, I came here to tell you that you have a grandson. You're a grandmother, and you need to start acting like one!"

"A grandson, huh...? He cute...? When can I see him?"

"When you clean up yourself," I scoffed.

"So you think ya better than me now, huh, Omar? You fixed ya life, gotta bitch pregnant, now you wanna try play like ya righteous. Fuck you! You ain't no fuckin' son of mines! You ain't better than me, nigga!"

My intentions were to forgive my mother, but looking into her wild eyes, and hearing her rant, made my blood boil. I needed to leave immediately and quickly made my exit to the front door.

She was still shouting at me like I was a stranger off the streets. It was the drugs taking over her actions and talking reckless to her own son. Her addiction always took over. It always fueled her rage toward society. I wanted to be used to it, but I never was.

"Get the fuck out my house, muthafucka! Don't come back 'til ya apologize to me!"

Barging out the front door, I decided to let my mother be for now. After twenty years, the addiction was still an important part of her existence. I stood outside my old home and looked around. Shaking my head in disgust, I knew it probably was a mistake showing up. I dried the tear trickling down my cheek.

"I still love you anyway, ma," I said aloud.

I walked down the steps, heading to the nearest bus stop. I got to the corner and two police cars sped by me like they were in NASCAR itself, with their overhead lights blaring, engine screaming. I watched the two marked police cars race down South Road, heading toward the projects on 164th Street. My curiosity got the best of me. I began walking in the same direction. A few blocks away, I could see there were more flashing police lights, and a small crowd gathering.

Heading toward the crime scene, I could see a bunch of locals gathered behind the yellow police caution tape. They were talking while observing the scene. Beyond the yellow tape, I saw the body of a young black male sprawled out against the concrete. His mangled carcass was grossly contorted in a pool of spreading blood for the neighbors to see.

"Damn," I muttered beneath my breath.

It suddenly registered to me. I knew the victim. It was Grudge, the same young kid who had made fun of Vincent being handicap at the Youth Center. Vincent had warned him about the dangers of hustling in the streets. I remembered his face. He was a fatal statistic.

There was a war going on. Two drugs that were making headlines in my community were meth and brown-brown. This brown-brown shit was becoming popular in the hood, especially amongst the teens. It brought these kids extra high and loss of reality. It made them kill each other without any feeling of remorse or fear. It was tearing my community apart.

America s
Soul

I soon heard a screaming mother running down the street. Her cries were like a banshee, ringing in my head. She wasn't the only mother to lose her son, and wouldn't be the last. The mother going berserk over her dead son was upsetting. It nearly tore me into bits.

Standing there, I felt helpless and angry because I was once that thug. The killer who was willing and ready to take a life for greed, gratification, and to uphold a reputation that used to be me. Now I wanted to be a part of the solution. My hood was being torn apart with this ongoing war.

I had a young son to care for, and I wanted a better world for him. His generation should be better for him. At the rate these murders were climbing, I feared that there would be nothing left for him to inherit from us, but the sins of his fathers.

11
Omega

He stared from a long distance at what was left of one of his meth houses. It was a smoldering mess. The house was burned to the ground and police had it taped off. It was money and soldiers lost. Sitting in the backseat of the idling truck, Omega was fuming. He sucked a couple of pulls from the Black n Mild cigar in his mouth. Omega's nerves were on edge as his eyes danced across the horrific crime scene.

"These pussy muthafuckas!" Omega cursed. "Tryin' to hit me hard, and put me out of fuckin' business, Rocky. They wanna destroy everything I built. What the fuck man?"

"We gonna get at them, boss. I'm a be on it," Rocky assured.

Omega knew from the get-go, that he had to hit the Jamaicans, the shottas, twice as hard. He had a bunch of young teens for soldiers, while Demetrius had King, and men who were skilled killers. Original Shotta, they were bred on destruction and violence.

Omega's mind was weighed down with heavy thoughts. He took a few pulls from the cigar before tossing it out the window. In order to achieve his objectives, Omega was willing to take the war to any lengths. The Mexicans set him up with the murder of a prominent judge. Demetrius and King were knocking down his door, thirsty for his blood. He refused to be backed into a corner.

"Get Biscuit on the horn. Let him know I wanna link up ASAP," Omega ordered.

"I'm on it, boss." Rocky said.

"I seen enough, Rocky. Get me the fuck up outta here!"

Couple hours later, Omega met up with Biscuit at an undisclosed location that only the trio knew about. On the top floor of a parking garage, they watched the evening sky gradually turning into dusk over New Jersey.

Biscuit pulled up in his sleek black Benz with Narmer in the passenger seat and 50 Cent's *Many Men* blaring. Biscuit parked and stepped out of the car to greet Omega clad in his expensive Nike Velour tracksuit and ice around his neck.

"Mega, what's poppin'…? I heard what happened to the lab, you know I'm on it fo' sure," Biscuit said, greeting Omega with dap.

"I want you to double up the muscle on every lab, stash house and business we got out there," Omega instructed.

"Fo' sure," Biscuit said, nodding in agreement.

"And ante up 'em niggas pay by a C-note. Make sure them lil' niggas stay motivated about business and tell 'em to stay fuckin' alert! If they even get a fuckin' small whiff of a problem, they need to hit you up ASAP."

"Fo' sure…"

"And I want you on the constant fuckin' hunt for that nigga, King. I want him dead. But I wanna holla at him first 'bout his boy, Demetrius. I want these niggas done, Biscuit. Your main priority is to kill these niggas, especially King. But I want your little brother Narmer on the stash and product. You think he can handle it?"

"Yeah, he good, Omega… He learned from me, and he smart."

"A'ight, I want him on the product while you be on that kill."

"That's all I need to hear." Biscuit smiled.

Once Biscuit received his instructions, he gave Omega dap, assured him things were going to be okay, and hopped back into his Benz. With *Many Men* blasting, he peeled off.

Omega got into his truck and instructed Rocky to take him to his next appointment. The meeting was with a woman, and he wasn't going to be in a rush for an exit.

It was two in the morning, Omega lay exhausted next to Judy. Sweaty, naked, they had a mind blowing episode between the sheets. The two had rented out another low-key room in the outskirts of Trenton, New Jersey. There they fucked until they couldn't fuck any longer.

On the nightstand near the bed, was a gram of meth ready for Judy. Her clothes were scattered across the floor. Judy's red, glossy eyes were proof that her addiction was growing stronger. She gently stroked Omega's flaccid penis until it grew erect in her hand once more.

Omega reclined on his back, and felt Judy's soft, manicured hand fondled him. Closing his eyes, he sighed, "Ahh…"

When her soothing tongue enveloped him, Judy slipped Omega's dick into her mouth, sucking like a porn-star. The drugs made her horny and bubbly. Like always, she wanted Omega to fuck her in the ass.

"You're gonna give me my treatment aren't you, Omega?"

Judy wanted to please him first. Deep-throated, her lips and tongue went to work saturating his nuts. Her tongue coiled around his mushroom tip, she kissed the tip of his hardened dick. Jerking him off, she sucked his dick. Omega's hands were in Judy's disheveled hair, forcing his hard-on further down her throat.

Judy gagged, but kept it professional. Her head rapidly bobbed up and down like a bouncing ball, causing Omega to squirm. Soon Judy was straddling him, pressing her thighs next to his sides, she slowly gyrated against him. She pressed her hands into his chest and felt his dick thrust into her like a strong rush of wind.

Judy jolted from the storm between her legs. Digging her nails into Omega's chest, she screamed, craving intense sexual gratification.

"Uh-huh…uh-huh, shit! Give it to me, baby," she wailed.

Cupping her ass and tits, Omega fulfilled every succulent inch of her below. Knowing how rough she liked sex, he smacked her ass and pulled her hair. Judy wanted it anal instantly.

"Fuck me in my ass," she said rolling off his erection.

On her hands and knees, Judy positioned herself. Her upper half lowered into the sheets and pillow, her ass arched and ready for Omega's quick entry into her juicy butt. Omega complied once again by pounding her out from the back while playing with her pussy.

"Oh shit yes! I'm coming!" Judy howled.

"Ah yes ugh…" Omega shouted, busting a nut.

He fell over on his back, being a bit winded. Judy sat up near the nightstand and snorted another line of meth.

"You need to take it easy wit' that shit," he warned.

"You need to come see me more often, and give it to me like how I like it. I told you a week ago that my supply was running low."

"I'm a busy man."

Judy snorted another four inch line like nothing. Omega looked at her with concern. She was slowly losing control, becoming a high risk. Judy was an NYPD sergeant, but was slowly crashing from an addiction she thought was under control. Omega wondered how much more abuse could her mind and body take.

Satisfied, Judy fell back on the bed. Her eyes were focused on the ceiling. Judy's long legs were dangling on the floor. Sweat poured from her naked torso like she was in a sauna. Omega started to get dressed.

"Baby, I got another favor to ask of you," he said, fastening his jeans.

Judy's head tilted toward him, her glossy eyes willingly looking over at Omega for instructions. Her chest moved up and down, making it seemed as if she was hyperventilating.

"What you need, baby?" she asked.

"I need you to use your resources and track a name for me."

"Who…?"

"King… I need aliases that he uses, his family, kids, where he rest. I wanna know where this muthafucka takes a shit at if necessary. I want you to go into that police database and pull up anything you can. Will you do that for me baby?"

"I'll try. All you have is King?" she asked.

"Yes…"

"Okay so you get your info and what do I get in return, baby?"

Omega reached in his jacket pocket and tossed another ounce of Meth near Judy. She snatched up the bag as if it was gold, her smile lit up the room.

"I'll have that for you within the week, if he's in our system."

"Cool…" Omega said, nodding.

Three in the morning, Rocky dropped Omega home. With his weapon in his waistband, Omega stepped out of the passenger side of the truck feeling exhausted. His home looked peaceful and quiet. Omega was satisfied that his family was alone and safe. He had set up a subtle procedure with Jazmin, instructing her that if she was ever being held against her will, that she was to keep the corner bathroom light on and only call from the house phone. Omega knew that if he ever came home to see that corner bathroom light on and his wife calling from the house phone, then there was problems. But everything looked normal tonight.

"Be here at noon tomorrow," said Omega.

"Sure thing, boss," Rocky replied.

Omega entered the house, knowing that his family was asleep. He walked up the winding staircase and entered the master bedroom. Jazmin was sleep, and their son snored next to her. Standing at the bedroom doorway, Omega stared at them for a moment then walked away. He went downstairs to his private den, closed the doors, and sat behind an expensive cherry oak desk. From his throne—a fifteen hundred dollar leather, high-back chair, he casually sparked a cigar and inhaled.

A ruthless killer, Omega came from a family of thugs and gangsters. He witnessed his older brother, Rahmel, kill a man. Since then Omega had blood on his hands. Omega remembered the incident as if it was yesterday.

Through the cigar smoke, Omega saw the incident clearly, just as if it was yesterday.

It was '89 and he was nine years old. Omega hid in the room as Rahmel was in the next room with another dealer. Omega listened and heard the heated argument. A fight soon ensued, followed by a loud gunshot. A man collapsed in front of Omega just as he stepped out the bedroom. He saw the smoking gun in his brother's hand. Witnessing death for the first time, Omega saw blood coming from the victim's chest. The eyes of the man were opened, but lifeless. At first, Rahmel was angry when he saw his little brother in the room. Then he reflected before he hollered at him.

"Yo Omega, get the fuck over here!"

Shocked and nervous, Omega shakily stepped over the body to reach his brother. The gun was at his side, and Rahmel showed no remorse. He pulled Omega close.

"You scared nigga?" Rahmel had asked Omega.

Omega bit his lips and shook his head.

"Don't lie to me, Omega."

"Yeah, a little," Omega uneasily replied.

"Yo, this is real life, Omega. That's death right there, you see that shit... It ain't fuckin' pretty, but it's the game. In the streets, you do what you fuckin' gotta do to survive and stay on top. A nigga try to come at you or play you, you handle a nigga the correct way. Always remember, it's gonna either be you or him. You fight your best so it's never you sprawled out." Rahmel directed Omega's head to the body on the floor. "Like that!"

Omega stood next to his ruthless older brother and slowly absorbed in everything his brother was telling him. He then stared down at the body on the wooden floor—a hole in the center of his chest and blood pooling. The sight frightened Omega, but he felt it was something he needed to get used to seeing.

A year later, Rahmel was convicted on numerous counts, including first degree murder and received a lengthy sentence. Omega was ten years old, but before his brother's incarceration, Rahmel had taught his younger brother almost everything there was about hustling, killing and the game. It was a tool of trade that Omega would always carry with him. Committing his first murder at fifteen, he shot someone in a stick-up of a local drug-dealer.

The dealer reached for his weapon, but Omega shot the man three times in the chest and head. Soul was there. He had his friend's back and was witness to the murder. Both were uncomfortable. Over a period of time, the streets and killing became easier for them—especially Omega.

Now he had money, power, victory over most of his enemies, and a war brewing out of control. Having built up an empire based on blood, sweat and tears, Omega wasn't ready to meet his downfall. He sat back in his chair puffing and thinking.

Even though his brother was a changed and righteous man, Rahmel's words from the past still replayed in his mind.

"Always remember, it's gonna either be you or him, you fight your best to never let it be you."

Exhaling, Omega observed the arsenal of weaponry on the wall. There were high powered guns, swords, knives and daggers. He harbored a fascination for weapons since he was young. Now he had money and collected them all. Some he even had the pleasure of using. Getting up with a determined look, Omega removed a chromed Desert Eagle from his display.

12
America

I looked stunning in my navy Donna Karan silk top and sported a pair of gold heels with a shimmering, gold mini skirt. Kendal and I were looking fresh at a Def Jam industry party in the city. Rubbing elbows with the record industry's elite stars and shot-callers made me a little nervous. The exclusive spot was buzzing with people—music moguls, rappers, singers and producers among the well-heeled crowd. Plenty of women came dressed in their fanciest, revealing attire, plenty of cleavage and legs. There was plenty of ice and designer gear, mixed in with fitted NY Yankees caps and street demeanor. The dignified types who were about business and making money were all there. Players were trying to snatch the next groupie to take home and fuck. I smiled and mingled with the ones that mattered to my career.

We drank champagne out of flutes at a upscale midtown Manhattan penthouse suite. Complete with a balcony that overlooked Central Park, the place offered a spectacular view of uptown. Lights bounced off thick marble floor; and the long glass countertops stocked with the best champagne and Cristal. Straight R&B music piped in through high tech speakers. The atmosphere was relaxing and I stood next to Kendal. Sipping on chilled champagne my throat was cooled. Kendal was looking nice in black slacks and a black Armani silk shirt. The Rolex he sported made an impression in the mix.

We were talking to one of the back up singers for Fantasia. I was having the time of my life. Like always, Kendal knew how to work the crowd. He was introducing me to rappers, producers and people that had influence in the industry. I blushed as he praised me.

"America is fast becoming the next best thing out there. She sings like Mariah and Whitney, with a style like J. Lo's. Right now we're working on opening up for Beyonce on her next tour," Kendal said to a record mogul who was actually listening.

Sipping champagne, I smiled and let my man handle his business. A steady flow of compliments kept coming my way about my looks and my voice. Men passed me and Kendal handed out business cards, and the ladies asked about my outfit and loved my shoes. I was getting the attention that I truly deserved and needed.

Kendal placed his arm around me, hugging me close and whispered, "This is how things gonna be from now on, baby. Lavish parties, lucrative deals and your name across the nation in lights... Look around. Did you ever imagine that we would come this far...? We're on the verge of signing a multi-million dollar deal and opening up for one of the hottest sensations in the business."

I smiled like a graduate on prom night. Then I took a deep breath and downed the rest of my champagne. Our hard work had paid off. I was going to continue working hard so I can become an icon like Janet or Tina. It was somewhat overwhelming, but I knew that I was able to handle the pressure that was to come. Smiling, Kendal kissed my cheek and said, "I'm going over here to talk to a few producers about some things. Have fun baby, and let's get it poppin'."

Kendal walked to the other side of the room, leaving me standing in the center of the attention, feeling like a million bucks. My voice, beauty, and style were slowly getting noticed by who really matters in the industry. Thanks to my devoted fans, the right kinds of people were starting to ask about me.

I went over to the bar for another glass of champagne. I wanted to feel a little buzz before the night was over. I took a few sips and saw Alimony walking in flanked by his entourage of men. He was looking fine in a black tank-top with his lean build showing through the shirt. He sported a Yankees fitted, some boot-cut jeans and fresh Timberlands. A long diamond and platinum chain with a colossal size pendant hung around his tattooed neck and the bracelet matching, the epitome of a gangsta rapper.

He was always eye candy and I had to admit that I liked flirting with him. I glanced around for Kendal, knowing how insecure he was with Alimony. I spotted him engaged in conversation across the room with the senior editor of Vibe magazine.

I left the bar area and walked to the outside glass balcony. A few folks were outside enjoying a refreshing spring night. I moved closer to a more secluded area and stood close to the railing, staring at Central Park from thirty five floors up. Sighing and smiling, I relished the breathtaking view of the city. Another sip had me thinking about my life.

This was one of those nights where I loved Kendal for everything that he'd done for me. I thought about our future. Loving the way he took charge of things, and wasn't scared to approach the most influential mogul in the business. So much confidence in himself, he knew he had a good product, me. It was such a turn-on to see him handle the business. My heart did a skip for him. He could have me anyway he wanted me tonight. It was gonna be a hot and steamy night together.

"I hope ya thinking about me, beautiful," someone said from behind me.

I turned to see Alimony with his smile on high beam.

"Nice, right?" he said, referring to the view that had me captivated.

"Yeah," I replied.

"It's good to see you again, America. You look really fly," he complimented.

"Thank you."

"So, where's ya not so better half?" he asked, taking shots at Kendal.

"Around somewhere," I smiled.

"Let him stay somewhere," Alimony joked.

His bling sparkled like the stars in the sky and he smelled so good. He had arms like a gladiator and a chest solid like rock. I knew if Kendal saw him talking to me, there were going to be problems.

"Why don't you let me take care of you, America? I know ya comin' up, ma... Fo' real, I can get you into places that you only dream about. I been in da game for a minute now, made my bones and shit. I know ya nigga is tryin' to do his thang wit' you, but I can do better."

"You think?" I chuckled.

"Baby, I can buy you whatever you want. Shit, you and me together in this business, we can be better than Jay and B."

"Alimony, you're something else. Now you know if Kendal see you here with me, he's gonna flip."

"Shit, let him. I never liked that nigga anyway."

"And why not…?"

"Cuz, that nigga ain't good for you. He too jealous, too insecure, and c'mon, if that nigga was handling his BI, then he ain't gotta worry 'bout nada. If ya know ya holdin' ya woman down at nights and keepin' her pockets right, she good money all the way. Ya feelin' me, luv?"

"So you think."

"Baby, you that girl, and I'm that dude."

Looking him up and down, I said, "You probably out here fuckin' everything out here that moves with your wild ass."

He doubled-over in laughter. Smiling he said, "Nah, I know it seems like that, luv, but I'm lookin' for that wifey to hold a nigga down, fo' sure. Too keep it real wit' ya, ma…. I luv your swag."

I laughed. "You're too much, Alimony."

"Nah, that's real rap. Yo, since that day we linked up at that event a few months back and you holla'd at me and didn't press a nigga because of his status. I knew you was da real deal. And then in the booth, when we were recording that track, yo, that shit I spit, it was just a rhyme, but on the real I wrote the rhyme for you and I definitely wanna work wit' you in the future."

"You're cute, but you don't even know me like that."

"I'm willing to someday and hopefully soon."

The game he was kicking told me Alimony wanted to get into my panties. I looked past him and spotted Kendal coming our way. He was looking upset.

"Twelve o clock," I said to Alimony.

"Huh?"

"Turn around," I warned.

He turned and I quickly stepped in between the two men and exclaimed, "Don't embarrass me here. I'm serious."

"What he want with you?" Kendal asked.

"We were just talking, that's all, Kendal," I said.

"Yeah, we were just talking," Alimony chimed.

Both men glared at each other and then Alimony was the better man by saying, "I'm a holla at you later, America. Think about what I said."

He walked away, leaving Kendal with mean inquiries about his business with me. I knew that Kendal was feeling some type of way about the two of us conversing, but he shrugged it off, and said, "Hatin-ass nigga. But we got better things happening. I just talked to the editor in chief of Vibe magazine and they are gonna do a piece on you. The interview is set up for next week Thursday, photo shoot to follow. Is that cool with you?"

"Perfect." I smiled.

Kendal smiled. "I see why you came out here. The view is gorgeous, just like my woman. In a year or two, we gonna afford some shit like this... Just the two of us in the city, dining and drinking wine... We're on our way up, America."

He put his arm around me and we took in the view together. The party behind us feeling like it was at a distance. It was a moment that I cherished with him and thought about our time together, but then my phone rang. I looked at the number on the caller I.D and had no recognition of it. I still answered the call.

"Hello..."

"Hey, America..."

Instantly I recognized the voice. I felt this sudden rush of thrill flow through me. It was Omar calling and hearing from him again almost put a smile on my face, but I contained my emotions and kept it nonchalant.

"Can you talk?" he asked.

"Yes, give me a moment..."

I removed the phone from my ear and told Kendal a lie.

"Babe, it's my Aunt, I need to talk to her for a moment."

He nodded.

I walked away and the guilt was gnawing. Kendal would be furious to know that my ex-husband was calling my phone. I went into the ladies' bathroom. Telling Omar to hold for a moment, I locked myself in one of the stalls and spoke to my ex.

"Hey, what's going on?"

"I just needed to hear your voice," Omar said.

"You okay?"

"I could be better..."

His answer made me a bit concerned. So I pried.

"Talk to me," I said.

"Can we meet up?"

"When...?"

"Tomorrow, if you're not busy..."

"Um...it's a possibility. Where...?"

"I'm gonna be at my cousin's gravesite around noon tomorrow, you can meet me there if you like."

I thought about it for a moment. I tried to keep telling myself that I didn't have feelings for him, but I truly did and genuinely missed him. My heart started beating like a race horse when he asked to meet up. I definitely wanted to. I thought about him and definitely wanted to see him myself.

"Okay, I'll see you there."

There was a short pause in our conversation. It felt like he had something important to say, but was hesitant. I waited for him to speak, and say something to me that would put a smile on my face.

"Later..."

Omar hung up and I felt some disappointment. I guess I wanted to hear him say he missed me. I had Kendal with his flaws, but he was taking me places that many only dreamed of, and Omar was my first love, my genuine love.

I sat in the bathroom stall for a moment and thought about Omar. I tried selling the idea of not seeing my ex to myself. The more I tried to ignore my feelings for him, the more my heart yearned for him.

Exiting the stall, my mind felt like it was doing sprints. I casually walked over to the sink. A sigh escaped as I stared at my reflection. I could hear the party going on behind the walls. Kendal was probably worrying about me.

I straightened my hair and touched up my makeup. Then I walked out the bathroom. Kendal was standing by the bar talking to a few people. Walking over to him, I kissed him on the cheek.

"It's getting late, baby. Are you ready to go soon?"

"Give me a minute, babe," he said.

I did and went back on the terrace overlooking Manhattan. The sights of the city became my private entertainment. Bright lights stretching for miles, and the bustling sounds below kept my thoughts preoccupied until we left.

Later that night, Kendal fucked me from behind. He had me in a curve clutching the headboard while thrusting deep into me. I opened up and gave it all to him. Mingling with the elite, talking business, and making it happen in the industry had made us excited. With Omar on my mind, my exhilaration was more invigorating.

"Oh shit, America!"

Kendal suddenly exploded. I had to admit it felt good. I tried to remain quiet, letting Kendal enjoy himself, but multiple orgasms got in the way.

"Ooh... Ah, yes!" I moaned.

I was on top of him, spent and feeling torn. My mind raced as if it was lost. I stared at my man. Kendal was exhausted from our session. Do I truly love him, or was I with Kendal because of my career?

The next morning I couldn't wait, I was up early. I wanted to look my best for Omar. Kendal had left for an early breakfast meeting with the brothers of AMG records in the city, and he'd be gone for a while. Dressed in a pair of tight fitting jeans, highlighting my curves, I stood admiring myself in a pair of four-inch, white, strapped wedges. Then I had some orange juice and fruit for breakfast. I walked out the door anxious as a expecting mother. I got in my white Lexus and drove to the cemetery on Springfield Blvd. It was after eleven in the morning and the day was warm with blue skies overhead.

It took me about forty minutes to get to the cemetery. I arrived five minutes before noon. I navigated my Lexus into the place and tried to remember where Greasy's grave was located. It had been a while since his funeral. Greasy and I never got along with each other, but his murder was uncalled for and my heart went out to Omar.

I parked and got out, searching the plots. Then I spotted Omar standing in the distance. A smile crept on my face. Skipping like a kid at play, I hurried to him. He had his back to me and stood over his cousin's grave silently. I felt uncomfortable at first thinking, Omar could be in the ground. There were plenty of nights I worried myself to sleep, thinking about him dying. I had nightmares of police at my door with gloomy news. It was prison for Omar, and not an untimely fate like his cousin, Greasy.

He stood in front of the plot clad in a pair of denim jeans, a snug T-shirt and some white Uptowns. He had this natural look to him, no bling, clean shaven and a fresh cut. My stomach felt like it had butterflies flying around.

13
Omar vs. Soul

Sadness coursed through me while I stood over Greasy's gravesite. I missed my cousin greatly. His time on this earth was too short. It could have been me in the ground, but God had blessed me. So much had changed in the hood. My relationship with America wasn't the same and my attitude had been transformed to a better place. I just wanted to chill and take things slow, but it felt like I was being compelled to make a difference. Young kids were dying, killing each other and the monsters behind it didn't care. I had been home two weeks and seen enough. Omega's name was ringing out, and so was his protégé, Biscuit. Those two were responsible for the murders and drugs saturating the community. They were getting rich off people's misery. I couldn't sit back and just watch it happen.

I needed to confront Omega. Maybe I could put some sense in his head, but it would be difficult. My cousin died violently because of Omega—his tongue ripped out, badly beaten, shot and stabbed.

Looking at his headstone, I closed my eyes and thought about the good times we had together. I continued to chill, but heard footsteps behind me. Turning around, I saw America coming my way. I smiled.

"Hey," she greeted with a warm smile.

"I'm glad you came," I said.

We hugged. She was close her body against mine. America's arms were wrapped around me and this must be what heaven felt like. I didn't want to pull away from her. Her perfume, her touch could weaken any man. I stared at her like it was the first time seeing her in years. America's beauty was overwhelming.

"You look good," I complimented.

"Thank you."

"It's been a while."

She smiled and nodded. There was a gap of time between us and it felt awkward with her. Even when I was incarcerated I still felt so close to her. But now she had moved on.

"How're you feeling?"

"Hanging in there..."

"I know you and Greasy were close."

"True indeed, you know we were. I see you're doing ya thang. I'm hearing about you... Kendal got you shining out there," I said.

"He's definitely business savvy."

"It's good to see you doing what you love to do. You always had talent, America. You were always a star in my eyes. I'm glad to see you're happy."

"And yourself...?" she smiled.

"I visited my moms the other day..."

"How did that go?"

I didn't answer verbally. The look I was wearing told her what she needed to know. The glint of anger in my eyes already answered.

"Oh, still the same, huh?"

"Sometimes I think I'd rather see her dead than disgracing herself the way she do. She ain't right, America."

"I know it's hard, Omar, but you been through harder."

"Indeed, you always knew me so well."

"Look at the time we put into each other."

It was casual chitchat, just reconnecting in a way we never did before. I wanted to be with her in ways that made my body and heart yearn, but I didn't want to break her heart again. Even though I'd changed my ways, I felt better seeing her happy than stressing over me.

"Are you hungry?" I asked.

"I could go for a bite."

We walked together, and I got into her white Lexus. She stepped her game up, from the crib to the whip America was now living in style.

We stopped at the nearest diner on Merrick Ave in Long Island. The place wasn't crowded and gave us a little intimacy. We sat in a corner booth in the back of the restaurant. I had waffles and eggs and America chose pancakes and bacon with a cup of coffee. We were so busy talking that our food just sat for a moment, getting cold. That awkward feeling that existed between us earlier was fading, and we talked and bonded again. Reminiscing and laughing about our son, we enjoyed ourselves, forgetting our past troubles.

"I can't believe you're a counselor now. Wow. That's good to hear, Omar," America said with delight.

"Yeah, I can't believe it myself. Mr. Jenkins was cool enough to give me my old job back with a bump. So I'm gonna take advantage of it, and won't mess things up this time."

"It's good to see you like this... Happy and with an objective," she said with a smile.

"I'm done with the bullshit, America."

"You deserve the best."

"You think?"

"Yes, I mean you lived a hard life, Omar. I should know, I trekked right beside you while you were living that life for ten years. It was hard, but you overcame."

"We overcame," I said.

"Yeah, we did come a long way."

She took a sip from her coffee and a few bites from her plate. I calmly looked at her, but inside, I was raging with passion. I took a sip of water to cool my throat then gazed into America's eyes.

"Baby, I'm sorry for everything. I'm sorry for the pain and uneasiness I put you through—"

"Please Omar, no—"

"Lemme finish, America. I was young, naïve, and took you for granted most times. I was caught up in these streets, but I always loved you, baby."

"Omar, it's okay, I'm cool. I done forgave you," she said, tears welling in her eyes.

"It's something that I needed to say, while we got the time," I continued. "I'm sorry that I lied to you about the gun, the money and the drugs... That night when we had that fight it ached me that I left you incomplete because of my foolishness. I had promised you that I would never return to jail. I got caught up over some nonsense. America, while I was in that prison, all I could think about was you and my son. I knew I let you both down. I fucked up and I vowed that when I came home this time, it was going to be for good and I was going to make things right. I'm good, baby... I am. I came home to less, but for some reason, I feel more complete."

There was a silence and I could see America's eyes through the tears. My own tears were falling on the plate in the food in front of me. I took a deep breath and continued.

"It was right for you to let me go. Yes it hurts, but it was the true thing to do. You needed your space from me. And now look at you, you're becoming a star. I just wished I was able to give you what you deserved. But no matter where we end up, I'm gonna always be there for my son and I'm going to always love you."

Unconsciously, I was holding America's hands across the table like I used to do in the past. Her touch against mines had me on cloud nine. America's watery eyes meant that she was touched by my words. I needed to apologize to her and let my true feelings be known.

"Omar," she started then looked away in the distance.

Pulling her hands away from me, her actions snapped me back into reality. I saw the uneasy look on America's face. She then looked at me with hazy eyes and continued.

"I love you, but I can't right now. I mean, it's been eighteen months and my life has changed. And I still think about those pictures of you and that girl that were mailed to me. You know how much that hurt? It broke my heart to see the man that I loved whoring with other women. Omar, I have forgiven you. Sometimes it's just hard for me to forget."

Her words tore my chest wide open, exposing an injured, lonely heart, but I couldn't argue. I sat back in my seat feeling defeated, and sighed.

"I understand," I said. "But can I ask you a question?"

"Yes..."

"Do you still see a future with me?" I asked painfully.

She didn't answer me right away, but the look in her eyes told me that there were still feelings there.

"Why do you make it so hard for me, Omar?"

"What you mean?"

"It's been almost two years and I thought I moved on. Then here you come released without any mention of it. And I'm nearing the peak of my career and you just make your way back into my world. I can't lie, I do love you and I think about you a lot. But what I fear the most with you is making the same mistakes over and over. It's like pushing forward hoping for the best but getting the same results."

"I know I fucked up, but I'm willing to give you your space and time. If it's meant to be between us, then it will happen. I really didn't expect to just come home and have you welcome me back with open arms. But you know it ain't feel right stepping out of 'em gates, not seeing you waiting for me. It was just awkward, but proof that my life changed and you've moved on."

"Ohmygod," America uttered.

I was surprised and saw the tears trickling down her soft cheeks.

"What's wrong?"

"I can't do this. I don't know… I look at you and… Ohmygod, I can't. Why do I fuckin' love you so much," America exclaimed, before rushing out the booth.

"America," I called out after her.

She hurried out the door and got into her car. I watched her from where I sat, wanting so very badly to chase after her. Something held me in my seat. I was unable to move, knowing there were issues that wouldn't work itself out overnight. Quickly, she peeled off. All I saw was the back of her white Lexus from my windowed seat.

14
America

I had to leave that diner in a hurry. The sudden rush that I was feeling for him left me confused. I wanted to separate myself from Omar. Meeting with him was a huge mistake. We had moved on. I should keep my distance, and only deal with him when it concerned our son. My heart, body, and the tears I was shedding for him, told a much different story. Seeing Omar up close and being in his presence had turned me on. The tears were evidence that I was still greatly in love with my ex-husband.

"Don't do it to yourself…" I kept repeating.

It will be a mistake. My mind warned me of the leap my heart was dying to make. The inside of my thighs were hot and wet from the contact he had made across the table. His apology was so heartfelt that I rode on his every word. It felt like a turbulent wave, but I wanted to keep riding.

I drove my Lexus four blocks from the diner, and stopped at a red light. The radio was mute, but thoughts of Omar rang aloud. I tried to compose myself. He didn't deserve another chance with me, but inside of me, I ached for him. Why was it so hard?

The light changed green and I drove off slowly. I knew it was rude of me to just leave abruptly, but I needed to clear my head. I drove another three blocks before braking for another red-light. I sighed heavily thinking about my options.

Tears came and I stared blankly at the red-light, trying not to look back. That thirsting for him just wouldn't leave me.

The light changed, and the car stayed idling at the intersection. Sighing deeply, I wiped the tears from my eyes. Then I made a U-turn and quickly drove back to the diner. I couldn't believe what I was doing. I was going back to my ex-husband.

Seeing Omar again at North Star's funeral rekindled something in me. It could only be quenched by him. I chuckled to myself while I drove. I wanted to be done and move on without him. With the quickness, I arrived at the diner.

Omar was exiting the front entrance. He was walking toward the bus stop and looked kind of detached. I sped up next to him, and rolled my passenger window down.

"Just get in!" I shouted.

He gazed awkwardly at me. Omar was trying to figure things out. He was also testing my patience.

"You sure?" he asked with uncertainty.

"Omar, please just get in."

He got into the car. Before he could even close the door, I threw myself at him. Pressing my lips against his mouth aggressively, Omar's tongue welcomed me. Our wet, sloppy kiss was so passionate it felt like ten years ago. His lips were soft. Omar's hands caressed me all over like a child with a new toy. I directed his hand up my thighs and placed it between my legs.

"Ah…ah…" I panted when he gripped my hot love-box.

We were about to get it on in front of the diner, but I collected myself and said, "Not here, Omar."

He smiled and finally closed the car door. I drove off thinking of somewhere inconspicuous. A few blocks away, on a side street near the train tracks under a thick shaded tree. There were hardly any vehicles on the block it was thin with cars, perfect for our rendezvous. With the tinted windows up, we crawled into the backseat like teenagers. My heartbeat raced with excitement while getting in positioning on my back. Omar quickly snatched my tight fitted jeans off.

Twisting in anticipation, I waited for him to pull his jeans down and enter me. My jeans and panties were on the floor and Omar was naked from the waist down. His erection looked more pleasing than ever. It'd been a while since he fucked me and for a moment, we looked at each other. His eyes peered deep into me and his body was speaking to me in volumes. Muscular and tense, his dick was hard and inviting. I raised my legs in the air, longing to feel him inside of me.

"You're more beautiful than ever, America."

I smiled, blushing like a school girl. Omar was able to peel back layers of me that most men dreamed of breaking through. He knew me so well, that sometimes it felt like we were one. I was completely naked to Omar.

"I missed you so much."

He positioned himself between my open thighs. I slowly felt him enter me and I caught my breath. Wrapping my arms around him snuggly, I felt his thrust in me like a crashing wave on a beach. I felt him rammed stiffly inside me.

"Ah!" I exhaled."

"Ugh yes, baby. I missed you too."

I felt every thick inch of his dick up in me, curling my toes. My shaven pussy openly greeted him and my manicured nails scraped down his muscular back. My back was against the warm leather seats, and my knees were pushing into the front seat. We were making love in the backseat of my car. Omar took me to that zone.

"I love you, baby. I love you," he said.

His thickness slid in and out of me. Hugging him tight, we sucked faces like young lovers. Omar was doing me like he missed me. My breath panting in his ear, he sucked on my nipples while relishing every inch of me.

"Damn, I missed this. Oh how I missed you. Oh you feel so good," he oozed with satisfaction.

"I still love you, baby. Fuck me!" I purred.

His rhythm style movement between my thighs had my legs quivering for me to cum. I gripped him with one hand, and dug my nails down his back. The other hand held on tightly to the back of the seat for support. Omar's thrust accelerated.

"Oh God...! Ah yes Omar! Oh!"

I closed my eyes and bit down on my bottom lip. Our bodies were sweaty from the constant friction and the spring heat with little air circulating inside of the car. It was steamy. I felt his dick swelling up in me. He was about to release, but me first. I let lose while he was inside of me, feeling that gratification of a quenched thirst. I let out a quick howl as my legs firmly tightened around Omar. Pulling him deeper inside I felt his beloved release and suddenly I erupted again. Through my sexual bliss I heard Omar growling.

"I'm coming, baby!"

I held him tightly, my body rocking with his ejaculation. It felt soothing to have him come inside of me. He shook between my legs then collapsed on top of me when he was done shooting his nut. We both were in a love drunk zone. I kissed his face, exhausted from a much needed fuck.

"I fuckin' hate you."

He chuckled and touched my face.

"You do? What now?"

15
Killer Season

Biscuit sat in the backseat of the Ford clutching a 9mm. In the driver seat was Rico, and riding shotgun another young soldier, eagerly awaiting Biscuit's orders. The trio sat in the cover of night, parked in a shaded area where traffic was almost non-existent. Their attention was focused on a three story building a short distance away. The block was quiet, most homes and businesses abandoned years ago. It was the perfect place for any illegal operation. The highway was close by, no neighbors in your business to gain suspicion and call police, and the nearest precinct was miles away.

Biscuit had put the word out on the streets and invested some serious cash to get the info he needed. The streets talked, he got word that King and Demetrius were running illegal guns up and down I-95. It was a part of a multi-million dollar a year international business for the Jamaicans.

The men sat for an hour watching and there was no activity. Biscuit was in the backseat inspecting his weapon. The block looked war torn and was nearly desolate. Biscuit stared out the backseat window and back at his goons, Rico and Torque, sitting up front.

"Yo, you know what they do in Mexico if they got beef wit' a nigga, or catch a nigga slippin'?"

"Nah…" Rico and Torque chorused.

"These muthafuckas will take a nigga, dead or alive and put the muthafucka in these large steel drums filled with fuel and set the shit on fire… Watch the muthafucka burn into liquid right in front of them. When that shit is done fuckin' burning, ain't nuthin' left of the muthafucka for police to identify... Muthafuckas' like vaporized and shit. They call the shit, 'Makin' Stew.'"

"Damn," Rico said.

"Yeah, that's some ruthless shit. Nice though, I'm feelin' that style of killing fo' sure. I'm ready to do that shit to these Jamaicans, especially King. I'm hurtin' to kill his ass!" Biscuit said.

"How many guns you think up in the spot now?" Rico asked.

"Don't know... But I tell you this, we run up in there, kill 'em all and snatch they shit, take over their operation... Not even tell Omega 'bout that. And have a little sumthin' for us to get rich off," Biscuit laughed.

"Huh? You wanna keep Omega out. I'm sayin' that nigga a powerhouse right now. He fuckin' crazy," Torque said.

"And you think I'm fuckin not," Biscuit exclaimed. "But I'm just sayin, it's a thought, my nigga, you know wit' the nigga bein' so wrapped up in this music career and politics. He might one day forget where he came from."

"I wanna fuck one of his bitches that be singing on his label," Rico joked.

"Nah, you know who I wanna get at? She got da bomb fuckin' body and da bitch is bad... America, yo," Torque said with a devilish smile.

"I seen that bitch around... She used to fuck wit' that clown-ass, nigga, Soul," Biscuit said.

"I heard that name before," Rico said.

"He a lightweight nigga... Still tryin' to make a comeback from a forgotten past... Had a few words wit' da nigga a while back and was 'bout to push this nigga's wig back, but Omega stopped a nigga," Biscuit said, shaking his head. "They used to run together."

"I heard the nigga spit before though. He a'ight... Kinda nice wit' the lyrics," Rico said.

"Fuck that shit, that music shit ain't no money for a nigga. Nigga's ain't no fuckin' Jay-Z," Biscuit said.

Rico and Torque kept quiet. Biscuit sat in his seat and looked around, then with an afterthought, he said, "Niggas fuckin' lose focus and forget where they at. They get caught up in fuckin' pipe dreams, and them the niggas that get caught slippin' and shit."

"Yeah, I hear dat. I hear dat, my nigga," Rico said.

A discolored white van drove past their beat-up gray Ford which looked like any other car dumped on the block. The men ducked in their seats for cover and watched. The van came to a stop in the driveway, near the entrance. No one got in or out.

"Here we go," Biscuit said.

Then three men stepped out of the van, and looked up and down the block. They didn't notice anything unusual except abandoned vehicles, including the one Biscuit and his goons occupied. Two men opened the back door to the van and started to remove large crates.

"Yeah, we on it," Biscuit said.

"How we gonna do this?" Torque asked.

"How else...? Shoot our way in, shoot our way out. Yo, they ain't gonna even see us coming," Biscuit said.

It was almost a suicide mission. No one had a clue as to how many heavily armed workers were inside. From the outside the place looked like there was not enough security. It was an easy take.

They watched the Jamaicans carry a dozen wooden crates into the building. Biscuit observed the last one being moved inside and said, "Let's go."

The doors to the Ford flew open, and all three proceeded forward cautiously. They moved down the street and planned to open fire if they were spotted. Biscuit led his pack to the prize. His eyes were fixed on the van and small warehouse. He slowed his stride and observed the block once again. Torque and Rico followed his lead. Both slowed.

"Sumthin' ain't right," Biscuit said.

The two men had puzzled looks on their faces. Before anyone could speak, Biscuit saw movement a short distance away. It was a small dark alley way overlooked by the men.

"Fuck! It's a set up! Run!" Biscuit shouted.

A loud shot roared. Boom! A shotgun blast abruptly slammed Torque violently against a brick wall. He was dead instantly. Gunfire erupted, Biscuit returned fire from his 9mm into the night. Rico followed suit, firing his gun hastily. The two men were soon overwhelmed by a half dozen of

King's men who were heavily armed with machine guns. Biscuit and Rico took cover behind a beat up Dodge.

"Shit!" Biscuit exclaimed.

"Di devil is 'pon ya, bredren… Ya meet him tonight. Ya hear mi, bredren? Gun down dem batty boys!" King shouted.

The Uzi King gripped brutally tore into the rusted Dodge Biscuit and Rico took cover behind. King rushed the car, his eyes red with rage.

"Yuh dead batty boi!" King shouted.

Biscuit and Rico fired back, but were outgunned and outnumbered. Biscuit panted, feeling his fate overcoming him. Suddenly, he was the hunted. Wide-eyed, Rico looked at him for direction. The Jamaicans continued their onslaught.

"Fuck it!" Biscuit said.

He gripped his gun tightly and rose to return fire. Quickly, he dropped one foe, hitting him in the chest. Biscuit took off running, machine gunfire whizzing by his ear and tearing up the concrete around him. Rico tried to follow, but King ran up on him and gunned him down fiercely, leaking his brains and stomach onto the sidewalk.

Kings' men chased Biscuit. With death on his heels, Biscuit sprinted down the street like a track star. Returning fire, he dipped down an alley and jumped over a chain link fence. Before he could make it over, two rounds ripped through his shoulder. He hit the ground hard. Biscuit endured the pain and continued running in search of safety.

In a nearby park, he found cover under low trees and shrubberies. He threw himself behind the trees and remained quiet. Police sirens wailed in the distance, they were nearing closer. It was his only relief. He tried to tend to his wounds. Biscuit's wounds weren't life-threatening, but his body hurt like he was.

"Fuck!" Biscuit cursed.

He hated himself for coming so close, but then being outsmarted. He had to lay low until he knew that he was clear of the threat and any cops wandering about the park. Two hours later, Biscuit lifted himself from his not easily seen location. He was bleeding, hurt and in urgent need to get back to the city. He broke into a car, quickly hot-wired it and made it back to Queens.

Once home, he got on the payphone and dialed Omega and Rocky.

"Who's this?" Rocky answered.

"Shit fucked up. Torque and Rico, they dead men," Biscuit said. "I need help... A fuckin' doctor... I'm shot, nigga!"

"What the fuck happened?" Rocky asked.

"Get wit' Omega, let him know shit is fucked right now!"

Biscuit hung up, stumbled to his ride and fell out into the front seat of the stolen car where he parked. His beef with King was now personal.

16
Omar vs. Soul

America's passionate cries were sweet music in my ears. It had been a while. The chime of her voice brought comfort to my heart. Her warm body made me calm, and her caring attitude for me made me love her even deeper. In my loving embrace, America's naked body twisted and turned. My tongue was deep in her like a drill in dirt. Her legs quivered against my cheeks as I tasted every sweet inch of her ass. The wrinkled sheets underneath us were saturated with obsession and sweat. She gasped and arched her hips into me. I cupped her butt cheeks and continued to eat her out—cleaning everything off my plate.

We were in room 219 it was a cheap motel room off the Conduit. It was a drab room with two full size beds. An old TV sat on a beaten up dresser. It wasn't my style, but I was happy to see her again and would have had her in the park. We met there separately, I in a cab, and she in her Lexus. For a moment it was all small-talk then we opened up and made love. It was our fourth sexual encounter together. We couldn't get enough of each other. Every moment with my ex-wife was spent in bliss.

After my rendezvous between her thighs, I climbed between her legs and thrust deep inside her. We fucked our brains out. Kissing each other fervently, we were caught in the afterglow. I rested between her legs, and America held me in her arms. Her breath was soothing in my ear, and her touch against my skin felt like a cool breeze on a warm day.

We stayed in the missionary position for a moment. She rubbed her thighs against my sides and stroked my face like a caring mother.

"That was so good, baby. I needed that," she said, kissing me.

America smiled at me with loving eyes. My mind was somewhere else. I didn't return the smile. The feeling was crushing me for some reason. Removing myself from between her legs, I sat on the edge of the bed, my back to her.

"Baby, what's wrong?" she asked in a concerned tone.

"Couple things..."

America came closer, embracing me. She kissed my neck and massaged my shoulders. Her touch traveled down to my chest.

"Talk to me, baby. I'm here for you."

"Are you really?"

The gentle massage stopped, and she looked at me with bewilderment. My comment had her confused.

"What happened? Did I do something wrong?"

"America, I love you so much, but this doesn't feel right," I sighed.

"What doesn't feel right?"

"Us... Me and you sneaking around like teenagers. We were together for ten years. I used to be your husband. We have a son together. All that has changed and I can't continue to do this with you. I came home to something different. I can't keep lying to myself like this. I love you America, but I can't love you like this. Fuckin' in a cheap motel... This shit was never us."

"Omar, you know the situation I'm in. My career... Kendal. I came a long way, and to just throw it away like that...? You think it's been easy for me?"

"I know it hasn't been too easy for you. If it wasn't for my error, you wouldn't have to make a choice. I'm the one that pushed you into his arms because of my foolishness, and I'm paying for it. But seeing you again, knowing that you're not my woman really hurts. You're the woman I'm ready to spend my life with, but right now there's too great a void between us."

America held me tightly. I felt her naked breasts against my back and knew she didn't want to let go. Even though I wanted another chance with her, my feelings were too strong for her. Jealousy began stirring up in me and was becoming hard to swallow.

"Omar, I just can't leave Kendal like that. There's a lot going on. I mean, it's hard for me to explain. I look at you and I love you so much, but..." her voice trailed.

"But what...?"

"You know how many times you've hurt me, Omar? I always came back to you. Now you're fresh home again, and I told myself that I'm not going to run to you again. I buried the feelings that I had for you months ago, and put all my passion in my career. The moment I saw you, those old feelings for you resurfaced. I hate myself for being so weak. I'm in a vulnerable position, Omar. I just can't pretend like it was yesterday with you."

"You pretended it was like that an hour ago when I was between your thighs."

"Don't go there with me, baby. You just can't come home and ask me to give up on everything that I've worked for."

"I don't want you to give it up. I just wanna know if you are willing to give him up, for us...? If you still believe in us...?"

I looked at America as tears trickled down her smooth brown cheeks. My heart ached for her in so many ways. I just wanted to escape with her and make it the way it used to be between us, but there were obstacles.

"Do you love him?" I asked her.

She hesitated with an answer. She wiped her tears and turned away from me.

"Please don't make me choose between you, and my career."

"I'm not asking you to choose between your career and me. Do you love him? Or are you only with him because of your career, America."

"When you went away, he's been there for me and our son."

"But I'm home now, and I'm here for my son. I'm not going anywhere, America. I'm here to stay, and that's a promise."

"What you want from me, Omar?"

"The truth and an answer... I'm not making the same mistakes again, baby. That life I used to live, it's forgotten, I don't even remember it anymore. But if God allows me to have one more chance with you, then I'm doing right by it. I'll fight for us, baby, if you want me to fight. I just can't be with you as my jump-off. You've always meant more to me than just some booty call.

I wanna be in your life full time or not at all."

"I know."

I rose up from her embrace and collected my things. I started to get dressed. America stayed seated on the bed, her nakedness and beauty reflected off me like the sunrise off a Caribbean beach shore. It was such an advantage to see. I didn't want to leave, but staying around with my feelings for her in the loop was becoming a disadvantage to me.

I tied my Timberlands and fastened my jeans. America started to dress also. I couldn't wait around.

"You need a ride back?" she offered.

"Nah, I'm good. I'll catch a cab."

"Baby, let me drive you," she persisted.

"I know you have somewhere else to be. It's easier for me to catch a cab."

"Well, let me pay for it," she sighed.

"America, I know you have money and wanna look out for me, but I don't need for you to take care of me. I have a job now, I can handle my own."

"It's good to see you on your feet," she smiled.

There was this brief moment between us where time felt frozen. It was early afternoon, and I had to be at the youth center by four. I had a group discussion with a group of teenagers.

America hugged me tightly and we kissed. We locked eyes and I asked, "Would you ever marry me again?"

My question fell on silence. I felt her heart beat against me, her grip around me loosen a tad. She closed her eyes and exhaled again. I added, "Do you trust me?"

"I believe you when you say that you're a fully changed man now. I need time to think it over."

I nodded then we hugged and kissed. Leaving out the door, I walked to the nearest cab stand with America heavy on my mind. I got into a cab and gave the driver my destination.

The center was my second home. Being a counselor, I had to be real with my kids, we had discussions about sex, gangs to drugs. I even talked about my past. When they found out that Omega and I used to be partners in crime, the questions came in droves. Around here, they idolized men like Omega and wanted to follow in their footsteps. My job was to prevent that, but there were a few in my group that were already under Omega's wing. I warned them about staying down, and told them about my cousin's death, and my imprisonment. Talking badly about Omega, I offended some of the teens who looked up to him. Donny was really upset.

"Omega's a lost fool," I said.

"You the fool man... Omega is rich and got respect out here. What you got man, huh?" Donny fired back.

"I got my well-being and dignity, Donny. I don't have to look over my shoulders anymore. I have a son who I love and I have my freedom. What he has, is not lasting."

"Whatever, Mr. Omar... You turned your back on your peeps," he retorted.

"You think I'm the one who turned my back on you or anybody else in this room? You got it twisted Donny. The ones who turned their backs on y'all and don't care for you, are the men out there killing and desecrating our community with violence and drugs... Treating you like pawns for their profit."

"And you used to be one of them. Now you think you're better than us," Donny smirked.

"I'm not better than you or anyone else in this room. I just woke up and came to my senses. That's all."

Donny was hardcore, a thug who came to my meetings because it was mandated by a judge. He'd caught a previous drug conviction and it was his first offense. At sixteen, he had been brainwashed by the likes of Omega.

I had been home for over a month and was a witness to the violence and drugs plaguing our youth. My heart was broken when I saw Cindy strung out on meth, and turning tricks on South Road late one night. That incident made me want to protest and fight the bullshit even more. She used to be a prominent college student, a good girl, but hung with the wrong crowd. She used to have a crush on me when she was at the center, but now she was a whore.

Speaking out against Omega, Biscuit and the rest of the violent drug crew became my daily chore. They were vicious and my war with them started at the youth center. It became my hub. Mr. Jenkins, Vincent and many others were behind me, giving support. We were determined to save our community and our teens. We held candle light vigils on the notorious corners for North Star, and the young men and women who lost their lives to violence. Hundreds of residents of the community came out to support our cause. We began staging protests in front of well-known drugs spots and stash houses. I was determined to put a stop to Omega's ill-gotten business by any means necessary. I didn't fear him and I didn't hate him. In my heart, he was still my brother, but he was the blind leading the blind toward a steep cliff.

I was making noise in the streets and I knew Omega had to be listening. Like back in the days, my name was ringing out, but it was for a cause now — and becoming active in my community helped to take my mind off America. It made me feel important. I felt needed.

After my session with my group, I walked out into the hallway and spotted Narmer with his girlfriend. Narmer looked at me, whispered something to his girl, and came my way.

"You tryin' a get fucked up, nigga?" Narmer asked.

"What?"

"You callin' out Omega? You think he ain't gonna come at you?"

"What he's doing is wrong."

"And who's gonna stop us? You…? Nigga, you don't hold weight 'round here no more. It's a new day. You hear me? You either gotta get yours or be gone. If you weak, you die."

"It's that kind of brainwash bullshit that has so many of you kids twisted right now. You're about to become a father soon, Narmer. Don't you care about seeing your son born? Don't you wanna be alive to see him grow up?"

"My little nigga gonna be a'ight, cuz his daddy is holding shit down in the streets. He got family who's gonna have his back when he grows up. My son ain't gonna be no punk."

"You think what you're a part of is family? That's not family, that's ignorance."

"Why you tryin to put us down all the time...? Nigga, from what I hear, you weren't any difference from us. Like you ain't got bodies on your hands?"

"And look what it got me, prison and missing the birth of my son."

"Yeah whateva nigga... All I know is you best to chill wit' all that noise out there 'fore you come up missing."

"Don't threaten me, Narmer."

"It ain't a threat, just a warning."

With his jeans sagging and boxers showing, Namer strutted over to his girlfriend.

"What was that all about?" Vincent asked, wheeling himself over to where I stood, annoyed.

"Nothing, Vincent. I was just out here trying to school a youngn'."

"And I assumed it didn't go too well by your look and tone," he said.

"It could've gone down better."

"C'mon, I'll buy you lunch," he chuckled.

My entire day had been spent debating with the kids about Omega and my past life. The youth center was slowly thinning out with the kids going home for the day. When I walked outside, it was seven in the evening. Exhausted, I just wanted to sleep. Right away I spotted the dark SUV parked across the street. Rocky was posted by the passenger door and I knew who was inside. He showed up sooner than expected. I walked to the vehicle and greeted Rocky.

"Rocky, it's been a long time. So you're his personal bitch now?"

"Just get in the damn truck, Soul."

We looked at each other for a moment. Rocky just came home from doing three years upstate for drugs and assault. I never had a problem with him, but we were never close.

He opened the back door. I stepped into the ride and sat next to Omega. He was smoking a Black-n-Mild cigar, and wearing a seersucker suit with the white V-neck underneath. He sported gold sunglasses and a diamond pinky ring.

"I see you're trying to get your grown and sexy on," I joked.

"I ain't here to share jokes with you, Soul," he said, puffing on his cigar. "You been home for over a month now, and not once did you come check ya nigga. You ain't got love for me anymore?" Omega continued.

"Been busy," I said.

"Yeah, I heard that you out here trying to ruin my image. You telling my young soldiers in the streets that I'm nothing. And you wanna be out there tryin' to protest my shit, fuck up my money wit' nonsense," he said heatedly.

"Wake up, Omega and take a look around you. Look what's happening to our community…"

"Community…? Fuck you see a community at, nigga? What I see, is the hood, and that's where you and me came up, Soul. That's what we know, these fuckin' blocks is what made you and me. Nigga, you should be out here gettin' that money like me, but look at you… Some broke down counselor who ain't got shit to show, but some words and time. I'm respected out here, nigga. I run this shit! Me muthafucka! But I guess you was too weak to ever fuckin' take it to the next level."

"I'm too weak? Look at you, Omega you're drunk off this war. This damn illusion you're living. It ain't nothing but a lie that's going to come crashing down on you… This is what you want, money, power and having our kids dying violently over your bullshit…? Addicted to your damn drugs that their future is ruined… Yo, this ain't supposed to be life."

"It was life for you and me comin' up, nigga! Ain't nuthin' changed. I'm a gets mines and do me!"

"We ain't never had anybody to tell us right from wrong. We never had our fathers growing up, Omega. We had nowhere to go, but to the streets. But you remember what it was like for us. Our mothers addicted to crack, our fathers not there for us, so we learned to become men ourselves."

"It just made me a stronger man."

"It made us stupid and naïve," I sighed.

I wanted to get through to Omega. I had known the man since grade school, and knew how hardheaded he could be.

"These kids have something that we didn't, Omega. They have a chance, opportunity, and mentors to steer them in the right direction. I admit my mistakes and my transgressions, but can you, my brother?"

"We're brothers, but you wanna fuckin' tarnish my name. And now preach to me like you my fuckin' mother!"

"That's right. You're still my brother, Omega. I don't hate you. I just want to help you," I pleaded.

"I need you to stay out my fuckin' business," he warned.

"And if I don't..."

"Then when you exit this truck, you become a stranger. I can no longer protect your well-being."

"You think I need protection from you. You forget where I'm from, Omega? I don't fear you or anyone in your camp."

He chuckled.

"You's a fool, Soul. You the one that needs to wake up. Where your bitch at? She ain't around anymore, huh? She left you for the next nigga. And if you ain't careful, you might end up confined to a wheelchair like Vincent."

"Really...? But this time I'm being careful, Omega."

"You of all peoples should know that I'm nobody to fuck wit'. Who you think help put Vincent in that wheelchair? S.S and me put work in on that nigga. Lucky muthafucka survived though. You might not be so fortunate. But if you keep coming against me we will find out, won't we?"

It was disturbing news to hear. There was a part of me that wanted to punch him in the face. I frowned at Omega, I needed to be the better man and slow my anger.

"I'm going to pray for you, Omega."

"Fuck you!" he exclaimed.

"Then I think we're done here."

Omega took another pull from his Black-n-Mild and spat, "Yeah, we done."

I started to exit from the truck, but I turned to him with an afterthought, and said, "Oh, I think you should know, your brother Rahmel made parole. So he should be home soon."

He took the news nonchalantly. Before I was completely out the truck, I heard Omega say, "He ain't no brother of mines anymore. Neither is you, Soul."

The door slammed shut. Rocky got behind the wheel and drove off. I stood there and sighed heavily. I knew that with him and me, it wasn't going to get prettier anytime soon. We had both changed in so many different ways. I was going my way and Omega his, but I knew that eventually our paths would cross.

17
America

It was almost the perfect day. Blue sky as far as the eyes could see, the weather was warm and comfortable. In a few days I was about to shoot my fifth video. Sitting by the pool in the backyard, I was being interviewed by Mindy Samson. She had been in the music industry since the days of Run DMC. Mindy was in her mid forties with a figure most women would kill for at her age. She was down to earth, had an uplifting personality, and some say that if Mindy reached out to you for an interview then you were definitely on your way.

I felt flattered when Mindy reached out to me for a private one-on-one talk with her. My son was playing near and letting mommy have her time with Mindy. Kendal was in the city on business and I was glad that it was just the two of us girls talking, no men around, except for my son.

We sat on opposite sides in deep cushioned seating chairs, cold glasses of lemonade between us. Mindy looked fabulous in her floral printed kimono sleeve tunic, her legs toned and sporting wedges.

"Girl, I love your shoes."

"Thank you," she replied.

I was wearing a silk khaki skirt, and a Dolce & Gabbana body suit with Burberry, ruby wood heel sandals. Dressed to impress, Mindy complimented me on my outfit.

"You've got what it takes and your style is impeccable," she said. "You've got what it takes, America."

I smiled. She had broken the ice and we hit it off instantly.

Mindy placed the tape recorder on the small table between us. Then she pulled out her pen and pad. I looked over at my son to see if he was okay. Kahlil was busy with his toys in the play area. I smiled.

"He's so cute," Mindy said.

"Thank you."

"How old?" she asked.

"Eighteen months. He's very good at nights too, sleeps well," I said proudly.

"You're one of the fortunate ones. I have three kids, and all my kids raised hell after birth. They were all night owls," she grinned.

"Kahlil knows mommy needs her rest. And how old are your kids?"

"My oldest, Sherrie, she's twenty-three, and my two sons, Markese is twenty-one and Michael is eighteen," Mindy said.

"You're the fortunate one, your kids are grown. I know that I have a good ways to go."

"Terrible two's is nothing to raising three teenagers, but that's a story for another day," Mindy said.

"And you made it through still looking good, girl," I chuckled.

"By God's grace," Mindy returned.

"I hear that."

"Are you planning on having anymore?" she asked.

I didn't know that Mindy had started our interview. It was so subtle. I looked down and saw the tape recorder was on and she was jotting a few things down in her pad. She was good. I looked over at Kahlil, watching him play then I answered, "Yes, I do. But my son is enough for me to handle right now. With my career taking off, I am so busy. But I can see having another one in five years or so. I want my girl."

"So what's it been like for you, America? Coming into this new found fame?"

"I'm enjoying it, Mindy. This is such God's blessing. I love every moment of it. I love to sing and I love to write my own songs. I've been singing since I was five. I won my first talent show at eight and from there on, I never looked back. I knew I wanted to be a star and I'm working hard at it. I'm in the studio day in and day out, constantly recording, writing my own material and sometimes ghostwriting for others."

"Busy girl…"

"I gotta be. Who else is going to do it for me?"

"So, your first album, even though it's independent, the buzz and love you've received for it, is overwhelming. The fans love you. Do you have any shows or tours lined up?"

"Actually, my manager is lining up something for me with Beyonce… But I've been out to doing the college circuits, clubs and other events. Every time I do a show, it's sold out."

"Beyonce…? Hmm, that's nice. You go girl…"

"I have butterflies in my stomach just thinking about opening up for her."

"She's nice, you remind me of her," Mindy said.

I felt my cheeks burning from blushing so hard.

"Besides singing, what else do you like to do?"

"I like being a mother. I enjoy painting, reading, and dancing. And one day I hope to get into acting. I'm a movie fanatic. And some nights, I like to get a few snacks, cuddle on the couch with my man, glued to a good movie. I love watching romantic comedies and action movies."

"You and me both, one of my favorites is *Hitch,* and I love *My Big Fat Greek Wedding,*" Mindy smiled.

"Oh really…? Me too, I love Will Smith, and Nia Vardalos was the best," I said.

Mindy agreed. We had so much in common. I took a sip of lemonade and tried to be myself during the interview. I knew that the piece on me was going to be read by thousands. It was the kind of exposure I needed to boost my stardom and career.

Mindy and I continued to talk. I felt relaxed around her sometimes I would forget that it was an interview. We spoke to each other like we were best friends that knew each other forever. She asked about everything, family, friends and where I was from. I kept it truthful with her. Forty minutes had passed and then the interview became a little more personal when she started asking about Kendal.

"So, with Kendal being your manager and boyfriend, are there any wedding bells for the two of you anytime soon?" she asked.

I didn't want to answer the question, but with Mindy Samson, you just couldn't leave her hanging. So I tried to downplay it.

"I don't know. We're both busy, have a lot on our schedule and who knows what the future has for us," I said briskly.

"So, is that a yes?"

"We'll see what happens."

Mindy looked at me for a moment. It felt like she was reading me, picking up on my vibes after the question. I took another sip of lemonade and hoped she moved on to another question. I wasn't in the mood to talk about Kendal.

"I got it. I hit a nerve with you on that one, huh?" she said.

"Not really a nerve... Kendal and I are good," I lied.

Leaning forward, Mindy stopped the tape and put down her writing pad. I figured something was up. I kept it casual and thought that maybe I fucked up somewhere. Maybe she was getting ready to school me about giving a good interview. Surprisingly, Mindy stared at me, woman-to-woman, and said, "America, you know what I see when I look at you? I see a lie."

"Excuse me," I replied, being taken aback somewhat.

"I see a woman that's trapped, but don't know the combination for her escape," Mindy continued. "I listen to your songs, and when a woman sings like you do, it means that she's passionate about something. When I mentioned Kendal, your eyes don't light up.... So that means your heart is somewhere else."

A nervous giggle escaped my throat.

"Girl, it's okay, I've been there a few times. I know the feeling. When I first came into this business, I married for money. I got started in the industry because of my first husband, but that marriage was a complete disaster. Now my second marriage, it was for love, and I gave him three kids... We divorced ten years later, but you know what? I don't regret it."

Sitting there quietly, taking in every word from Mindy, I thought I loved Kendal, but I was just blinded by the success and things he was doing for me. I felt obligated to be with him because of how far he took my career.

"What I'm trying to tell you, America, you're a very talented and beautiful woman. You're going places regardless of who you're with. To be with someone because of a career decision is only going to make things worse for you. Money might be able to buy you companionship, but it can never buy real emotions. I know we went off track a little, but that's just the mother in me."

"Thank you."

Mindy and I went on with the interview and it was fun. Her personality and attitude inspired me. She was so positive. After she was done interviewing me, she stayed around for two hours and we had cocktails, some more girl talk and really got to know each other. I told her about Omar.

By late afternoon, Mindy got into her Porsche Cayenne, waved and drove off. I beamed. It was a good day and the advice Mindy Samson gave me, stuck to me like glue. I cooked lunch for my son and spent some time with him. It was our day together.

Kahlil was taking a nap and I sat by the pool working on my next song. The cool evening breeze was pleasant. I had a drink in one hand and a pen in the other, thinking about the next hit to come up with. I put the pen to the pad and thought about Omar as I wrote.

> Is it true, ooh, is it true,
> the way I feel about you,
> you know that love is so special,
> I don't mind, don't deny, seen it in the eyes…
> cuz I remember a time, between you and I,
> I was your girl, you was my man 'til our dying day,
> your love washing down on me like warm spring rain.
> I'll walk a thousand miles,
> lift you up a thousand times,
> find it in my heart to forgive you,
> cuz I dedicate my soul, my love, my life to you…
> baby, you're all I'm lookin' for,
> so I'ma take step back, take a deep breath,
> and become the reason why …
> I'm your angel, your sweet angel.

I was tempted to call Omar, wanting to hear his voice and talk to him.

He was right about us creeping around. Omar was my drug, my addiction and it felt like I was coming to a crossroad. The issues with Kendal had to be resolved before I continued seeing Omar. That tingling between my thighs and the devoted feeling in my heart were putting me in a risky situation. Like Run DMC said, 'It's tricky'. I gave in to temptation, picked up my cellphone, and dialed Omar's number. When he picked up, my panties got wet and my heart melted.

Several days had passed since my interview. I was talking to Omar daily and even convinced him to come visit me at my home while Kendal flew to L.A for the weekend. He wanted me to fly out with him, but I gave him an excuse and stayed in New York. I waited for Omar that morning. I wanted to go all out for him, and with Kendal away, I felt that it was safe to play. I made sure my home was in order and spent the morning working on another song.

Omar had been spending quality time with his son, it was the greatest thing. I heard he was doing a phenomenal thing at the center with at risk kids. He was trying to help make Jamaica, Queens a better place. He had changed for the better and I was in awe.

Waiting around for him, I felt like a kid on Christmas Eve. It was almost two in the afternoon. I sighed with concern that he might not show. A few days ago, I was at the spa, getting dolled up just for him. Today all I was wearing was a silk robe with pleated kimono sleeves, and a wrap-around belt.

At a quarter to three, I heard a car pull up. I looked out the window and smiled when I saw Omar getting out of a cab. He made his way to my front door and I hurried to greet him. Before he could ring my bell, I opened the door with an inviting smile and a warm hug.

"Hey baby," I greeted cheerfully.

We had a warm, lengthy embrace and I kissed him deeply. I led Omar into my new home and he looked around. It was his first time seeing the place in Long Island and I could tell he was immensely impressed.

"Nice, really nice, America."

"Thanks baby."

"You came up."

"Are you hungry, Omar?"

"I'm good."

The way I was feeling I would have cooked on the grill by the pool, butt naked if he wanted me. I smiled at the thought.

"What you smiling about?"

"Nothing," I answered teasingly.

I looked Omar up and down, noting every inch of him from head to toe. He was fine in his strapping white tank-top that highlighted his thick chest and exposed his muscular defined arms. He sported a pair of designer cargo shorts, a Yankees fitted and a pair of fresh white uptowns.

"You're looking good, Omar."

"You too," he smiled.

As we chatted, I flirted with him a little. He took a seat in the great room on my plush sofa, and kicked off his sneakers.

"You're getting comfortable, huh?" I joked.

"Yeah, it's easy to relax in a place like this," he said.

"It is."

Then I saw a change in the look on Omar's face. He went from smiling and looking around to suddenly being bothered. I knew Omar and his demeanor when there was something heavy on his mind.

"Baby, what's wrong? Why the sad look all of a sudden?" I asked.

"America, I wanted to give you all of this. This is exactly what I wanted for you. A nice home outside of the hood... I wanted to provide for you, make you happy. But I kept fuckin' up. It looks like your boy beat me to it. He's the better man for now."

Hearing him say that made me want to comfort him. I went to him and slowly straddled him as he sat on the couch. I kissed him on the lips and said, "You are the better man, Omar. I mean, yeah this place is nice... but it's not everything. Besides, what you're doing with them kids, trying to keep them off the streets and making a stand against the violence out there, and you being a father to Kahlil…you're the better man and will always be in my eyes."

He smiled when I kissed him again. Omar's warm lips caressed mine, I felt my pussy trickling. His warm embrace made me treasure the way his strong hands touched my body. I was ready to untie my robe and expose all of my glory to him. There was nothing to worry about. Kendal was away in L.A for two days, and Khalil was with my aunt. It would be our special moment together.

"I shouldn't be here with you," he suddenly uttered.

"And why not…?"

"I'm in this man's house. It just doesn't feel right."

"It's my house too. I'm helping pay for it, so? Besides, since when did you care where you fucked me? It's never bothered you before."

"It does now. I'm not that dude anymore, America."

"So why did you come?"

"I really miss you, America."

"Well I missed you too, Omar."

My pussy grew hotter in his lap, letting him know that I was horny. I missed Omar. Grinding my body against Omar's muscularity, I saturated his oral cavity with kisses. Then I slipped my tongue into his mouth, enjoying every minute.

"You don't have to worry we're alone for days," I said.

"I ain't worried."

"That's my man talking," I teasingly whispered in Omar's ear.

He perked up, and I felt his hand sliding up my naked thigh. It rested on the curve of my ass underneath my robe. I nibbled at his ear and felt his touch between my legs. Slowly untying my robe, Omar cupped my breasts and his lips touched my nipples. He made circles with his tongue.

"Oh yes, Omar!" I gasped as he shoved a tit into his warm mouth.

My body was writhing and the robe slowly fell from my shoulders. Now I was aching to be fucked. Omar's staff was at full attention underneath me. He was ready. I reached down for his belt buckle and undid it with the quickness. He got out of his pant, gripped my waist, and thrust himself inside of me.

I was gasping for air. The feeling of his huge member opened me up like a doorway. Holding on tightly to my man, I began riding him slowly.

"Ugh…"

"Yes…"

We both grunted and groaned. My hips and thighs nestled against him. His strapping chest was pressed against my breasts. Omar's hands were tangled in my hair. His body was like a sledgehammer slamming into me. Omar fucked me right. My silk robe fell to the carpet and I was completely nude.

We made love on the plush sofa. Then I guided him into the warmth of my bedroom. Omar came out his clothes, climbed between my legs and laid pipe in my juicy, inviting pussy.

"Oh shit! Damn!" he cried out.

Omar exploded in me, I thought he tore my sheets because he was shuddering and gripping the bed so tight. Breathing against me like a runner out of breath, I held him close. Massaging his back, I gently kissed my ex-husband. We were in the missionary position, where we recovered for a while. My inner thighs were wet and tingling. The bedroom sheets were soiled with his sweat and my lust. I cherished the moment.

He rolled off my stomach and rested on his back. I wanted to cuddle, so I threw myself on top of him and laughed. We both shared such a wonderful moment even though I knew it was fucked up to have him in the home that Kendal and I shared. He had sweated in the same bed. When it came to Omar, I could never think rationally.

Minutes passed, but for me, it felt time stood still. His dick had worn me out, and I wanted to take a nap. Omar was just in his own zone, thinking about something, and I didn't want to bother him. He was a busy man with a lot on his mind. Staring into his eyes, I fell in love with him all over again. I loved the commitment he showed to the youth center. It was a measure of his growth. When he spoke about his work, the passion of his words touched me and my heart would skip a beat. I was completely vulnerable around him. I started kissing his chest, and my hands roamed all over his statuesque body, feeling on him.

"I love you so much, Omar."

"America, I love you."

Tears welled. Omar reached out and wiped them from my eyes. He smiled. I smiled back through cloudy eyes and exhaled with satisfaction.

Time passed and neither of us moved from the bed. Lying in each other's arms, we chatted and I revealed my true feelings for him. I was shocked when he brought up Omega in the middle of our chitchat. I didn't want to hear his name, but Omar needed to share that during our pillow-talk.

"He got a beef with me. The other day he was waiting for me outside the center. We had words, but I wasn't reaching him."

"That's because he can't be reached. Omega's a fool. Some men won't change. The devil has his soldiers too, you know? You just need to stay away from him, Omar."

"That man's my brother, America. I just want him to understand what he's doing to our community is fucked up. He got these kids dying out here. It wasn't that long ago that I was doing wrong myself, but I can't sit back and just watch."

"Baby, he's not your concern. You need to be focused on the kids. You need to just do you. Don't stress yourself."

He let out a heavy sigh and looked at me. My head was against his chest and I toyed with his nipples.

"It's gonna get ugly, America. I can feel it," he stated, being calm.

"Forget all that, baby. Just feel me today, okay."

I stretched my hand down to his package, massaging his family jewels. I wanted to get his mind off his problem. My lips circled his bulging rod. I took him into my throat and gave him a pleasant blowjob. He was harder than steel in my mouth and I liked the way he squirmed when I sucked him. Kissing on his mushroom tip, I was getting down and dirty with him.

"Spray it in my mouth, baby," I begged like a sex-starved vixen.

"Oh, yeah… What?"

"I wanna taste you," I pleaded.

He grunted and turned while I continued sucking him off. About ten minutes into pleasing him, his cellphone went off.

"Don't answer it."

"I need to," he said, reaching for the disturbing instrument.

I sat up while Omar talked.

"Yeah," he answered, looking around at me.

I waited for him to finish. I wanted to finish him off the right way. There was a look of frustration on his face then Omar exclaimed, "What? When...?"

Something seemed to have gone awfully wrong. He talked for another minute then hung up.

"What's wrong, baby?" I asked with concern.

Omar glanced over at me with a sad gaze staining his grill. He swallowed hard before speaking.

"That was Vincent," he said with furrowed brow as if deep in thought. "He said that another teen from the center was found murdered last night. He said it's really bad."

"Ohmygod," I uttered.

"I gotta go, America."

Omar started to get dressed and our time together came to an abrupt end. He quickly threw on his clothes, called for a cab, and made his way for the exit before I could blink. I followed behind him. I wanted to drive him, but he wanted me to stay home.

"Omar, please be careful," I shouted from the doorway.

Watching him leave so suddenly, without a proper goodbye, felt like someone hit me in the stomach. But I understood. The violence in my old hood was becoming a serious problem. I saw my old block on the news a few times and it was always a murder or drugs.

I plopped down on my couch, turned on the TV, and tried to distract myself. It wasn't working. Thinking about Omar and his problem with Omega bothered me. I knew what Omega was capable of doing. He was a dangerous man, and I didn't want anything to do with him. I prayed for Omar and I prayed for myself. I sat watching the news and tried to ease my mind. My feelings for Omar was growing and the situation with Kendal didn't seem to be getting any better. I debated back and forth if or when I should tell him. I couldn't hide it from Kendal any longer. He needed to know.

Monday morning came and I was taking a warm shower, getting ready for the day. I planned on meeting Mike One at the studio for a two hour session, have lunch with Joanna then pick up Kahlil from Aunt Genes' place. I wanted to take him to the park. It was a beautiful day.

I stepped out of the shower and heard the front door slammed. I knew that it should be Kendal coming home from the airport. I quickly dried myself off, and hurried out the bathroom.

"That's you, Kendal," I called out.

"Yeah, I'm back baby," he replied.

From the top of the spiral staircase, I saw Kendal. He was in a dark blue button down, black slacks, and carrying a duffle bag over his shoulders while making his way up the stairs. He smiled at me in my towel with my hair wet.

"You miss me, baby?" he asked with a greeting smile.

"How was the trip?" I asked.

"Business was good, but I'm exhausted," he stated.

He dropped his duffle bag, pulled me into his arms, kissing me passionately. I returned the kiss, but I didn't want to take it any further with him. Kendal felt me up under the towel and I knew what he had on his mind. I gently pushed him away and said, "After that long flight, I know you need a shower and some rest. Go get situated, baby, I'll be here."

"Yeah, you're right. I gotta surprise for you, baby. We're on our way. You got fans out there waiting to meet you, America. I'm setting up some events for us and within the summer, we should be out there handling business."

"That's what's up," I smiled.

"But let me take this shower and when I get out, you can treat your man to the right homecoming he deserves," Kendal said.

He kissed me again and disappeared into the bathroom. I went to the bedroom, put on some clothes, walked downstairs and into the kitchen. After pouring a glass of orange juice, I grabbed my book and went outside on the patio. I was enjoying the sunny day and staring at our thick tree-lined fence separating our property. We had privacy. Our next door neighbors were some distance away. My home looked and felt like it was a place out of a high-end real estate catalog.

One hour later, I was still sitting with my thoughts to entertain me. I thought about Los Angles, I couldn't wait to be out there. I wanted to experience the west coast and their ways of doing things out there. Ever since N.W.A. and *Straight Outta Compton* and Snoop Dogg's *Gin & Juice,* I wanted to visit the west coast, and L.A became one of the top cities hot on my list to visit.

The peace around me was uplifting. Stretching out in one of the lawn chairs, sipping on orange juice, I soon heard movement in the kitchen. Kendal was preparing a cup of coffee. I chilled and opened the pages to a good book.

Just as I got into the story, Kendal joined me on the patio. Shirtless, he was wearing a pair of shorts and sandals. He took a seat next to me and asked, "So what you do while I was gone?"

Fucking my ex-husband and falling in love, I thought. "Oh, I've been busy with work. I finished a few songs while you were away," I lied.

"Oh really…? Nothing special happened?"

"Not really… Just me and my son," I shook my head and replied.

"Oh okay. So did you miss me?" he repeated.

"Of course, baby," I answered nonchalantly.

"It doesn't feel like you did, America. I mean, I'm home now. You know I need some of that good loving." He smiled.

Placing his hand on my thigh, Kendal rubbed me soothingly. He studied me for a moment. Maybe he was trying to catch a hint of infidelity in my eyes. I gave Kendal no reason to suspect me—not now anyway. I had washed the sheets we fucked on and sprayed the couch with Febreze to get rid of any smell of another man in the house.

"Damn, baby, at least you could have cooked breakfast for your man," he said.

"I didn't know you were hungry."

"I am… I'm starving. The meal in first class was okay, but it wasn't enough to fill me. I need some food and some of your loving. Hmm, now that'll do."

He moved in closer to me, his hand on my thigh traveled further up. I wasn't in the mood for sex. I just wanted to relax and get my day started. Kendal wanted to change my agenda. He reached between my thighs, and I subtly tried to shift my body.

"Baby, your coffee is ready," I said, hearing the whistle.

He got up and went into the kitchen. I stood up, collected my things from the patio and walked into the kitchen while Kendal was busy making his coffee. I tried to move by him hurriedly. To my dismay, before I could exit from the kitchen, Kendal grabbed my arm and pulled me close to him. With his hot cup of coffee on the counter, he nestled me into his arms and nibbled on my neck.

"Damn, I miss you so much, America. I love the way you feel, baby," he said.

He grabbed my ass, cupped my tits and tried to raise me up on the counter and get himself a quick fuck.

"Kendal, I have a busy day," I said, offering slight resistance.

"I just need a few minutes with you, baby. I just need to be in you right now. I've been thinking about you for days," he said.

His touch became more aggressive towards me. I felt his erection poking through his shorts. Kendal was like an octopus on me, his hands all over on my body. He tried to undress me, but I continued to resist. Kendal became aware of my resistance and took a step back.

"America, what's up with you? I mean, I haven't seen you in three days. We ain't fuck in a week. I'm horny baby. Why you being all selfish like that?"

"Between Khalil and writing, I'm just tired, and I have a busy day today. That's all"

The look in his eyes clearly showed his doubt. He sighed and continued to look at me.

"What you been doing this weekend, baby? Just break down your day to day for me. I wanna know," Kendal said to me seriously.

"What? Are you kidding?" I spat.

"I just wanna know what got you acting funny all of a sudden. I mean, you ain't trying to give your man any ass right now. That's obvious. So my guess is, you gotta be fuckin' somebody else," he said angrily.

"How dare you, Kendal, I'm tired of your fuckin' accusations," I hissed.

"Accusations...? America, I'm out here busting my ass for us, so you can get ahead and be a star in this business. You can't even be fuckin' real with me right now! I'm not stupid America," he shouted.

"I never said you were."

"So why are you trying to play me like I'm a chump?"

"What are you talking about, Kendal?" I retorted.

"When were you going to tell me that you have been seeing him again, huh?" he shouted.

"Yeah, you think I didn't know that since his release y'all been hooking up. You think I don't have sources that let me know what's up..."

"You're spying on me now?"

"You're the one keeping secrets, America. Are you fuckin' that jailbird?"

Playing it off, I chuckled in disbelief then said, "You're unbelievable."

"No, you are! You're a fuckin' liar, America!" Kendal shouted and stormed into the next room.

I thought our argument was over, but Kendal came back into the kitchen and dropped what seemed to be some pictures on the kitchen counter.

"If I'm unbelievable, then explain these," he spat.

I looked down at them and was shocked to see that he had recent pictures of me with Omar. There was one of us having dinner together and another with him walking me to my car, and others showing me with him. Then I saw he had one of us kissing.

"Did you fuck him?" Kendal asked.

I sighed then shouted, "Kendal, you bastard! You fuckin' had me followed?"

"I'm glad I did... Here this nigga is not even fresh home and you up this nigga's ass like a wedgie. I did more for you than he ever will. I'm the one who was there for you when he was locked down. And this is how you fuckin' repay me?"

"You're impossible, Kendal. Ohmygod! I can't believe you had people following me. Are you crazy?"

"I—I am. Crazy to ever trust you... I fuckin' love you, America. You don't love me. You love that ex-con more than you love me. And he don't do shit for you but cause you problems. You ready to fuck up everything that you worked so hard for, just to go running behind his trifling ass?"

I stood there, breathing hard, trying to calm the bitch in me. Feeling like I wanted to go upside Kendal's head and fuck him up. I kept my cool. Our argument continued into the great room. We went at each other, cursing and shouting loudly. Sounding ugly, we were shouting and yelling at each other. I refused to admit to having sex with Omar. I was so upset about the pictures I started throwing things in the house.

"You know what just admit it America, you fuckin' him, right? You probably fucked him over the weekend while I was gone. That's why you ain't trying to give me any. That jailbird done probably stretched out the pussy already. You'd rather be out there being a whore to a jailbird, than trying to handle business."

I slapped Kendal so hard that my hand stung. His cheek quickly turned red. I glared at him and was reaching my boiling point.

"Fuck you!" I cursed.

"No, fuck you!" he retorted.

Kendal went over to the sixty-inch plasma flat screen, and slipped a disk in it. Picking up the remote, he pressed play.

"Bitch, explain this!"

"Oh..." I gasped wide-eyed at what I saw.

My breath laid still, my body became motionless. The rendezvous with Omar from the previous day was all caught on camera. Kendal had a recording of us getting it on in the couch. The picture of us, clear as day, was displayed on the wide screen like some type of porn movie. He turned the volume up of me and Omar together. The sound shot through the living room with me confessing on video.

"Oh shit....I love you, baby. Fuck me! Fuck me! Oh God, Omar, I fuckin' love you so much."

I watched me riding Omar with zest, sweating and smiling teasingly for him. How could something that was so good turn out to be something so hurtful to watch? I was pondering, struggling with my thoughts. I heard the executioner's tone in Kendal's voice.

"Does this work for you or do you want more? Huh America...?"

I shot a wicked stare at him. He was teary eye and was hurting too, but I didn't give a fuck about his sniffling ass. He had disrespected, spying on me without my knowledge. He had cameras placed throughout the house, had people watching me. I wanted to hate Kendal so bad. Although I was in the wrong myself, I felt no pity.

He fast forwarded the video and there were me and Omar in bed. Kendal saw and heard things I said to Omar that I never told anyone else.

"Turn it off!" I screamed.

"Why? It's you right? But I'm the one that's wrong. I'm the one being played for a fuckin' fool! You got what you want from me, so now it's back to your ex, huh?" Kendal shouted.

"It's not like that, Kendal."

"Then what's it like, huh, America...? You fuckin' tell me! What's it fuckin' like then!" he screamed, throwing the remote into the TV.

The screen was shattered and the remote smashed into pieces. Kendal then turned over the wood and glass coffee table, breaking it and charged at me. I saw the rage in his eyes, but I didn't budge. Knowing that this moment between us was inevitable, I stood my ground.

"I didn't want you to find out this way," I started.

"I love you, baby. I really do. I want us to work, but this nigga comes home and turns our world upside down. And the fucked up part about it is you're allowing him to do it!"

We stood there. Our words cutting each other sharply like sharp samurai swords against soft skins. There was going to be a lot of blood flowing. I understood that Kendal was upset, but the spying on me and the video was the proverbial straw that broke the camel's back. He shouted and screamed, but I knew he still wanted his way. He didn't want Omar to win. His ego couldn't deal with losing me to an ex-con. This is the point where I had to let Kendal know I was never his to keep in the first place. Our angry, cold silent staring was interrupted when Kendal spoke.

"Did you ever love me, America? I mean, love me... Like you love him?"

I looked at him. The truth was too much for him to bear, it would crush him. I loved Kendal, but I wasn't in love with him like I was with Omar. He held me down, helped me get started, but the spark for him didn't set me on fire. Omar's did.

"You wanna know the truth?"

"Just fuckin' tell me."

"I love you, Kendal... But there's something that Omar and I have together that I just can't explain to you," I admitted.

"So I'm the fool?"

Kendal wiped his tears. He stepped further away from me. He reached for his briefcase, his hands rummage inside. I stepped back, thinking that it was about to be a murder or suicide in the house. My heart raced and my mind went spinning. For a second, I even rationalized that I deserved to be killed. Kendal, to my surprise, pulled sheets of papers and dropped them onto the broken coffee table. I stared at him, I was confused.

"I got you the tour with Beyonce. It was my surprise. She's lookin' forward to working with you even doin' a song with you. I was in L.A wrapping up some business for you, because I love you. But I don't get that love back."

For a couple of heart rending moments, he watched my reaction. Then he added, "I even negotiated a film deal with an independent company that begins shooting next year. I met up with some peoples, and they really loved you. But I see now, you just took me for granted. I hope Omar can look out for you the way I did. America, I'm through."

Kendal walked out the front door, leaving our home and my heart in crazy shambles. My mind scrambled wildly, it felt like I couldn't breathe. I stared at the contract he had worked so hard to put together for me. My tears dropped as I stared at the sheets of paper. I plopped down on the couch and felt torn.

"Oh God," I gasped.

18
Omar vs. Soul

A teenager's funeral was a scene that I never wanted to get used to. Pinero was a young, Spanish male, sixteen years old from the neighborhood that ran with Narmer and his crew. It was late Wednesday evening at Gilmore's funeral home on Linden Blvd, where his family and friends were crying their hearts out. Cars and people lined the block. A few police officers were in attendance, and the halls were packed with mourners.

Pinero used to come to the center on the regular. He had a charming personality and was one of Vincent's favorite kids from the group. Pinero was well liked by everyone but the girls loved him. Rumors were that he got caught up in the drug war. Pinero was kidnapped and tortured by the Jamaicans. They shot his friend, Dino. He survived, but Pinero was taken in a dark van. Twenty four hours later, he was found dead and mutilated.

The mortician suggested a closed casket funeral, because of the disfigurement to her son's face, but Pinero's mother, Ms. Rodriguez, refused. She wanted everyone to see what the Jamaicans did to her son. Everyone in attendance would witness the horror and pain that her son endured. His captors had broken his fingers and he had fractured ribs. His teeth were missing and his testicles had been found in a jar.

Thinking that it was complete overkill, I walked up to the open casket and the sight of him made me cringe. Pinero's whole right side of his face was completely melted and almost burned away. His right eye was missing. Even though Pinero was just a child, the Jamaicans had tortured him for information. He had no close connection to Omega or any of his lieutenants. His brutal death was meant to send out a message to whoever was listening. The war and violence was getting worse, more deadly.

The city had assigned a task force to combat the gangs and drugs. They wanted to put a stop to the violent drug organizations in Jamaica, Queens. Pinero's murder was nationwide news. His tragic end brought attention to the neighborhood. Influential men like Al Sharpton and Jessie Jackson were now saying enough is enough. The media had picked on this tragedy and the extra coverage was bad business for Omega's organization. I had stepped up protests on the streets. The shutting down of meth labs continued. Everyone was now aware of the dangerous drug, brown-brown. The news station did a special on it. The once naïve public was informed about the cocaine and gunpowder mix the kids were using to get high. The deadly concoction was making them go nuts.

"'Brown-brown' is snorted and its growing popularity among young teens, have authorities concerned and parents worried. What was once used in West Africa, given to child soldiers in an act of war, has now reached the shores of our country and into the streets of our urban cities..." The anchor woman for ABC said.

At the funeral, I was interviewed by the media people there. I spoke out on everything that was wrong with our system. Letting the public know that I was a reformed gangster, I talked about my past. I refused to be quiet and threats didn't scare me. My fear and motivation was seeing my son caught up in this mess when he grew up. People were applauding my work at the center. I was becoming a force in my community and I had an army of people behind me who were tired of the bullshit.

Pinero's death and funeral was a tipping point. Standing in the back of the room, I watched while the memorial service took place. The young men and women from our community outreach program came out in droves to show their respect.

The slow-paced gospel song played while the congregation sang a catchy song.

"This little light of mine… I'm gonna let it shine. This little light of mine, I'm gonna let it shine…"

Pinero's mother was escorted by family members to the podium. Clad in a black dress and clutching a framed photo of her son, her heartbreak was evident. Like too many before her, Ms. Rodriquez was weeping for her son. She took a deep breath and addressed the other mourners.

"Look at my baby, look at him. He was my son, my joy and I miss him. I just wanted to say to our young generation today, don't turn your head from him, don't you dare… Y'all come up here and look at death. Look at what these streets did to my son! Look at him!" she exclaimed with fury. "I shouldn't be burying my son like this… Deformed and gone from me. No. I was supposed to watch him grow. But they didn't just take away my son they took away my future. He was my only son, my only child… And this is what they do to him. Look at him! This is how we do each other, huh? Killing and maiming for what…? Tell me. I want him back, I do. I want him home with me right now."

The room was silent. Tears were falling. Many wiped them away and continued to listen. I was one of them. My heart sank hearing that mother speak out the way she did. It took courage. She needed the hurt she felt to be communicated to all. I hoped the teenagers in the room saw the damage the streets and violence did to a home. Hoping that something was getting through to them, I prayed on.

Then I turned and walked out into the foyer. The woman's cries for her son haunted me and I needed to leave. I wanted to chill, have a drink somewhere, and have a moment for myself. The evening's heat was overbearing and the emotionally charged atmosphere was affecting me negatively. There were more kids, more people in the foyer. I saw familiar faces, but didn't take the time to greet anyone.

Outside Gilmore's funeral home, there were more gangsters than in a penitentiary. They were smoking and sipping on liquor, lingering out front of the memorial service like they were in front of a club. It was like party and bullshit, I was so disgusted.

Narmer and his friends were there. I spotted a face I knew was the heart and reasoning of the violence and chaos with our teens in our community. It was Biscuit, Omega's errand boy. His name rang out loudly like church bells on a Sunday morning, but there wasn't anything holy about him. His left arm was in a shoulder sling, and he stood next to Narmer. He was only eighteen years old, and he had more bodies to his name than an Iraqi soldier.

We locked eyes and my disapproval of him was apparent. Everyone was scared of him. He was a young killer and crazy. But his violent rep didn't move me. He had no right to be at this funeral. My disrespectful look caused Biscuit and his crew to confront me. I stood my ground. Biscuit was in my grill with his angry stare and spat, "What the fuck you lookin' at nigga?"

"You," I returned boldly.

"You tryin' a dis me, Soul? You need to stay the fuck outta the news, ya hear me, nigga! Fo' real, we don't appreciate you running Omega and our name into the ground like you do. You might end up dead. Omega was your fuckin' boy," Biscuit continued.

"You're an abomination, Biscuit," I stated strongly.

Biscuit slowly lifted his shirt, revealing the 9mm he had tucked in his waistband and said, "I'll show you an abomination, muthafucka."

"You see that young boy in there laid up in the casket…? You killed him. You're responsible for that boy's death. You come at me, Biscuit, and I'll make sure you pay for your sins."

"Nigga, what…? You threatenin' me?" Biscuit barked, causing a scene.

He started at me, but Narmer quickly stepped up and grabbed his arm, pulling him back.

"Biscuit chill… not here," Narmer said.

"Yeah, step off, Biscuit. I ain't the one to mess with. I ain't scared. I used to be you," I said.

"Nigga, you ain't never been me. But you gonna know me fo' real, nigga! You gonna know me," Biscuit shouted.

Narmer continued to drag Biscuit further away from me. He looked at me and I saw something in Narmer's eyes that told me that he needed reaching too. He was about to become a father. I hated to see another young father become separated from the birth of his child.

With Biscuit gone, I felt a little better. I looked around and saw a few eyes on me. I heard the whispers. One of the kids from the center approached me and asked, "Mr. Omar, you okay?"

I smiled. "Yeah, I'm good."

"Why you talk to Biscuit like that? Everybody knows he's crazy. He could've killed you, Mr. Omar."

"He's only a punk."

I was about to go back inside. But suddenly I heard numerous gunshots ringing out. The sound came from a few blocks away. People ran and the cops quickly became alerted. The crowd became startled, lights were flashing and police radios began crackling. There was more gunfire, but nobody knew which direction they came from. People got in their cars and ran in the funeral home while police tried to maintain order.

I ran in the direction where the shots were coming from. Following behind police, I ran for two blocks and approached the gruesome scene. It was Biscuit and his crew, they were hit. I assumed, ambushed by waiting enemies. Their car was riddled with bullets, windows shattered and shot out—doors opened, blood and a body in the driver's seat.

My eyes widened seeing Narmer on the ground. He had been shot. I didn't know how badly. I looked around for Biscuit, but there wasn't any sign of him. The police quickly had the area sealed. I heard more police sirens in the distance, getting closer every minute. I couldn't believe it, even at a funeral, there was no respect, no peace. It was really ugly out here.

People were baffled, but many including me, were very upset. Witnesses reported that a brown van pulled up beside the car, opened fire then took off. It was confirmed, two dead and Narmer was rushed to Jamaica hospital. There was no sign of Biscuit among the bodies.

Shaking my head, I walked away, needing to get a drink. I was tired. Bodies kept piling up. If the violence didn't stop soon, the government could declare Marshall Law in our hood.

I sat sipping on a Corona and tried to relax in the Lenox Lounge, one of my favorite spots in Harlem. It was my escape from Queens. When I was deep in the game, I used to come here and listen to the different jazz musicians. I like the history and knowing legends, Billie Holiday, Miles Davis and John Coltrane performed and had left their mark in the Lounge. It felt good to be around something like that.

Like my father, I was gifted with playing instruments and writing good lyrics. Music was soothing, and I loved jazz. My time and energy went to the streets and I regret never pursuing my musical career further. I couldn't dwell on what I should have done. I had to move on up and really think about my future.

One of the reasons I came to this spot was to see a live performance. Tonight was a quiet night and the crowd was light. I didn't mind. The relaxed atmosphere was refreshing and it gave me a chance to think.

Queens was becoming a very violent place. Pinero's funeral made the news. The shooting was aired on every news channel in the city. Businesses in my community wanted to leave and residents had for sale signs displayed across their lawns. Once the money and people left, funding and other organizations would soon follow, leaving the youth center in a critical situation. The kids living in the surrounding neighborhoods needed other places to learn and be creative instead of home and school. The streets were swallowing up most of our youth, but we continued to fight for them. They needed choices and we had to keep as many programs as possible available.

Sitting back, I glanced up at the screen mounted over the bar. I took a sip from my beer and watched the Yankees beating the Red Sox. Checking the messages on my cellphone, I saw two from America. She'd left a crying message about having an argument with Kendal. She informed me that Kendal knew about the affair. She went rambling on and on to my voicemail. America wanted me to call her right back. It was the type of drama that I didn't need in my life right now. I loved America, but I had too many things going on at the moment. I wanted her back, but at what cost? She had her music career and I wondered if I would only get in the way.

I was chilling and downed my third bottle of beer. The small crowd dwindled even more by midnight. James Brown was playing on the jukebox. I saw the female bartender rinsing glasses and kept on eyeing me. She had her eyes on me since I walked into the lounge. Her pretty face lit up when I smiled. She returned my smile, but that's how far I kept my flirting. The last thing I needed was to get caught up in a love triangle.

I was ready to leave when a familiar face walked in. I thought that maybe I was followed, but I really didn't care. We both knew of each other, but never had officially met. He walked in with a small group, all in business suits. I kept my eyes on him, observing everything about him. He looked sharp in his suit, and was laughing with his friends and seemed to be the alpha male in the group. I didn't know if I had a beef with him or not. I didn't want any problems with him, but I was ready for anything.

Kendal was talking by the bar, ordering drinks and suddenly saw me. His smiling face quickly changed to a frown. He whispered something to one of his friends then started walking in my direction. I sat, sipping and waiting for his bullshit. He stood over me, and our eyes locked. We both were in love with the same woman. It was an awkward moment.

"Soul, right?" he asked.

"Kendal...?"

"Yes..." he nodded. "I heard you was a jazz man, but didn't know you frequent this lounge," he continued.

"It's one of my favorite places."

"I come here often too, but never saw you around. Can I buy you a drink?" he smiled, offering an oak leaf.

"I'm good," I said, raising my Corona.

"Well can I have a seat so we can talk?"

I gestured for him to sit. I was cool and didn't feel threatened. Our meeting was inevitable. Kendal sat, looking nonchalant. He didn't explode into me. I guess from a distance it looked like we were old friends talking. Kendal called the waitress and she quickly came to my table.

"Yes, let me get a rum and coke," he ordered. He then looked at me and asked, "You sure you don't want anything stronger? I'm buying."

"Nah man, I'm good."

Kendal smiled, went into his pocket, and pulled out a huge bankroll of twenties and fifties. He slipped the waitress a twenty and told her to keep the change. She was grateful and hurried off to get his drink. He was ego-tripping.

"Business is good," he smiled.

"I see."

There was a brief moment of awkward silence between us. Then Kendal grew some balls and got brave, testing me.

"Look, I'm gonna cut the formalities with you and be straight up. You need to stay away from her. America's been doing fine without you in her life for almost two years now. Here you come, fuckin' things up between us."

"I'm not doing anything. And if you can't control your woman from straying then you're not doing something right."

"Nigga, I'm the one that been here night and day when she was in tears over your fuckin' ass. I helped her through many difficult situations. I'm the one that got her music career poppin, held her close when she needed lovin'… I been a father to your son," he smirked.

It was a low blow. He was lucky I didn't come across that table and slap him like the bitch he was. I kept my cool because I realized that he was just trying to rile me up. I wasn't going to give him the satisfaction.

"Yeah, well I'm home now. And believe me I'm not going anywhere, yo. I'm here to stay. My son has his father now, so good-looking out, but you fired, my man. And America, I guess we need to let her decide. I'm not worried about that at all, sometimes seniority rules."

Kendal frowned and said, "You think you're the shit, huh? You think that gangsta attitude is going to keep playing out for you with her…? You're a jailbird. You fucked up with her back then, and you're gonna fuck up with her again. She doesn't need you. I'm the one in her life now. Accept that."

I chuckled. This clown–ass, bird nigga was a funny dude. My icy-cold stare met him in his seat and I could see the bitch in him rise up. I was letting him off easy.

"You feel threatened by me, Kendal?"

"I'm not afraid of you."

"You should be…"

"Fuck you!"

I held my tongue and tried to talk some sense in him.

"Look, I'm not here to fight with you. I'm passed all that gangsta bullshit.

I found something more worth fighting about."

"Whatever. If you care about America, let her go. Give her a chance to let her live. Cuz she don't need you. She needs me."

I shook my head, chuckled a bit and mumbled, "You're a joke."

"Excuse me? What?" he spat.

"You heard me."

"Look, I'm able to provide and do for her. You have nothing man. You fresh home with what...? A fading rep and some pipedreams for yourself...? I made a lot happen for America. I did for her what you couldn't do?"

"And I got what you'll never fully have—her heart." I said, throttling him.

If this was chess my last statement would be checkmate. It was real life and this was a homerun. Kendal remained quiet chewing on his loss. The waitress walked over with his drink. We both knew it was time for him to be ghost.

"I'm warning you, stay the fuck away from her!" he shouted.

His friends by the bar looked our way, trying to see what the commotion was about. Kendal stood up, snatched his drink from the waitress, downed it like a sailor and stomped off. The waitress stared at me with a quizzical look. I sat back and smiled.

Kendal and his friends didn't stay long. They were out the door ten minutes later. I left after they did. I called America's cellphone. She answered, excited to hear from me.

"Hey baby," I said.

"Can we talk?"

"When and where?"

19
Omega

Omega sat behind his cherry oak desk in his downtown Brooklyn office where he ran his record company. He had a few gold records displayed on the walls of his office and a few pictures of him with different celebrities. Lavishly decorated, the place had quality leather furniture, two wide screens mounted opposite each other, parquet flooring and large bay windows from floor to ceiling. It was high-end enough for Omega's business.

Reclined in a leather chair, his expression was very unhappy with the article he was reading about his record company. Insiders were labeling him the Suge Knight of the industry and comparing his label to the infamous Death Row. His business had declined in the past months because of the ongoing violence. The alleged strong-arm tactics to get business done and bad press made him a mark. The media dogged Omega's company with accusations like his artists being cheated out of their royalties, bootlegging within the company and the label having cooked books. North Star's death was raised, and people were saying that it wasn't safe to work with Omega. The FCC was scrutinizing his business and the FBI had opened an investigation. Then the payola scheme surfaced for Omega not too long ago. It was Murder Inc. all over again.

People knew that Omega used extortion and intimidation to get ahead. He was one of the most feared men in the business. His earnings were phenomenal, but the executives knew that doing business with Omega came with a cost. Every major distributor was turning away from him. This made it even harder for his record company to sell any records he was producing. Slowly Omega recognized that he was being blackballed.

Everything he had fought so hard to achieve was crumbling before him. Omega was hurt even more, when he turned on the news. His once-best friend, Soul was helping to derail his organization by speaking out negatively about the business and Omega. He had to reconcile the problem or he would lose more money due to the bad press and negative campaign.

Stress was written all over Omega's face. Sighing heavily, he tossed the article aside. Swiveling his chair around to the windows, Omega peered out into the Brooklyn streets. It was a clear and sunny day, but it felt dark where he sat. Not only was his legit record business in trouble, but profits on the streets were dwindling. The war had taken its toll on earnings. There was a NYPD Task Force kicking in doors and making arrests.

Omega had law enforcement trying to pin charges on him, while Demetrius and King gunning for him. The streets were a shaky ground. He had a few cops on his payroll and they warned him of the troubles that were coming his way. Judy put the word in his ear when she said, "Slow it down, boo. You're hot right now. And I'm not going to be able to do much for you soon. The IAD watching everybody…"

His pride, his ego didn't allow for his enemies to win. Refusing to give up, Omega would die trying than to admit his defeat. He had soldiers on the streets that were riding for him. His reputation was notorious and he knew how to maneuver when trouble came his way.

But the Mexicans had him worried. They phoned, informing Omega that they needed to meet with him. Omega agreed. He felt that his office was a safe place to meet. It was near the city, in public and he had his office scanned for any bugs on the daily. He didn't need the feds listening in.

It was noon, outside his window downtown Brooklyn was bustling with people and traffic. The noise outside carried into his window. Omega shut it. He went over his books, ran some figures, but no matter how many times he crunched the numbers, business was still slow and fucked up.

"Fuck," he muttered.

Omega sat in the office until his meeting. At 1 p.m. the receptionist buzzed Omega. He put the paperwork on his desk into a neat stack, collected himself and sat upright waiting for the Mexicans. Now in business mode, he was ready when the thick office doors swung open. Escorted by his receptionist, two men clad in dark suits walked inside. One of the men was a liaison for Falco and the cartel, the other man, muscle. The receptionist closed the door as she left, and the liaison walked to Omega.

"Have a seat," Omega said.

"That won't be necessary," the five-eight, immaculately dressed man with the dark goatee and darting eyes said.

"Your name...?" Omega shrugged.

"I'm here for my employer, that's all. I'm here to inform you with news from my employer. We'll no longer render services to you and your organization due to difficulties on your end."

The news took Omega by surprise. He rose from his seat and barked, "What the fuck you talkin' 'bout?"

"It has come to our attention that a federal investigation may be pending against you. The bad media coverage and your ongoing war with the Jamaicans, is a threat to my employer doing business with you," the man said nonchalantly.

"Muthafucka, you listen, I've been showing Falco and ya niggas a lot of love. I made ya Mexicans muthafuckas plenty of money over the last two years. And you come into my place and wanna diss me?"

The second man by the door reacted to Omega's shouting by gripping his holstered gun. He glared at Omega, waiting for a reaction. Omega shot him a cold stare and said, "You need to tell your bitch security over there to fuckin' chill. I see him reaching... Ain't no beef big man."

"It's only business, Omega, nothing personal. Until the situations on your end are resolved, we feel the need to disrupt any communication with you."

Omega sat down and let out a loud sigh. He felt the urge to put a cap in both their heads, but he knew it would be stupidity on his end and he would have signed his death certificate for murdering one of Falco's essential men.

"That's fuckin' it?" he exclaimed.

"One more thing... We require your loyalty and silence if things shall we say, end up inadequately and badly for you."

"Muthafucka, I ain't no snitch, if that's what ya implying," Omega spat.

"We've taken certain measures on our end to ensure that my client's well-being is protected," the man said, opening his briefcase and dropping a CD on Omega's desk.

Omega looked down at it and asked, "Wha- what da fuck is this?"

"Insurance," the man said, closing his briefcase.

"Have a good day," the man said, before exiting the office with his security on high alert.

Feeling nothing but displeasure, Omega watched them leave. The Mexicans walking out meant his control and ties to the streets would soon dry up. Omega didn't have any product to push.

"Muthafuckas!"

His rage rang down the hall. Omega looked down at the CD on his desk, took it out of the case and examined it. Curiosity got the best of him. Placing it in the DVD drive, he pressed play. Soon he was watching a video of him executing a federal judge.

"Those back stabbing muthafuckas!" Omega exclaimed.

Omega quickly shut the video off, removed it from the drive and broke the incriminating evidence into two pieces. He plopped down in his chair, picked up his phone and tried to reach his number one enforcer.

Police in riot gear were patrolling the streets of Queens and Brooklyn. They made routines searches of anyone who looked suspicious even the beat cops were seen making more arrests to bring the violence and murders down. The task force was kicking in doors, making arrests and snitches began talking, trying to elude lengthy prison sentences.

A week went by without any murders or violence. Known drug spots looked abandoned, and the citizens of a torn community plagued with war and violence felt a little bit easier. With the mayor vowing to make his city a better place from crime and violence, activists targeted the troubled communities with pickets, large gatherings, refusing to be ignored.

In a dark underground Queens' basement, half a dozen men gathered around a beaten man, his wrists were bonded to an old dining room table. He was naked, his arms were outstretched. The swollen eye, missing teeth, bruises and razor cuts across his back were the result of severe beaten he had endured.

His name was Brian Brown, a businessman, who unfortunately did business with the wrong people. He was Demetrius' drug money launderer. Brian was in his mid-thirties and greedy for cash. He was responsible for transfer of funds from multiple businesses linked to Demetrius. Brian laundered millions of dollars for his employer. He was the mastermind behind the complex system of shell companies, holding companies and offshore bank accounts that fronted Demetrius' holdings.

His clothes were torn off him, glasses shattered on the ground. Each man in the room beat on him manically. He was a sucker for beautiful women. Brian was led astray by one of Omega's beautiful associates. His chase for lust and greed became his downfall. Now Omega had his hands on one of Demetrius prime players—the money man to his organization.

"Please, please... I don't know anything," Brian pleaded.

"Shut-da-fuck-up!" Biscuit shouted, punching Brian in his face, and bruising his jaw.

"Ah... Ugh no," Brian wailed.

Biscuit was angry and more brutal to the man. There was a warrant for his arrest and he had to keep a low profile. Word had gotten back to him that there was a snitch implicating him in two brutal murders. It gave detectives a reason to turn up the heat on Biscuit. He was a dangerous felon, and over a dozen precincts was waiting for Biscuit with a tremendous hard-on.

Biscuit was angered by the fact that he couldn't visit Narmer in the hospital. Cops were watching his brother's room and investigating the shooting outside Gilmore's funeral home. Although Biscuit was worried about his little brother, he went on with his business. He took his anger and frustration out on Brian, leading to the deep razor cuts in the man's back.

Tired of beating on the helpless victim, the men waited for Omega to show up. Rocky and a second goon flanked Omega as he walked down into the basement. He looked over at Brian's beaten body and asked, "What you got from him so far, Biscuit?"

"He's a tough coconut, fo' real Omega. We been goin' at this muthafucka for an hour and he still ain't really talking," Biscuit said.

Omega stared at Brian with cruel intentions and approached the man. He was tight and needed some leverage. He needed something to give.

"You gonna talk, muthafucka! You definitely gonna talk, cuz I know you know something. I need this nigga Demetrius, King and his niggas dead and stinkin'! You hear me muthafucka?" Omega shouted in Brian's swollen face.

"Please, I'm just his accountant. I don't know anything," Brian cried.

"We'll find out, cuz I'm gonna go at this all night. I'll give you a blood transfusion to keep your ass alive to experience more pain. You hear me, muthafucka?"

It was very rare that Omega got his hands dirty with violence and murder. This was getting too personal for him and time was running out. He looked at Rocky and said, "Yo, pass me that shit."

Smiling, Rocky passed Omega a long cattle prod. Omega took the dangerous instrument in his hand and stood over Brian's naked, bruised body. He then charged the cattle prod. The crackling sound it made caused Brian to cringe and whimper.

"Talk to me," Omega warned.

"No... Please, no," Brian shouted.

"A'ight, you think I'm playing," Omega said.

He attacked Brian's bloody, razor cut back with the prod. Brian's screams echoed loudly. Omega struck him again, but Brian didn't give out any information. Omega became furious. He looked at two of his goons and instructed, "Yo, spread his fuckin' legs!"

Quickly his men did as told, holding apart Brian's legs as far as they could go. Brian squirmed and tried to resist, but his wrists were bonded, and he was unable to put up much of a fight. Suddenly he was vulnerable to the most unthinkable attack on his manhood. Omega readied the cattle prod between his spread legs and once again said, "Talk to me."

Brian whimpered. Omega grew impatient and thrust the prod into Brian's rectum. There was a piercing scream that could probably be heard for miles.

"A-a-a-h-h-h-h shit! Oh-oh-oh-oh-oh…!" Brian screamed.

"Talk to me, muthafucka!" Omega shouted.

Brian was in too much pain to say anything. Omega thrust the prod into his anus again. This time he held it against Brian's nuts, causing burning of his skin at the contact points.

Biscuit, with his arm in a sling, stood on the side smiling at Omega's innovative style of torture. He never took his eyes off the brutality. Omega passed the prod to Rocky and crouched down in front of Brian's fading eyes. His body was limp and the smell of burning flesh stank.

"Listen to me, nigga. I can make the pain go away. C'mon, my dude. Just holla at me, let me know sumthin. If not, it's gonna go on and on until there ain't nuthin' left of you to torture. But you a tough fuckin' cookie, I respect that," Omega said.

Brian's breathing was light. His eyes were barely open. The silence on his lip was frustrating Omega. He looked up at Rocky and said, "Hit the muthafucka up the ass again."

Rocky was ready to oblige, but Brian uttered, "No, please… Okay, I'll tell you what you need to know."

"That's my nigga," Omega said.

He leaned in closer and waited for the information. Brian's breathing was sparse. Omega snapped his fingers quickly, and said, "Talk, nigga. Fuckin' talk!"

"My office… A lockbox with everything you need to know about Demetrius," Brian informed.

"Now we gettin' somewhere, but that's not enough," Omega said. "Rocky, hit him again.

Rocky didn't hesitate to shove the prod into Brian's ass repeatedly. The agonizing screams continued. The smell of burning flesh gradually overwhelmed the men. It took another hour for Omega to finally extract all the information he needed for Demetrius and King's demise. Brian, in his work as Demetrius personal accountant, had all the private information to the kingpin, including personal home addresses to his residences in Jamaica and New York. Omega was ready to react. He organized a plan and wanted to strike his enemies all at once.

When he was done with Brian, Omega had Biscuit shoot the accountant in the back of the head twice. He wanted him to dispose of the body mob style—chopped up and tossed in the Hudson.

Omega needed air and exited the gloomy, smelly basement. Biscuit followed behind him. Omega lit a Black n Mild, and Biscuit was soon in his ear.

"Yo, we need to get at your boy, Soul. His mouth needs to be shut permanently. Lemme get at that nigga, Omega. He fuckin' up our business wit' his badmouth talking about us," Biscuit said.

Omega took a pull from the cigar, looked at Biscuit and said, "I'm a handle Soul, you just stay on the fuckin' hunt for King and his goons. You already fucked up wit' your arm in a sling. Don't fuck me again, Biscuit."

"I got you, Mega. Don't worry about that shit, fo' real, I'm on it," Biscuit assured.

"You better be, Biscuit. I can't afford anymore mistakes."

"One hundred, my nigga," Biscuit said, nodding.

Omega and Rocky got into the truck and drove away, leaving Biscuit to ponder about many things—especially the snitch that was linking him to two homicides.

Omega was in his den, taking swigs of E&J. He had a lot on his mind and one of the problems was Soul. The two had been friends since grade school. Omega quickly devised a plan to put his former friend down. It pained him, but he knew it needed to be done. He planned on taking care of business in the morning. Omega took another swig of E&J and sat back in his chair.

Jazmin walked into the dimly lit room, her belly growing bigger as the weeks went by. She was wearing pajamas. She let out an exhausting sigh, went up to her worried man, and took a seat on his lap.

"I thought you would be sleep," Omega said.

"I heard you down here, thought you might need some company," Jazmin said.

Touching Omega gently and kissing on him lovingly, Jazmin tried to comfort her man. Omega looked unfazed by her affection. He took a few more sips from the bottle. Jazmin was not pleased.

"You need to chill with that, baby."

"Or what?" he snapped.

"What's wrong with you?"

"I got a lot on my mind."

"And you're ready to take it out on me?"

Omega looked at her, and then he unexpectedly informed her, "We need to move again, so start packing ya shit."

"What? And move where?" Jazmin replied angrily.

"It ain't gonna be safe for you here anymore. Shit is bad out there, Jazmin, so don't argue with me."

"I'm tired, Omega. Look at me, I'm gonna drop your seed in a month, do I look like I'm in the condition to just get up and leave?"

"I don't give a fuck what you think. I'm selling the house. And I'm gonna find us a better place. A safer place," he said.

"And you think just by us leaving, it's gonna make things better? No, it's not. I don't see you anymore. I don't even know you now, Omega. I'm stuck here in this fuckin' house alone everyday, with your son and you're out there doin' I don't know what. I'm tired. I'm fuckin' tired! Your son barely knows you, and will it be the same way for this one in my belly? You think I don't know, I watch the news, Omega. I know what's going on. I hear what they say about you. I've been reading about you."

"You knew what the deal was when you fuckin' got wit' me. It ain't shit brand new to you, Jazmin. So stop fuckin' actin' like that. I'm a gangsta first and I'ma do me! But I'ma end this war wit' the Jamaicans. So you ain't gotta worry about me."

"Baby look, let's just go somewhere, far from here. Let's start over we have enough money to live comfortably. You can sell your company, get something for it, and we can leave New York and go somewhere far... Just us and the kids," Jazmin pleaded.

"What? Fuck I look like to you, Jazmin? I don't run from no fuckin' body. I'm a finish what I started."

Tears in her eyes, Jazmin looked at her man and said, "And that's your problem, you only think about yourself. Fuck you!"

She stood and rushed out the room. Omega said, "Fuck that confused bitch." Then he took another swig of E&J.

Losing himself in the bottle made it easier to mull over many things. Like dominos, one by one, he knew his enemies would fall. He leaned back in his chair, closed his eyes and felt the urge to fuck something. Jazmin was bloated and moody, Omega thought about his cop bitch, Judy. He dialed her phone number and his call went straight to voicemail.

"Fuck it. I'm out!"

Alone, he drove to the city. Two hours later, Omega was deep in pussy — having a threesome with two voluptuous females in an upscale apartment. Omega was fucking his brains out while Jazmin was left crying herself to sleep.

Omega woke up the next morning and his cellphone was ringing. Two women were naked against him, sprawled out from their all-night fuck frenzy with the rising music mogul. The two big breasted and swelled ass groupies, who had seen Omega's face on the news, in magazines and heard of him, couldn't wait to bed the man down. They had porn-style sex and a bottle of grey goose had them wasted.

The sun was high in the sky, and Omega slowly awakened with his 9mm exposed on the nightstand. A wad of cash was next to it. Omega's clothes were scattered all over the room. It had gotten sloppy last night. He quickly observed his surroundings, shoved one of the bitches sleeping against him to the side, and reached for his phone.

"Yo, speak to me."

"Yo boss, where you at?" Rocky asked.

"In the city…"

"What you doin' in the city?"

Omega ignored the question and asked, "What you callin' for, Rocky?"

"I'm at the house, we got that thing today, remember?" Rocky reminded him.

"A'ight, give me an hour. Stay wit' Jazmin she needs the company," he instructed.

"I got you, boss."

Hanging up, Omega quickly secured his belongings. He got dressed and retrieved his gun and money from the nightstand. He left the two women sleeping and eased out into the hallway. He headed to his parked Benz which was ticketed for illegal parking. Omega snatched the ticket from his windshield and tossed it to the curb.

He jumped into his Benz, started the ignition, and sat back in the pig-skin seat. It was another sunny day, but he was thinking about another drug connect. The Mexicans weren't the only suppliers in the game. He was going to meet with the Columbians in Washington Heights. If the meeting went well, Omega would be able to push the product back on the streets. It would be inferior to what the Mexicans were supplying him with, but he had the remedy for that.

Omega's phone rang again. He didn't recognize the number, but still answered the call.

"Who this?" he abruptly answered.

"Omega right?" the caller asked.

"State your business fast," Omega said.

"We need to talk. It seems that we both have a common problem that needs to be dealt with," the caller said.

"And what problem is this?"

The caller stated his business and it appealed to Omega. They had met previously. This time he had Omega's ear. He had set up a meeting with the caller at his downtown Brooklyn office in a few hours after he had met with the Columbians. Tires screeched as he raced to begin his busy day.

His discreet meeting with the Columbians went good. They were ready to do business at a cheaper rate, and Omega needed to get product out to his workers in the streets immediately. He walked into his office and plopped in his seat. Biscuit and Rocky followed behind him. Biscuit had walked in through the back entrance of the building, because the men didn't know who was watching the building. Omega wasn't about to take any chances being charged with a conspiracy. The streets were hot, Biscuit was on top of everybody lists—law enforcements, the Jamaicans and old foes.

"You sure you wasn't followed here?" Omega asked.

"Mega, you gotta stop being so fuckin' paranoid. I'm good. I'm watching my back out there, I ain't bringin' no heat nowhere around here," Biscuit said.

"Just to be safe, don't come to my office anymore, Biscuit. I can't take the chance," Omega ordered.

"Whateva, man," Biscuit retorted.

"Nigga, fuck you upset for? This is my place of business, Biscuit. You understand that, nigga? I don't need the fuckin' headache here. I got enough of that fuckin' shit on the streets," Omega barked.

"A'ight, I'm good. You the boss…"

"Yeah, I'm the fuckin' boss, Biscuit. I gave you one fuckin' job to do, find King and do what you do best. But this nigga is still out there causing havoc on my business, making my fuckin' name look bad out there," Omega shouted.

"Nigga, I'm fuckin' tryin'!" Biscuit exclaimed.

"Nigga, you ain't tryin' hard enough, nigga still alive right," Omega snapped.

Rocky stood silently, watching the two go at it like a ping pong match. He knew that it was best to keep his mouth shut and not get involved.

"Fuck you, Omega! I'm the nigga bodying muthafuckas out there, gettin' my fuckin' hands dirty. I'm the muthafucka wit' pending indictments on me, while ya ass sit pretty in that fuckin' leather chair and eat off the blood I been spillin' for you on these streets... You better fuckin' recognize Omega...fo' real nigga," Biscuit shouted.

"You need to slow ya roll, youngin'," Omega warned.

"Or fuckin' what?" Biscuit dared.

Omega quickly stood from his chair, and was about to get into a heated confrontation with his top enforcer, but the buzzing from his secretary halted his action. He pushed for the intercom.

"What?"

"Your four o clock is here," she informed.

"A'ight, send him in," Omega said.

Omega tried to calm himself down. He glared at Biscuit and said, "You chill, nigga?"

"I'm good, just don't fuckin' disrespect me," Biscuit warned.

Omega looked at his young warrior and saw the rage in his eyes. He smiled and said, "You hold that feeling in you now, and put use to that shit on the streets. Now get the fuck out my office... Both of y'all, I got business to talk about."

Rocky and Biscuit started to walk out as Kendal was entering the office. Kendal locked eyes with Biscuit. The street soldier recognized the young producer. He wondered what Omega's business was with America's boyfriend.

The door shut behind Kendal, and Omega gestured for his guest to have a seat. Kendal nervously sat opposite Omega. He wanted to get straight to the point. Omega already was on fire.

"What the fuck brings you my way, Kendal? We from opposite sides of the tracks," Omega said.

"I just wanna holla at you about your boy, Soul," Kendal said.

"And what about him...?"

"I understand that he's become a problem to the both of us," Kendal continued.

Omega leaned back into his chair. He already knew what Kendal was suggesting. He stared at Kendal.

"He's my problem. But again, what issue does a square muthafucka like you have wit' Soul?" Omega asked. Then it finally registered. Before Kendal could answer, Omega said, "You muthafucka…? America…?"

"I love her, man," Kendal admitted.

"And you ready to kill for her?" Omega questioned.

"If needed…"

"That nigga's like a brother to me. We came up together and did shit on these streets that you can't even imagine, choirboy. So what's to stop me from fuckin' ya shit up right now, have my boy out there, body ya ass for even thinkin' of that shit?" Omega threatened.

"Because, like me, Omega you're a man of business and understanding. We're both young black men trying to succeed in this music business. We might have different backgrounds, but we both came up and made it happen for ourselves. But what's similar about us… We ain't trying to let anyone tear us down. Now I know about the problems you're having with the industry. Your reputation precedes you, and you're not even Diddy or Russell."

"You're not fuckin' funny."

"All I'm saying is you do us this favor, you know… Kind of make Soul disappear and I can make it worth your while," Kendal hinted.

"You think I need money from you?" Omega asked.

"I'm not talking about cash. I'm talking about I'll arrange for you to have the master recordings to a few of America's song. She's becoming a rising star, about to do a fall tour with Beyonce in a few months, and with ownership of something so valuable, in a year or two, you'll be the envy of this industry when America's become a huge star," Kendal said with a knowing smile.

"You fear Soul that much, huh? You chanced coming to me to put a hit out on him."

"He's just in our way."

"You come to my damn office to get the big bad wolf to do your dirty work for you? Ya too scared to get your fuckin' hands dirty, huh? You think that I'm some fuckin' puppet on a string…?"

"Nah…"

"Let me ask you sumthin," Omega said.

"What's that?"

"You ever had a gun pointed at you, muthafucka?" Omega asked.

He quickly removed the 9mm from his desk drawer and took aim at Kendal's dome. Kendal's eyes widened with fear. He sat frozen to his seat, gripping the armrest tightly.

"I'm sorry, I didn't mean any disrespect," Kendal pleaded.

"You didn't mean any disrespect? You come to my fuckin' office and talk shit about a nigga I grew up with. In the past, you never wanted anything to do wit' me when it came to music, kept that bitch America to yourself, didn't want to do a collaboration wit' any of my artists ... But when it comes to foul play, some gangsta shit, now all of a sudden I'm the nigga to do business with...? Fuck you!"

"I can just leave. I'm sorry," Kendal said, shaking and looking nervous.

"Yeah, you fuckin' are," Omega spat. "I can handle Soul my own way and in my own time. And besides, once you got blood on your hands, there ain't no washing it off. Nigga, get the fuck out my office before I really get mad and change my mind... Have ya ass carried out instead."

Kendal quickly got up and rushed out the door like the room was on fire. Omega put the gun away. He knew of a better way to handle his problem with Soul and he refused to become some duty boy for Kendal.

Kendal walked out of Omega's office very frustrated with his pants wet. If he had the heart and balls to off Soul himself, then he would have done it. Kendal wasn't that caliber. He was about business, not the streets. He was from the suburbs of Long Island, but moved to Brooklyn to live on his own, away from his family and their influences. He'd experienced living in Bed-Stuy to be more connected with the urban environment for his career and songs. He wanted to fit in and in his heart, he wanted to be Soul. Kendal yearned to have for a reputation as a gangsta. Moving to Brooklyn wasn't enough. He wanted to be respected among his peers, especially with America. Kendal felt that she loved the gangsta in a man more than anything

else. Jealousy filled his heart and Kendal was blinded by hate for a man he envied.

Rushing from the building, Kendal ran into Biscuit. He was still lingering outside the office smoking a cigarette. Biscuit stared at Kendal, approached him assertively and asked, "What's ya business wit' Omega that got you peeing all over yourself?"

"Why should you care?" Kendal asked.

"Why shouldn't I?" Biscuit returned. "I'm a business man myself for the right price, we need to talk."

Kendal stared at the young man who face showed immaturity, but his eyes told a different story. Biscuit's eyes displayed a vicious young man aging way before his time. He made Kendal extremely nervous, but Kendal was willing to sit down and talk. He treated Biscuit to lunch.

20
Betrayal

Officer Judith Wagner had a long and stressful week. She sat in the locker room of the 113th pct quietly putting on her uniform. She could hear the men outside the locker room. They were loud and vulgar as usual. It had become routine. She didn't mind. Judy played just as rough. Opening her locker, Judy removed a small cellophane packet of meth. Nervously, she sprinkled the gram of meth onto the back of her hand. Using a small thin straw, Judy inhaled. A rush shot through her immediately and she was now set to start her day off.

Five years on the job, and the past two years she had fell in love with Omega and had done many illegal things for him—even persuaded Judy to kill a rival in the industry who was getting in the way of his business. One late night on a dark street, Judy had pulled the man over in his drop-top BMW. Before the driver could reach for his license, Judy had blown his brains all over the cream leather interior. Rushing back to her squad car, she took a deep breath and sped away. Omega paid her in both cash and drugs.

Her transgression was finally wearing on Judy. She was tired of being Omega's pawn and slut whenever he needed. Judy wanted to be clean, check herself into a rehab program, and resign. She didn't want to disappoint her father, now a captain in the Bronx. She tried to keep a low profile, hide her addiction and heinous crimes.

Her life was turned upside down when she found out she was eight weeks pregnant. There was no doubt in her mind that it was Omega's child growing inside her. They had unprotected sex numerous times while she was high.

She had thought about an abortion, even contemplated suicide. Judy wanted to change her life, start anew. She removed her registered Glock 17 from its holster and pressed it against her chin, all she had to do was squeeze. No one was around to stop her. They would hear the shot, but by then, it would be too late. Tears ran down her face. There was no way she could become a mother. Her life was too fucked up. Meth had taken control over her life, dominating her day and night. She was powerless, felt used, and abandoned. This would be a disgrace to her father.

Judy placed the gun back into its holster and quickly did another line of meth. She collected herself and continued getting dressed. She slammed her locker shut, stood, adjusted the equipment on her belt and sighed heavily. Judy walked to the bathroom, and splashed cold water on her face.

"Another day," she said to herself, staring at her reflection in the mirror.

She splashed more water on her face and walked out the locker room. The precinct was busy for the day. The drugs and murder rate had many officers on high alert. The mayor's office wanted results, and this led to many changes in the precinct.

Judy walked into the room and was ready to attend roll call, but the presence of three IAD officers in the room caused her to be on the alarm. She noticed the awkward looks she was receiving from fellow officers. Their eyes told the story and Judy immediately knew something was wrong.

IAD instantly came in her direction. Looking stern, they were about their business. Judy stood still waiting for them to apprehend her if they had any charges on her. She wouldn't fight them. She was ready.

"Officer Judy Wagner," one of the IAD suits questioned, but already knowing the answer. "You need to come with us."

"What's this for?" she asked.

"You need to come with us," the IAD officer said.

Two men began relieving Judy of her gun and shield, and they quickly escorted her from the Queens' precinct to their own location for questioning. Her father, Captain Wagner, was notified and he planned on meeting his daughter down at IAD headquarters in the city.

An hour later, Judy sat in the room alone at the department on Hudson

Street, the west side of New York. She was stripped of everything and didn't know the severity of the crime they were charging her with. She knew she fucked up.

Half-hour after her arrival, three detectives walked in. One of them quickly spoke.

"The only reason we didn't take you out your house in bracelets, is because of your father. He's a respected man. So don't continue to bring shame on his name and make it easy on yourself."

"I'm detective Harrison, this is detective Shapely, and that's detective Bronson, and as you know, this is the Internal Affairs Division," Harrison informed.

Judy remained quiet. She saw two FBI agents in the hallway just before the door shut. Swallowing hard, Judy tried to keep her composure.

Two investigators sat across from Judy, the third stood near the doorway. One of the men slid a thin manila package over to Judy.

"Go ahead, take a look," Harrison said.

Judy removed a couple of eight by ten, glossy photos from the package. They were all of her, taken under surveillance with Omega and doing a few other illegal activities. Her hands were caught in the cookie jar. IAD had everything on her, from her meth usage to her other various crimes they had recorded.

"You're dirty, Wagner... We have a search warrant for your home, your locker and if we push, we'll look into your father's history, go through his files, see what we can come up with," Harrison threatened.

"You can't do that, he ain't got anything to do with me. Leave him alone," Judy retorted.

"Make it easy on yourself and him. Cooperate with us, tell us everything you know, and we'll help you salvage what's left of your life and freedom. But you make it hard and I swear we'll dig. And your father, he's going to have to give up them captain bars with all the bad public relations that will be put out there," Harrison said. "Now give us the names of the other dirty cops Omega has on his payroll."

Judy knew that snitching on other cops was always bad, but she loved her father more than anything else. She didn't want his career to be destroyed.

Judy buried her face into her hands, let out a heavy sigh and said, "Okay, I'll tell you everything."

With the promise of leniency from the DA, a maximum of a three year sentence and probation, Judy began singing like a bird. Her testimony about her crimes went on for three days, with the feds, IAD, and DEA recording it all. Judy implicated herself in murders, drug use, extortions and trafficking. They had it all on record and the grand jury was ready to seal indictments for over two dozen men linking to Omega's crew, dirty cops, and other associated gangs. Slowly, but surely, three different bureaus were bringing together a strong case on one of the most deadly and ruthless criminal organizations in the streets. It was the beginning of the end for many men.

21
America

Inside the soundproof booth, I waited for Mike One to find the right track he wanted to use. With the headphones on and my eyes glued to the floor, I was thinking about my song. Breathing deeply, I tried to relax. There was a lot going on in my life and singing was one of the ways that I expressed myself—music was my manifestation. A ton of songs were waiting for me to do. Some were already completed and songs floating in my head everyday. I didn't need a therapist, I was ready to become Mary J. Blige in the studio— *No more drama*.

It had been a week since the argument with Kendal. I hadn't seen or spoken to him since he stormed out. Even though I was concerned about Kendal, I couldn't get myself worked up about him not calling. He was devastated about my affair with Omar. We both owed each other an apology. He did me wrong, but my actions weren't any better. My feelings for Omar were so strong that when I'm with him, everything was upside down.

I tried not to lose focus on my career. Since my fight with Kendal, I was writing songs daily or I was in the studio singing. The heartfelt talk I had with Omar amount to our reconciliation. If I rekindled my relationship with Omar, would Kendal still be there for me with my career? It was a naïve question that I had to ask myself. I wasn't too quick to make a decision about my love life. There were so many things to ponder—Kendal had the money and power, but Omar had my heart and desire. It was an age old question do I go with wealth or love?

"A'ight America, you ready to do this?" Mike One asked through the intercom.

Nodding, I gave him two thumbs-up.

"Let's go platinum, babe," Mike One joked.

"Two times over," I replied with a smile.

He chuckled.

After another deep breath, I had the perfect song coming from my heart. The beat dropped. It was bouncing and definitely appealing. The snares kicked and the melody of the piano flowed.

Standing tall, I moved confidently to the microphone. My head to the beat and went in. My eyes were closed as I sang.

> *You make good things happen to me...*
> *They say that you and I are ridiculous,*
> *But I'm a still love you, gonna trust you,*
> *Your sweet tunes dancing me to home,*
> *There's no need for me to wonder,*
> *I'm home...cuz I hate to see you go,*
> *Seems like I can't never tell you no,*
> *One kiss is joy, even if it's only for one night...*
> *Oooh, if it's only for one night...*

I tried to stop the tears from trickling while I cut loose in the studio. I wrote the song a few days ago while thinking about my trying times with Omar and my battle with Kendal. It took about forty minutes to write and I called up Mike One after finishing. We agreed on a schedule for a studio session. I needed to release my Whitney Houston of the eighties in the booth. I listened to the beat ride then looked up and saw Mike One bobbing his head. When he gave me two-thumbs-up, I knew I was definitely on point.

While singing, Kendal walked into the studio. I was in shock. He locked eyes with me and smiled. My lyrics traveled into that microphone like electricity, jolting anyone that listened.

The track was about four and half minutes long. The lyrics meant something to me. I wiped the few tears from my eyes, took a deep breath, and collected myself. The smile on Mike One and Kendal's face proved that they loved the track.

"Damn girl, you rocked that shit. I need a cigarette after that," Mike One said over the intercom.

I laughed easily because the song released pent up emotions I was feeling. Kendal stood behind Mike One. He was handsomely wearing a proud smile, and was looking good in a pair of dark slacks, wingtip shoes and a silk button down shirt. Kendal started talking to Mike One and I took a quick break. I stepped out of the studio, to greet Kendal.

"Hey babe," he greeted pleasantly.

We hugged and then Kendal asked, "Can we talk?"

I nodded.

"Yo Mike, can you give us a minute?" Kendal asked of him.

"Sure," Mike One agreed, leaving the studio to give us some privacy.

"Have a seat," Kendal suggested.

I hoped that it wasn't another one of his marriage proposals, because the answer remained the same. The studio was quiet and we sat near each other. You could hear us breathing. Kendal looked at me with sincerity. He reached for my hand, held it gently and had his eyes fixated on mines. I was nervously waiting for what he had to say.

"America, I'm so sorry for my actions. I messed up, I know it. I had a lot to think about this week. I know that I need to trust you more. I will, I promise. No more spying, no more insecurity issues with me, and I'm ready to give you some space if you need it. I'm not trying to push you away. But you hurt me, baby. You did. I love you so much that I promise from now on, there won't be any further distractions between us. I guarantee that. I'm going to handle things the right way, if you let me... And your affair with Soul, it's already forgotten. But it was a mistake, right?"

I didn't answer him.

"You still love him?" he asked.

I was silent. I didn't want to answer him. Kendal looked at me with watery eyes. He was so apologetic and caring, that I wanted to hug him. He was a good man with issues, but was he the right man for me? Kendal took my silence as an answer.

"I see. Do you still love me?" he asked.

I took a deep breath and knew Kendal needed to know. I gazed at him, keeping my hand in his and uttered, "I'm pregnant!"

It looked like I had just knocked the wind and breath from Kendal. His grip loosened from mines.

"Wha...what!" he stuttered.

"I'm pregnant," I repeated.

"You sure?" he asked despondently.

"Yes."

"By who...?"

I had stopped taking my birth control once I started messing around with Omar. I knew that I had fucked up. I counted back to my last cycle. It was too close to know who the father was. I had been with both men during that frame of time.

"I don't know."

It looked like the life was slowly draining from his eyes. He finally freed my hand and stood. Kendal seemed aloof like he was trying to hold back his tears.

"Kendal..." I called out.

He closed his eyes and walked out of the studio. Slamming the door behind him, I heard him yell. The loud thud sounded like he had punched the wall. Mike One came back in right after Kendal stormed out. He had a puzzled look on his face, stared at me and asked, "What's up with Kendal?"

I dried my tears and held my breath. It felt like I was on the outside looking in on myself. I had taken the home pregnancy test three times. All came back positive. Then my doctor confirmed it. I was six weeks pregnant.

Mike One saw my tears and asked, "America, you okay?"

"I gotta go," I said getting out my chair and quickly exiting the room.

I raced over to Aunt Gene's place. I needed to talk to her, also spend time with her and my son. She raised me since I was young. Aunt Gene knew everything about me and was such an inspirational woman in my life. I went to her for everything.

We sat out on her patio in the backyard, drinking cold iced tea and having girl-talk. I was stretched out across my Aunt's lap as she fidgeted with my hair, braiding it for fun. I looked up at the stars painted across the dark sky. The second week of summer felt like the perfect night. The cooling breeze, full moon, and relaxing ambiance made me feel like I was in a different world. Flowers were displayed on Aunt Gene's patio. Her backyard was covered with tomatoes, cucumbers, cabbage and anchovies. She loved to have her hands in dirt, growing her food naturally.

I had on a pair of short jean shorts and flip flops. I didn't want to move from the warmth of my aunt's touch. I told her about everything. When she heard about my pregnancy, she sighed and hugged me tightly.

"Are you ready to have a second child?" she asked.

I shrugged.

She was a little upset that I didn't know who the father was. Aunt Gene had warned me about sleeping around and said, "You're not just hurting yourself, Pecan. You cannot continue to toy with the hearts of these two men who love you. Love is a very dangerous emotion."

"I know Aunt Gene."

"Pecan, you're a grown woman doing very good for yourself. You'll make mistakes, but you need to learn from them. Omar, I've been seeing him on the news lately. I'm glad to say I'm proud of that man. He's really trying to make a difference. He seems like a man who's learned from his mistakes. Now he's filled with God's blessing in him," Aunt Gene smiled.

Hearing her talk about Omar like that made me smile. Then she continued.

"Kendal, I really don't know him that well, but I see the love for you in his eyes. But he still has some growing up to do. I can't tell you who to be with, Pecan. You've got to make that decision for yourself. Prayer and faith can help. Don't be blinded by another man's riches."

"I hear you, Aunt Gene."

"Let me tell you something, wealth is not what we have. Wealth is who we are. And who we are depends on what direction we choose to travel. Pecan that moral compass can only point you in the right direction. I can't make you go there... It has to be your choice. I'm pointing you in that direction, keep God close and he'll guide you."

"I will, Aunt Gene. I will."

Aunt Gene smiled and hugged me lovingly. We continued to sit and talk on her patio till it was two in the morning. Afterwards, I went into the bedroom where my child was sleeping. I nestled next to him, kissed him and whispered, "You're going to become a big brother."

I fell asleep feeling at ease and peaceful. Talking to Aunt Gene was the perfect remedy. My cloudy vision was finally clearing, and I felt the sunshine was about to shine brightly on me.

22
Omar vs Soul

I was surprised when the news channel, NY1, came to me and told me that they wanted to do a small feature on me—dubbing me the New Yorker of the week. Over the past three months, I had been making so much noise in the community and helping with the outreach program. I was trying to stop the violence, but it wasn't an easy task. I had been described as articulate and charismatic. Many kids looked up to me, and respected me. The media were interested in a reformed gangsta becoming a positive activist in his community.

There was an article of me in the Daily News titled, *Reformed Thug Brings Hometown Love...*

I was on two news programs and even met with Al Sharpton. It was an unexplainable feeling. Slowly, I was becoming a motivational speaker, speaking in the auditoriums of local schools and centers. My mug was coming familiar throughout Queens, Brooklyn, Harlem and Long Island for the right reasons. It was ironic. Sometimes looking into the sea of faces, I saw the old me—troubled young men and women from all backgrounds. I would reflect on my old life, from where I been to where I'm going. I wanted to write my memoirs. I wanted to tell my story, from the ugly to the now.

The good thing happening was waking up from a dream. My life couldn't have changed this much, so soon. Sometimes it felt like it was only yesterday when I caught my first body. I was nineteen and out on the streets wilding with Omega and our crew.

This dude named Buddy was my first kill. We had continuing beef over drugs and money. One night Buddy came at me with his .380 but missed. I needed to retaliate or my reputation would be questioned. Omega and I hit back—three in the morning, we had caught Buddy slipping, seated in his black 85 Benz alone, and sipping on a bottle of Mad Dog, laying in the cut on one of the back blocks. I ski-masked up, cocked back the .45 I carried and crept up to Buddy in his ride. Before he even knew what was up, I had put four hot shots in his chest, left him slumped over the wheel.

Homicide detectives picked me up a week later. The system tried me, but never convicted me. This was way before CSI. There wasn't enough evidence or any witness to my crime—they had to let me go. I had nightmares about Buddy for months, but then the pain went away and I kept doing me.

Over the years, I did a lot of bad shit. Shot many men, but none of them lethal, mostly hitting them in the arm, ass or legs just to prove one point—don't fuck with me. Once, Omega and I beat the shit out of two Dominicans with metal baseball bats. Put both men in ICU at Long Island Jewish Hospital. I stole cars, sold crack, I did heists, robbed other drug dealers, and was an accessory to three murders Omega committed. I caught my second body two years ago, trying to save Omega's life outside of his club.

My past life was wicked, and I would think, why me God? Why me? I mean, there were times when I knew I didn't deserve to live. I didn't deserve to have America by my side. I was a bad, treacherous man. But I was here on a second chance, unlike many men either dead or doing life. I couldn't help thinking, when will I reap what I sow? Maybe I already did.

Every day I was finding time to get in my son's life. There were days where I was so busy, I didn't know if I was coming or going. Rahmel always said that a man needs to set a foundation for himself, or else he'll fall at the first shake.

Vincent and me, we were a duo, we had stories to tell and the kids who showed up at the Center were listening. My story kept becoming more complex with each passing day. I got the news about America being pregnant via phone. She called me with the news and I didn't know what to think. She explained to me that she wasn't sure if the baby was mines or Kendal's—that hurt. I wanted her back in my life, but I wanted Kendal completely out of the picture. He was a fraud, a shady dude, a wolf hiding in sheep's skin. I didn't trust him.

I wanted to remarry America, be a family again. We were talking, slowly working things out. Her pregnancy and having two men in the picture was a hard pill for me to swallow. I wouldn't leave or abandon America. She was my sunshine, my rock when I needed her through my difficult times.

Omega called and informed me that he wanted to meet up with me on one of the rooftops of 40 projects. I was leery about meeting with him, but he told me that it was urgent. He assured me that I'd be safe, and I agreed.

I went to Jamaica Hospital and visited with Narmer first. He had gotten word to me through one of the kids at the Center. He was fortunate. Narmer was going to be okay. The bullet traveled through, and missed all his vital organs. Narmer was shook. I hoped that it would be a wake up call for him.

It was late afternoon and he was laid up in bed, his right arm bandaged, face a little bruised. There was a single cop standing outside his room. Narmer was handcuffed to the bed. I was given permission to visit him. When I walked into his room, he greeted me with a slight nod of his head and turned off the television.

"Yo, shut that door," he said.

I did, walked to his bed, and asked, "Why did you call me up here?"

He looked upset about something. There were no roommates in the room with him. It was only us two to talk about whatever. His movements were limited because of the handcuffs. Narmer raised the bed upright and adjusted himself into an upright position.

Narmer looked like he was struggling to tell me something. I saw the pain and worry in his eyes. At first, he didn't look me directly in the eye. Maybe he felt guilty about something.

"What you gotta talk to me about?" I asked.

"Yo man, how you get out?" he questioned.

"Outta what... The life...?"

"Yeah yo..."

"I just got tired. I didn't have an appetite for it anymore. I lost a lot fuckin' wit' the game… I told myself, no more."

"They charging me wit' attempted murder and gun possession. DA tryin' to hit me wit' a mandatory fifteen if I'm convicted. I can't do that time, Soul. I'm scared man… Lying on that fuckin' concrete wit' two shots in me, bleedin' did sumthin' to me. And my fuckin' brother, he runs off and left me to die," Narmer said.

"Brother…?" I asked with raised brow.

"Yeah, Biscuit is my older brother. We keep that shit on the low, cuz we know how shit be. Word gets out, and niggas come at me to get at him."

"I had a talk wit' my baby moms. She upset wit' me. She talkin' 'bout she gonna have the baby and move down south wit' her grandma if I don't leave the streets alone. She talkin like she 'bout takin' my son away from me. That's my seed, Soul. Lorraine talkin' 'bout leaving me… I never told her this to her face, but I love her. Can you talk to her for me, Soul? Convince her to stay?"

"That depends, you done wit' the bullshit?"

He was quiet for a moment. Then looked away from me, sighed heavily and stated, "I took a plea."

"Word…?" I said, being caught off guard.

"They know I'm kin to Biscuit, that's why they comin' at me hard. They offered me a deal, to give up my brother for a lighter sentence. They tellin' me I'll do two or three years, probably be back out in time to know my son. I fuckin' gave up my brother, Soul. What kind of man am I?"

"A brave man," I said.

Narmer was in tears. He was hurt. I knew it must have been hard to give up family. His son came first. Narmer said, "They gonna grand jury my ass in the morning, take my testimony. Shit is fallin' apart, the feds, the cops, they on us, man. They got surveillance, recordings of shit, informants. They on it, Soul…"

"What goes up must come down."

"They gonna come for me, man," Narmer said nervously.

"Who…?"

"Who you fuckin' think…? Omega and his crew, they know everything. Omega got connections everywhere."

"You just chill, Narmer. Just hang in there. I'll talk to Lorraine."

Narmer laid back and he couldn't shake the worried expression.

"Thanks," he said.

Then he added, "I'm a fuckin' snitch."

It was the same old saying, you reap what you sow. Now it was coming back on Narmer and he was feeling it. I always hated snitches, but with my renewed mind, it was the best move for Narmer. Biscuit needed to be locked up for a very long time and the walls were finally coming down on Omega and his crew.

It was after midnight when I drove my rented white Pontiac into 40 projects. The summer heat was searing and I wore a pair of beige shorts and a wife-beater trying to keep cool. The projects were quiet and the cops were out on the streets in large numbers. There were a large number of arrests being made. The gang units of the police were also patrolling the neighborhood with arrests warrants for over a dozen of Omega's men. Word was out that there was an informant in the crew. I heard that his identity was really low-key.

I took the elevator to the top floor and walked up to the rooftop where Omega was waiting. He had three other men on the rooftop, they all were muscle, and they all looked at me like I was enemy number one. They were armed and deadly.

I walked to where Omega stood. He was at the center of the rooftop, smoking a Black n Mild, and trying to look like the boss of all bosses. His rise was dwindling, and because of bad press, his label was losing its luster. I hated to slander my former running mate and brother, but I was doing what needed to be done. There had been too many funerals, and I had heard enough mothers crying. Someone had to save the children, I was thinking as Omega stared at me with contempt. Never nervous, I approached him with an air of coolness about me.

"You an ign'ant muthafucka, Soul!"

"You call me up here to tell me that, man?"

"I'm here to warn you! Shut ya fuckin' mouth, Soul. You causing too much trouble for even you to handle right now. You gettin' in my fuckin' way and it's gonna get ugly, my nigga."

"I told you, the war needs to stop. I'm not shutting up."

Omega quickly removed a 9mm from his waistband, aimed it at my head and said, "Then how about I shut you up right now, nigga," he threatened.

"You really that stupid...?"

"Nigga, you know I don't give a fuck! Just take your bitch, and get the fuck outta town, Soul. I'm warning you. I don' give a fuck how far we go back, my nigga."

"When does it end, Omega? Look around you. Is this your Utopia? Kids dying, drugs prevalent among our teens, murder? Cuz you know what, it ain't mines. And if I gotta die on this rooftop then so be it. I found something worth dying for. How about you...?"

"What happened to you, nigga...? You was a real muthafucka, Soul. You and me, we coulda took over this muthafuckin' city, been kings and shit."

"I am a king. And what's real with me is finally opening my eyes and waking up from this shit."

"And you blame me for this. These little niggas out here got a choice. I don't force a got-damn thang on nobody."

"You influence them, Omega. You might as well pull the trigger on them yourself!"

"Fuck you, Soul! You fuckin' pushin' me, my nigga," Omega said, coming closer with the gun pointed at me.

"You ever think about Greasy?" I asked.

"Nigga, don't bring him up. His death wasn't on my hands."

"It wasn't...? The Jamaicans tortured him trying to find you. He was butchered cuz of this game!" I shouted.

"He was family to me too, Soul."

"And how much more family gotta die before you see this shit ain't us anymore? Look at you, Omega. I knew you since grade school and you gotta gun to my head. And you trying to hold on to something that's falling apart. You shooting dope without a needle. You're addicted to this shit, man."

Omega gazed at me with intensity in his eyes. He lowered the gun and said, "What else I got? Huh? This is all I know, Soul."

"You can walk away, my brother. You still got me, man. I'm still a friend to you. Rahmel will be home in a few days. You still got family."

Omega stood there, he looked over at his three goons, including Rocky and replied, "Nah, I'ma finish what I started. I'ma end this war wit' them fuckin' Jamaicans and get back on my feet. I'm not gonna bitch out like you did, Soul."

"It ain't gotta be this way," I sighed.

"Nigga, there ain't no other fuckin' way!" Omega shouted.

I hated that I couldn't get through to him. His ignorance was thick like the walls in Fort Knox.

"So you made your choice, huh?" I asked.

"Yeah, and you made yours. You got a week, Soul. After that, my goons gonna be out for blood," he warned.

"And how long you think is it gonna last for you, Omega?" I asked him.

"If I die, then so be it. But I ain't running and I ain't scared."

With frustration in his voice, Omega angrily replied, "You got blood on your hands too, Soul. You remember that incident two years ago."

I did and it was something that I wanted to forget. It remained a burden on my mind.

"It was to save your ass, you remember that."

"It don't matter. If I go down, then you go down. Murder is still murder, Soul."

My eyes were fixed on him. I refused to be blackmailed by him. I casually said, "You do what you gotta do, Omega. And I'm gonna keep doing what I gotta do."

I nonchalantly walked away, leaving the bitterness and the angry glare of his goons. I took the stairs down, jumped into my rental and took off.

23
Omar vs. Soul

It was a blissful moment for me. A perfect lullaby to our day, America was snug in my arms, and her laughter rang beautifully in my ear. She helped me keep my problems with Omega off my mind. Her pregnancy wasn't leaving a strain on our relationship. It felt good spending some quality time with her and my son. We went to the park as a family then went out to eat. Sitting together in a diner, my son in a highchair felt really special.

"Da...da..." Kahlil struggled to call me daddy.

"He called me daddy. He called me daddy!"

"Keep your shirt on, hon. He's been saying mommy and now you're here he's trying to holla at you," America said, smiling.

This was a *Cosby* family moment. I felt so lifted by the attempt. Kahlil made my day.

"You daddy's boy, ain't you Kahlil?" I said, giving him a piece of French toast.

"Omar, that's too big for his little mouth," America cautioned me. "He's mommy's boy," she smiled, wiping his face.

My boy had called me daddy and smiled at me. It was the proudest moment of my life. I held America and my son in my arms, and didn't want to let them go. I was having the time of my life with them.

"I love both of y'all so much," I said to them.

"I love you too, daddy," America said.

Later that evening, America brought me back into the studio. I spent some time recording with her. It felt good to be behind the microphone, hearing the track and spit a rhyme to the beat. I was charged up and had a bunch of new rhymes that I wanted to spit. I had so much on my mind, that I was ready to flow. America and I were the perfect duo. It had been a long time since I was in the studio. I never lost it. It was a perfect day, standing side by side with America, hearing the beat play. My head bouncing to the beat, I locked eyes with America's beauty, and her angelic smile had put me in a place that I always yearned to be—paradise. I gripped the microphone and laced the track.

I had started rhyming something different—poetry form, with that love in my heart for her.

> She makes my heart beat fierce and had my breath lay still,
> I looked in her eyes and her beauty gave me this at ease feel,
> she stood tall in them four inch heels,
> her brown skin was smooth like cool,
> her smile was catching with this gracious exchange of conversation,
> I was just caught up in this profound admiration that had me besieged with this overcoming sensation,
> that I had to step to her with a smile,
> and approach her with an intellectual line and leaned back,
> cuz I wanted to capture her heart, her beauty,
> her warm eyes and that entire nice smile.
> She gave me her name,
> I told her it was exotic and atypical…
> she was far from typical….America,
> Ohmygod…looking like one of God's miracles,
> now this cutie got me becoming lyrical, cuz I'm feelin' you.
> She done passed up on so many others,
> but I felt blessed just to get her number,
> her touch got me tingling, her mind is so intriguing.
> I shy away with just the thought of us being complete,
> couldn't help to wonder with her, what will tomorrow bring,
> was willing to wait around and see

America had smiled, she touched me in a flirt and then she went on with her nice little rhyme.

> *His look is so divine, his body so refined,*
> *like appetizing wine,*
> *I had to look up and thank heaven,*
> *for droppin' that handsome man of mines.*
> *My God, lookin' so tailor, cut like a Mandingo,*
> *swing like a vine. I'm fixated like hypnotized,*
> *you got me dizzy boo.*
> *You know you got me feinin' you,*
> *cuz his touch is x-rated,*
> *his lovin is never underrated,*
> *his flirt gotta bitch ready to squirt,*
> *his kiss got me ready to give birth,*
> *cuz he's my America's Soul,*
> *I love his flow of words, we missed,*
> *we hit, together all the time Jay wit' the Z…*

America sang with a smile. I gave her a hug and a kiss, but I knew that I was the better lyricist. I loved spending every minute with her. We had the perfect day. First I had breakfast in the morning with her and my son. Then we spent a few hours in the studio during the afternoon. We went cruising downtown in my rental. I was her willing chauffer for the day.

Last summer found me incarcerated, but I was looking forward to spending this summer with her. I wanted to travel with her and start recording with her. My list of things was so long that I don't think there would be enough hours in the day.

America noticed my upbeat attitude and it turned her on even more. We decided to get a motel room for the evening. I wanted to spend some quality time with her uninterrupted. We checked into this cozy, single bed, motel room on N. Conduit Ave. It began raining, so I covered America with my jacket and fitted Yankee and we whisked ourselves into a second floor room. Once inside, she slowly slid out of her wet clothing. Dropping her tight denim shorts to the floor, she stepped out of them and threw her arms around me. Our wet kiss went down fervently. The way her soft wet breasts pressed against my chest, made me so hard like the man of steel. America had a naughty smile, purred in my arms and said, "I see someone's excited."

Gripping her round ass, I sucked on her hard dark nipples, ran my hand between her wet thighs and made her come out her panties. I undressed myself and soon after she was butt-naked on the bed. We caressed each other from head to toe.

I positioned my face between her quivering thighs, finger fucking her first. Her pussy was ready for some tongue licking. She was panting while I toyed with her clit. I tasted her for a long moment, inch by inch—ass and all.

She pressed her fingers into my shoulders and deepened the thrust of my tongue. I climbed between her inviting thighs and we fucked like young teenagers with the hard summer rain cascading off the window. The lightning flashed and the thunder roared outside. It felt like the storm had entered the room. America's moans were as loud as thunder. The bed shook from our strong fuck and we both came in sync.

After that intense episode, America nestled in my arms. The storm raged on outside, with the skies gray and gloomy. The night was still young. I was in seventh heaven. We opened up to each other and it felt like old times again. I told America about everything, whatever was on my mind. It came out to her. She knew about the blackmail by Omega. I told her about the murders. I told her about the women, the drugs, and the violence in prison.

She wasn't upset with me, she was already familiar with much of my past, because she'd been through it with me, but the things that she wasn't sure about, I openly revealed to her. I even told her about the abortions that I made a few women get, even my affair with Alexis.

"I'm ready to change, baby. For that to happen, I gotta confess to you all my past wrongdoing."

"I know," she said.

America continued holding me close to her. I felt her heart beating against my chest. I felt loved. I felt that this was my last and final chance with her. She was forgiving, understanding, and we both wanted to make it work. America was so into me that she wasn't even thinking about her issues with Kendal. I wanted it to stay that way.

"I made my choice, I'm going to end it with Kendal, and whatever happens, it'll happen," she sighed afterwards and continued. "I love you, Omar. I do so much. And I believe in you, so you better come correct this time."

"Baby, I already am."

Her beautiful stark naked frame was next to mine. I pulled her closer, kissed her neck and pressed my lips against hers. The conversation was even more exhilarating to me than sex. She poured her heart out to me. America accepted me back into her life. I was the luckiest man on the planet. My eyes lit up with a smile.

"I love you, America."

"I love you too, Omar."

For about half hour, we were joined in each other's embrace. Then America remembered that she had forgotten her purse in my car. We were in such a rush to get a room and please each other, that we forgot some of our stuff in the rental. America needed to get her cellphone and other things. She wanted to call her aunt to check up on Kahlil.

"Baby, I'll get your things for you," I offered.

"No…You stay here and relax yourself, baby. Because when I come back, I need you to be fully charged for round two," she laughed.

"You sure…?" I smiled.

America kissed me on my lips, and said, "You did enough for the day. I got this. Besides, I gotta use the ATM in the lobby."

"Okay, but I like doing things for you."

"You'll get your chance, Omar."

America leaped from my arms, and began throwing on her clothing. She wore my jacket and Yankees fitted because of the rain. It was coming down in buckets and the weather didn't look like it would clear up anytime soon.

"Look at you, tryin' to look like me," I said, admiring how she looked in my gear.

She smiled, stuck out her tongue at me and said, "Yeah, it must be nice being you, cuz you got me, and you know I'm popular."

"Yes you are, but they can't have you like I can."

"I know."

America walked to the bed and passionately kissed me on the lips. She said, "That's because I love you. Behave for now, and I'll come back and get naughty with you again."

"You got it."

She smiled and we looked at each other it felt like I was falling in love with her for the first time. She exited the motel room, leaving me to lie around and think about our future. It looked really bright. I wasn't worried about Omega. I had been through enough hell, and Omega's threats didn't worry me. I saw the insecurity in his eyes when we met on the rooftop. I didn't see a man. He was a scared and confused little boy hiding behind success that wasn't lasting.

I chilled in the silent room with my thoughts for about five minutes. I closed my eyes and for once, had pure thoughts. It was like I was going in the right direction. I finally felt God's favor smile on me. Then there was an abrupt sound of gunshots echoing from outside the motel room.

Rattled, I jumped up, leaped from the bed and rushed to the window. Frantically, I tried to see outside. The heavy rain blocked any clear vision I had of the streets. I raced for my jeans and quickly put them on. Then I ran out into the hallway barefooted and shirtless. My heart was beating like African drums were in my chest. I ran for the stairs, flew down them and raced outside.

"Please God... Please..." I cried out, fearing the worse.

The motel clerk was already on the phone dialing 911. The shots were loud and had to come from a very big gun. I ran outside in the rain shirtless and headed to where the rented white Pontiac was parked.

My breath was coming hard. There was a knot in my stomach and I was praying America was alright. I got closer to the rental, and knew something was very wrong. Running to the car at full sprint, the heavy rain drenching me, my entire world collapsed. The windows were shattered, bullets holes in the door, and America slumped in the driver's seat. There was blood everywhere. I stood frozen in cold shock for a moment then I hurried closer. Swinging the car door open, I pulled my baby into my arms. I could tell she was lifeless, her face and hair matted with blood. She wasn't breathing.

"No, no, no, no... Baby, please, get up! Get up! Get up! Please... Get up!" I cried, clutching America in my arms.

The rain started to wash away some of her blood. Her eyes were closed her voice was silent. She was slipping into the darkness. I gave her mouth to mouth, fervently trying to revive her. America was unresponsive. I held her in my arms, crying hysterically, my tears blending with the rain. Hearing the sirens getting closer, I held her even tighter.

This couldn't be happening. Not now Lord. Closing my eyes, I prayed harder, wishing it was a nightmare. When I opened my eyes, I was in the same predicament. Clutching the woman I love in the pouring rain. She was bleeding and I was crying. A police car arrived then a second, followed by a third. The officers jumped out of their cars and rushed to where I was sitting. They were alarmed at finding me with America dead in my arms.

Quickly the place was flooded with cops and EMS. I stood aside while a detective questioned me, but I was too distraught to even comprehend the questions he was asking. My teary eyes steadied on America's body lying on the gurney while the paramedics tried reviving her. They had the right tools and proper training. A female paramedic worker confirmed what I already feared.

"She's gone," she said.

"Oh God!" I screamed.

Falling to my knees, I cried, just wanting to die along with her. The detective tried to console me, but his efforts were fruitless. My entire body felt like putty. I was stuck on the cold, wet ground.

This couldn't be it. This couldn't be my life. America had been violently ripped away from me. My baby didn't deserve this. I was lost. Why God?

A few hours later, Vincent and his wife came to the hospital where they had brought the body. Vincent looked at me with sadness in his eyes. I was distraught, angry and wanted answers. Some monster out there had shot America with a 50 cal handgun. The bullets mangled America's body. It had to be a hit.

Vincent rolled up to me and took my hands as I sat hunched over. My elbows were pressed into my knees and my face buried in my hands. His wife sat close to me and put her arms around me.

"Soul, I'm sorry man. I'm sorry for your loss," he said remorsefully.

"What you apologizing for…? You ain't killed her!" I spat.

He looked at me, reading my thoughts. I was ready for action. America probably wasn't the target. I had to be. She was getting into my rental, wearing my jacket and hat and I knew from a distance in the pouring rain, the killer could have mistaken her for me. I was furious. I knew that Omega was behind her murder. Guilt clouded my mind.

"Soul, let the police handle it," Vincent suggested.

"Fuck the police. Fuck it! Fuck this shit!" I shouted.

I had startled Vincent's wife. Other eyes were looking at me with curiosity. My tears began welling up again and I cried, "She's gone, man. She's fuckin' dead. You know she was pregnant. They killed her and my child."

Tears came from Vincent's eyes. Then his wife started weeping and hugging him.

"But I'm gonna see what's up, man. I know who's behind it," I shouted.

Vincent grabbed my wrist before I could walk away. He held onto me firmly, locking eyes with me. He then said, "Man, fight that rage, Soul. Fight it! It ain't worth it. I know how you feel."

"Do you?" I barked. "You got your woman alive and by your side."

I jerked my arm from his grip and walked away. Vincent shouted, "Soul, think about your son. Think about him, man. He already lost one parent. He doesn't need to lose another."

Vincent was right, but I kept walking away from them. Drying my tears, I was controlling myself from doing the unthinkable— committing murder.

America's Soul

America's death made the news. I sat on Vincent's couch with puffy, red eyes. Hearing the news about her murder, like it was an event and them tying America's death to the other murders which had occurred was very troubling. I felt disgusted. Many knew about America, she was popular, but they didn't know her like I knew her—to them, she was an upcoming singer who got caught up in a deadly drug war. My America was a forgiving, lovely, beautiful, and a caring woman. She was so talented that I knew one day she would outshine Beyonce, Mariah, and Rihanna. Now she would never get that chance.

Vincent and his wife were there for me. They played a huge role in me keeping my sanity and prevented me from exacting revenge on Omega.

"You came along way, Soul. Both you and me, we came far, man. And you made a vow to stay out of prison. Don't break it, my friend. I know you're hurting, but just think about your son. He's gonna need you more than ever, and the youth center gonna need you too," Vincent said.

Reluctantly my anger subsided, and I began thinking rationally. America wouldn't want me back on the streets. She would want me to continue doing what I was doing and even get back in the studio. I owed that loyalty to her. I spoke to Vincent then the detectives came to the house, and I gave them details about what happened. They had a witness who saw a black Ford Taurus flee the scene and that the shooter was a young, black man in black hoodie. It wasn't much of a lead for the detectives, but I prayed that they would catch the murderer. America and I needed justice.

Word traveled quickly, and almost immediately a large shrine was set up for America where she was murdered. Dozens of folks and fans of hers came out to pay their respects. Many activists continued to speak out against the violence. There was a ten thousand dollar reward for any information leading to an arrest in her murder. I felt that everyone was doing their part to get the suspects involved. I got on camera and spoke out strongly and decided not to let her murder deter me from doing what was right. I fought with myself everyday. I knew it was easy to pick up a gun and hunt in the streets for her killers, but I didn't want to be a hypocrite.

Her funeral was huge. Thousands along with a few celebrities showed up to show their respect. I was teary-eyed during the whole thing, but remained cool and strong. She was placed in a beautiful eighteen gauge casket with a white shade and pink finish. The Lord's Prayer was decoratively positioned in the head panel. She was buried in a Long Island cemetery next to her mother. Sadly, I was thinking that my woman could finally rest in peace.

It was difficult to see her Aunt Gene in tears. She took America's death hard. I held her in my arms and swallowed my pride while watching Kendal get behind the podium to speak about America. I just looked at him, hating the fraud that he was. Out of respect for America and Aunt Gene, I let the man speak his peace.

"I loved her," he'd said. "We were going to get married and have a baby. But I know that she's in a better place. I know she loved me as much as I loved her. She's going to be missed. She is and will always be everything to me."

He was crying. I wanted to intervene and say my peace, but I continued to console Aunt Gene and myself. I knew the truth

The call came in the day after we put America to rest in the ground. I was sitting despondent and alone in my room when my cellphone rang. I didn't recognize the number and was going to ignore the call, but my instincts told me to answer it. I picked up and heard Omega's voice.

"Soul, Soul I didn't do it, man."

"What? Nigga, you got the nerve to call my phone?"

"Listen, Soul... You and me, we got our differences since you came home. But her blood ain't on my hands, my nigga. You need to know that and you need to know sumthin else," he said.

"What?"

I began listening attentively as Omega explained that Kendal came to him about putting a hit out on me because of his jealousy. Omega told me that he refused the hit and threw Kendal out his office, sparing his life. He suspected that Kendal reached out to Biscuit. Biscuit probably had a hand in America's murder. My blood boiled even more, because I knew Biscuit hated me and it gave him a motive. I wanted to break Kendal's neck.

"Why you telling me this...?"

"I just felt it was sumthin' that you should hear. Despite my feelings toward that woman and you, there was no need for it to go down like that. She was too talented. I knew how much you loved her, Soul. I just thought you should know the truth," he said with sincerity in his voice. "You do wit' that info what you want. But I'm out of it," he added.

"Thanks," I said.

I heard a dial tone. Omega had hung up. It angered me. I was angrier at myself for failing America again. I felt that if I hadn't gone to prison then Kendal wouldn't even have been a factor in America's life. He wouldn't have had the chance to squeeze in on my woman. My absence provided the opportunity then when I returned home, I became a threat to the relationship. That led to her eventual demise.

Kendal needed either two things to happen to him, get his asshole spread open in prison or have his blood spilled in the streets. Either way, he was done.

24
End Game

Omega sat in the prestigious midtown Manhattan lawyer's office and received the grim news about the warrants and subpoenas being issued out to him and his men. The FBI had enough information via informants and wiretaps to unleash indictments for various crimes. Charging Omega under the RICO act was a possibility. His organization was falling apart.

"So that's it? They gonna come for me, cuz of a fuckin' snitch, huh?" Omega questioned his expensive lawyer he kept on retainer.

Robert Goldstein was good at his job and had a reputable image with his clients who were mostly high-end drug dealers or corporate thugs. He won cases and got favorable results for them. Robert Goldstein was a man of resources. He had acquired a mole in the courthouse. He illegally purchased copies of sealed indictments to aid in the defense of his drug lord clients. The info would sometimes give him the edge in federal cases.

Goldstein knew Omega's chance of winning a jury trial was bleak. The Grand Jury had its case. The D.A would seek life without parole if Omega was convicted. The information and crimes that the D.A had stacked against him from murder, racketeering, extortion, money laundering and many more, it would be almost impossible for Goldstein to have any charges dropped or to convince a jury of twelve to decide on Omega's acquittal of his crimes.

"My advice, you turn yourself in, don't make them come look for you and take a plea, Omega. The D.A wants your connections. They want your main enforcers, especially this Biscuit. If you're ready to give them up, they'll work with you for a lesser sentence," Goldstein said.

"You want me to become a snitch. It ain't happening," Omega said. "I fuckin' pay you good money to hear this shit?"

"Omega, my hands are tied. They have an informant, strong evidence, and the violence and murders in Queens. There's negative media coverage of you, and with the wire taps, it's a no-win situation for us," Goldstein informed his client.

"I can't do that," Omega said.

"You pay me to help you and I'm helping you, Omega. People will cop out, start pointing fingers, and you're going to be the main subject. Now if the D.A can get a conviction of someone over you maybe a supplier or political corruption, then they'll work with you. I can't do a damn thing if you're not willing to cooperate. I can work the system in your favor, pull some strings, maybe call in a few favors, but you're going to do some time. How much is up to you."

Omega ruled the streets for several years, took over the empire by force and now he was falling on his sword. He eyed his lawyer. Omega hated losing. Once he was incarcerated, the Jamaicans would take over his territory. He wanted to end the war with King and Demetrius' blood spilling out on the streets, but the FBI was getting in the way.

The walls were closing in on him. If he gave up the Mexicans it would seal his doom. He declined the snitch label. Rahmel did eighteen years, becoming a rat didn't run in his family's blood.

"You do what you gotta do… Take it to trial if needed. But fuck the feds and DA. I ain't no fuckin' snitch."

Robert Goldstein let out a frustrated sigh and said, "You're making it difficult."

"Shit's been difficult for me my whole life. I really don't give a fuck."

Irritated, he got up and walked out his lawyer's office. Omega was met by Rocky in the lobby.

"Everything good, boss?" Rocky asked.

"Just get me home."

Omega arrived at his New Jersey home an hour later with a for sale sign displayed across the sprawling manicured lawn. He told Rocky to pick him up in the morning. Inside his home, Jazmin greeted him with kisses. She saw the strain of frustration on his face and instantly knew that his meeting with his lawyer didn't go well.

"What did he say?" she asked with concern.

"Nuthin' that I can't handle," he said.

"And if you can't handle it, then what's going to happen with us?"

"Listen, don't fuckin' worry 'bout my business, Jazmin!" Omega barked.

"So when should I begin worrying, huh? When the FBI kicks down our fuckin' door and drag you out of here, or when the Jamaicans kill you, huh, Omega? Is that when I need to start worrying?"

Omega angrily turned in her direction. He was ready to backhand her, but checked himself.

"Look, I got everything under control."

"You're full of shit! I don't even know why I got wit' you in the first place. They gonna kill you, Omega. Don't you fuckin' understand that? Let's just leave here. We can get out the country and start over," Jazmin pleaded.

Omega had enough money to flee the country and live comfortable with Jazmin and his kids, but he was against that. Omega was a man that never ran from trouble a day in his life.

"I ain't goin' no fuckin' where. This is my fuckin' home, my city! I'm not being forced out, so fuck you!" he shouted.

"You know, you ain't nuthin' but a scared bitch…"

That smart remark caused Jazmin to receive a hard slap across her face. She stumbled over the marble countertop. Blood trickled from her lips. Omega's recent display of violence toward her had her at her wit's end.

"Oh, so you're a big man, huh, hitting your pregnant woman makes you even a bigger gangsta, huh!" Jazmin mocked.

Omega removed his gun and pointed it at Jazmin.

"You need to shut the fuck up!" he warned.

Jazmin collected herself and stood upright, she stared down the barrel with bold eyes then said, "I can't do this anymore."

"You gonna fuckin' leave me...?"

"Look at you. You have a gun pointed at the mother of your children. You're insane. I can't... I can't do this with you anymore."

Omega put the gun away and walked out the room. Jazmin was left shaken in the kitchen. Her relationship with Omega was slowly fading. She made plans to leave for North Carolina to live with her mother. This was a life she could no longer live. All the glamour, the money, wasn't worth it.

Omega walked into his private den and immediately got on the phone to conduct business. It was now or never. He made a phone call to some outside contractors and set up a hit. The men he called were very expensive, but they were professional hit-men who knew how to track and kill. He gave the information that he coerced viciously from Demetrius accountant, Brian, and started putting everything in motion. He was becoming sloppy, slipping up. Omega never conducted illegal business from his home. The landline was not secure. He was becoming desperate, and his angst led to mistakes.

Rocky pushed his truck south down the New Jersey turnpike. He soon made his way into Delaware and navigated his truck through the quiet city streets as evening descended. He pulled into the parking lot of a Wilmington shopping mall. It was nearly empty. It was far enough from home and he felt that this would be it for him.

Rocky pulled up behind a gleaming black Dodge Charger. He quickly got out his truck and entered the backseat. Two federal agents sat in the front seat, sipping coffee and waiting.

"Hey Rock, what you got for us?" the driver asked.

Rocky pulled a small tape recorder from his pocket and passed it to the agent. He had been wired for sound for months. Rocky had turned federal informant a month after his release from prison. His P.O was about to pull his parole for violation until the feds took over and knew Rocky could be of use to them. For eight months, Rocky gave the feds everything that they needed. This allowed them to gradually build a tight case against Omega and his organization. In exchange, Rocky and his family would be placed in the witness protection program after his testimony.

"I got everyone on there, Omega, Biscuit, and other goons. He had a meeting with the Columbians to get a new supplier about a week ago. But Omega's fuckin' up. He's not as cautious as he used to be."

"Good, that's better for us," the agent said.

"And he knows his time is up?" the other agent chimed.

"I'm out though. I gave y'all enough and the heat is coming down. I'll testify. I just can't do this anymore. They know there's an informant out there so niggas actin' paranoid. They can question me anytime and find the wire on me. I just can't take that chance," Rocky said.

Both agents shook their head in unison.

"We have our indictments. We have our case," the agent said.

"What about Biscuit? Do you have a line on him?" the other asked.

"He got every cop in the city looking for him. I heard that he's the one responsible for killing that singer, America. He's on the run. Last I heard of him, he fled upstate somewhere. I think Poughkeepsie. He got family up there. Ah, I think an older sister."

Both agents were jotting down notes as quickly as Rocky spat the info. With the countless hours of wire taps that they had, Rocky had become a critical informant for their investigation. The feds had enough verification to kick down doors, and hit everyone simultaneously.

King and Demetrius were the feds next line of target. Demetrius had fled to his hometown in Jamaica, leaving King in charge. It was difficult for the agency to attain an informant for the Shotta posse. They were smart and really loyal. When a shotta posse member was arrested, he remained silent and became bitter. They were brutal toward law enforcement—hating cops and feds with a passion.

Rocky gave the feds everything he knew about the Jamaicans. It wasn't much. He wasn't on the inside and could only describe his run-ins he had with them. The agents were grateful. Rocky was promised immunity for his crimes. He helped bring down a much bigger fish. It was the end of the road for many men.

Getting back in his truck, Rocky exhaled loudly. He looked at himself in the rearview mirror and didn't care if he would be labeled as a snitch for the rest of his life. He just wanted a whole new life with his girlfriend and baby daughter. He didn't want to go back to prison. It was easier to give up friends and men that he once called his brothers. He had his taste of freedom and wasn't going back to jail for anyone. Starting his truck, Rocky drove back to his home in Brooklyn.

It was breaking daylight in the city of Poughkeepsie. Night had become dawn, and the sun slowly painting a ray of sunshine in the sky. The summer heat had arrived and the suburban streets were still asleep. Midway between New York City and the state capital at Albany was the city of Poughkeepsie. It was a city suffering from severe socioeconomic turmoil, and a symbol of urban decay in the Hudson Valley.

For the past two weeks, it became a safe haven for Biscuit. Queens had become too hot for him to stick around. Mistaking America for Soul, he gunned her down, and fled. He had fucked up the hit. The cops were everywhere. Multiple arrests were being made on a daily and snitches and informants were all pointing fingers. Considered armed and extremely dangerous, Biscuit had several warrants out for his arrest.

The task force was hard at work, cleaning up corners and making raids on well known drug locations. Taking back the city streets from drug crews that ravaged communities for months, was their agenda. The mayor held a press conference on the arrests. Commending the police involved, he promised a better and safer summer for residents.

Over a dozen FBI agents working with the local police swarmed outside the Mill Street projects. Heavily armed, they were wearing bulletproof armor. They knew that Biscuit was hiding out at his older sister's apartment.

Biscuit sat on the couch watching early morning cartoons with his three year old nephew. Tina, his sister, was getting ready for work and was leaving her son with Biscuit for the day. He came cheaper than a babysitter. She looked at the time. It was almost seven o clock and Tina was running late for her shift at the factory.

Biscuit was shirtless, sitting in his boxers and house slippers, a 45 close by. Biscuit was paranoid and woke up early every day since he was there. Peering out the windows, he would watch the streets, observing all of his surroundings for hours. Queens was too hot for him. There were too many enemies, and the police had made him the most wanted.

"Alvin, I'm going to work now. Make sure Jayson eats his breakfast," Tina said.

"I got him, sis. We gonna hang out for the day," Biscuit replied.

"And don't be putting any guns in my son's hands. You hear me, Alvin?"

"Sis, I got him. And what I tell you about callin' me that?"

"It's your God-given name. I'm not calling you Biscuit. Mama named you Alvin and I'm gonna call you Alvin," Tina said.

Biscuit let it slide because she was family, anybody else would have gotten a bullet in their head. He watched his sister scurry around the apartment rushing for work. He went into the kitchen and poured himself a big bowl of cereal and before he sat down, he pulled the blinds back and stared out the window for a short moment. The block looked quiet and he was satisfied.

He went to sit back down, unaware that a covert operation for his arrest was underway. A swarm of cops and agents were just a few feet from rushing into his sister's apartment.

Tina gathered her things, kissed her son goodbye, and walked out the door. A few steps out the door, cops grabbed her. Her mouth quickly covered to prevent her from screaming. Tina was hastily secured into a nearby corner out of sight. She was afraid, but the lead officer warned that everything would be okay if she cooperated.

"How many inside?" he asked.

Nervously Tina looked around, fearing for her son and brother's life. She didn't answer him immediately.

"Look, think of your son. How many inside...?"

"Just Alvin and my son," Tina answered.

He nodded, getting the team ready for entry. The tactical team that came was ready for anything. The lead agent informed Tina to knock on her door and let Biscuit know that she had forgotten her keys. A tactical team would be close by ready for entry, remaining out of Biscuit's sight. Tina didn't have a choice. She walked to her apartment door and did as she was told. Knocking a few times, she shouted, "Alvin, it's me, open up. I forgot my keys."

Biscuit dragged himself up off the couch with his weapon in hand. He walked to the door, looked through the peephole and saw that it was Tina. He started unlocking the door, relaxing his guard and saying, "Damn sis, you a hot mess right now."

The door flew open and Biscuit caught a quick glimpse of the nervousness that his sister had in her eyes. Before he could react, a team of eight men in their heavy body armor stormed the apartment, yelling and shouting. Biscuit tried to run and was trying to get a shot off. They were on him too fast. He was thrown against the wall and quickly overpowered.

"Get down!! Get down!! Gun! Gun! Gun!" one agent shouted.

They subdued Biscuit with extreme force. He was no match for the cops quickly storming the apartment.

"You muthafuckas! Get the fuck off me! Get off me!" Biscuit shouted, resisting his imminent arrest.

Biscuit fought, spitting and tried to bite the cops, but he was restrained in heavy bracelets and gagged to prevent him from spitting. In tears, his sister watched a half dozen agents manhandle her brother. Twenty minutes later, they hauled him out of the apartment without any serious incident. Biscuit was in handcuffs and would be transferred back to New York City for processing and his arraignment. It was finally over for him.

Parked across the street from the heavy police action, King and two Jamaican hit-men sat in a black Yukon. Watching from tinted windows, they saw Biscuit being guided into the backseat of an unmarked car by two FBI agents. King observed with contempt as his prize kill was captured by the police.

"Ras claat, bredren. Dat mon lucky, yuh hear. Him was gwan meet him maker today," King hissed through clench teeth, while gripping his Uzi.

A loaded Beretta was on top of the dash. The other two men put away their automatic machine guns. They were eager to spill Biscuit's blood. All three men wore dark fatigues and were high as antennae. Having gotten the word about Biscuit's staying in upstate New York, they came to kill him. The state police and the feds had shut the block down. They were too late.

"King, dat man still can be touched, yuh hear me? I don't give a fuck 'bout FBI, me blast off on dem blood claat police... Just say da word, yuh hear. Me down for whatever," the Jamaican goon said.

"Chill brethren... Chill," King said to his wolf. "We gwan tend to other business. Drive."

The driver started the car and made a slow U-turn, going the opposite direction. Biscuit had nine lives, but his freedom was no longer his.

The next morning, Biscuit sat handcuffed to a steel desk in a barren small room. He was angry, his face knotted in a scowl. He cursed and carried on like a mad man.

"Fuck y'all muthafuckas! I'ma fuck ya niggas up. Ya fuckin' hear me! Fuck ya'll!"

He yanked at the thick chain that had him confined to the chair and desk. His wrist was bruised from the pulling. He refused to cooperate and give up any information.

Two agents entered the room and Biscuit began spitting and cursing at them. One became so furious at Biscuit's actions that he hurried over to Biscuit and slammed his head against the desk violently. He had split Biscuit's head open and exclaimed, "Listen, you little muthafucka! We ain't playing with you, you fuckin' hear me?"

Blood was dripping from his forehead, Biscuit smirked and spat, "Fuck you!"

He tried to charge for the officer, but was restricted to his seat. Biscuit had serious mental issues. He was suicidal and was HIV positive. His health status was revealed to him when he was an inmate at the Crossroads Juvenile center in Brownsville, Brooklyn.

Biscuit was a special ED student and special needs child growing up. Since he was eight years old, he had been abandoned by his mother and placed in foster care. He began doing violent crimes when he was ten—fighting, burglaries, selling drugs and assault. He did a few months in the detention center. His first week inside, he was raped and abused. Two older teens held Biscuit face down on his bunk. They gagged him while the third young male stripped away Biscuit's pants and aggressively forced himself inside Biscuit's rectum. He soon ejaculated inside of Biscuit, exposing the fourteen year old to the HIV virus.

Biscuit became even more angry and disturbed. He hated himself for being weak and vulnerable. A few months later, he caught up with two of the teens that raped him and he murdered them maliciously, shooting both teens straight through the eye. Murder was his passion and he vowed never to be vulnerable again. He wanted to be feared. He was the walking dead and just didn't give a damn.

The word quickly got out. Biscuit was locked up and the residents breathed a little bit easier knowing the young killer, Alvin Coolidge, AKA Biscuit, was off the streets. His brother Narmer was set to testify against Biscuit if necessary.

Alone and ashamed, Kendal sat in the dark bedroom of his Long Island home. He couldn't believe that America was gone. Biscuit killed her by mistake. He regretted hiring the thug and so badly wanted to rewind time and correct his mistake. When the horrifying news reached Kendal, he collapsed and cried out. His jealousy and hatred for Soul had caused him a great loss.

He had invested so much time and love into America, that Kendal felt his hard work was in vain. His career and image in the industry was ruined. His name was tarnished. News had gotten out about him hiring Biscuit to kill Soul, but America caught the bullet. It became front page headlines. Alimony and his goons, Soul, the police, it was only a matter of time before they all came for him. Kendal couldn't imagine spending his life in prison.

Kendal sat on the bed, gripping a loaded gun. The urge to blow his brains out was welling inside him. Tears of pain and lost stained his cheeks. His eyes were red with grief. There was a loud banging at his front door. Kendal got out of his bed, and peeped out the bedroom window. Police cars were parked outside his home. This is it, he thought.

The police continued to knock and Kendal sat back on the bed. The gun was still in his hand. His mind was distraught. Loud knocking continued, growing stronger and more impatient.

"This is the police, open up! We have an arrest warrant. Open up!" an officer shouted.

Sitting quietly, Kendal ignored them. He closed his eyes and heard the cops beating down the door, yelling and shouting. Kendal stared at the chromed handle weapon and took a deep breath. He could hear the cops rummaging through his home, their steps getting closer.

Soon they were upstairs, moving through the hallway, shouting and searching. He heard them outside his bedroom door. Kendal swallowed hard. Placing the barrel of the gun under his chin, he closed his eyes and whispered a prayer. The bedroom door crashed open, and half dozen cops barged in just as Kendal pulled the trigger.

Blam!

The bottom half of his chin exploded, splattering blood and fragment of his face throughout the neat room. Kendal's motionless body lay contorted on the bed.

Dusk was settling over the quiet Brooklyn Street where Judy called home. It had been a very long and trying day. She was suspended indefinitely from the police department and many of her friends had turned their backs on her. They found out about the conspiracy charge that she was caught up in with a major drug kingpin. She was facing serious prison time if tried and convicted, but she took a plea from the DA for a lesser sentence and gave up five other dirty cops in her precinct. Overnight, Judy became a marked woman.

She wanted to terminate her pregnancy. She couldn't have Omega's baby, and wasn't ready for kids at such a tumultuous time in her life. Her father was angry with her and the IAD was pressuring her. Judy stepped out of her blue Ford Taurus and slowly walked to her home. Her mind was burden with so many things, that all she thought about was suicide. She had shamed her father and their family's name. She wanted to reconcile with her father and planned on having dinner with him the next day.

Judy walked into her dark apartment and was ready to get some sleep. But she was violently grabbed from behind and thrown face first into a wall. Intense pain surged throughout her body.

"What the...!" she screamed.

She couldn't see who was attacking her, and tried scrambling for safety in the dark. She felt a boot making brutal connection to her ribcage. Darkness cloaked her attacker and Judy hugged the floor with her nose bleeding. She was shocked by the sudden assault.

The lights to her apartment came on, and the invaders became visible to her. Judy's eye widened with fear. She stared up at King and two other Jamaican goons clutching machetes and guns.

King glared at her with a dark, deadly stare. His long twisted dreadlock looking like a lion's mane around him, he was shirtless. Judy could see his many battle scars and tattoos across his chest and torso. King was scary and intimidating. He clutched a machete in one hand and a Glock in the next.

"What the fuck y'all doing in my apartment...?"

King rushed toward Judy, dropping the machete, and keeping the gun. He grabbed Judy's hair aggressively and shoved the gun into Judy's mouth.

"Yuh da blood-claat bitch who set me brother up! Me gun is bi-sexual, yuh hear, bitch? Lie to me and I will rape ya and blow yuh bomba claat brains out and slit yuh blood-claat throat!"

"Oh shit! No!" Judy whimpered as she stared into King's murderous eyes.

The other men looked ravenous and deadly. They stood in the background with their long sharpened machetes awaiting instructions from King.

King wanted to slaughter Judy in so many ways. She was the one feeding Omega the info which had led to his younger brother's gruesome murder. He was ready to butcher Judy. Before he gave the order to his goons to work on Judy, King wanted info.

"I don't know anything," Judy exclaimed.

King didn't believe her. He yanked back her hair strongly again and exclaimed, "I'm nuthin' nice so yuh need to talk…"

Judy continued to cry, but King didn't care for her tears. He wanted answers, death, and butchery on everyone involved in the death of his little brother, Node. King reached for his machete, and gripped it tightly.

"Me hear yuh pregnant. Me gwan give yuh an early birth," King threatened, moving the machete close to Judy's belly.

She saw evil in King's eyes, and even though she had contemplated an abortion, she didn't want to lose her baby to a machete-wielding Jamaican. He was ready to strike, but Judy fought back, kneeing King in the genitals with tremendous force. King doubled over in pain.

"Ras claat! Yuh bitch!" King wailed.

Judy freed herself from under King. She jumped up and ran for the bedroom. King's goons opened fire on her and gave chase. The shots were loud, echoing throughout the apartment. Judy caught two slugs in her shoulder. She stumbled, but still managed to escape into the bedroom. Slamming and locking the bedroom door, her adrenaline was on high. She quickly removed her off-duty weapon from a nearby drawer, and with lightening speed, she had the gun ready to fire.

Hurt, scared, and bleeding, Judy's breathing was intensified. Her nerves were shaky. Having witnessed the damages these goons caused, she didn't want to be gutted and butchered like their other victims.

Seconds passed and the bedroom door came crashing down. King and his goons were rushing in for the kill. Judy opened fire on them repeatedly. Striking King in the face and stomach twice, he fell. His two goons quickly rushed Judy, wielding their machetes at her wildly. The first strike fatally cut Judy across the neck. Her blood rushed like a fountain. She dropped the gun and fell back on the bed, grasping her open throat with her eyes fading.

The Jamaican goons jumped on Judy like lions on a prey. Their machetes viciously sliced Judy's tender brown skin. They hacked and cut into her from head to toe, leaving her stomach opened like the doorway.

When the goons were done tearing Judy apart like Lego. They left her bedroom walls and bed covered in blood and torn flesh. The goons stopped to look down at King. He was down on the carpet bleeding and dying. King was dead.

"Him gwan, bredren..." one said.

They both raced off leaving King and Judy's body.

25
Omega

Sitting in his eighty thousand dollar Benz alone, Omega was deep in thoughts. Something wasn't right. Rocky wasn't there to pick him up in the morning. He called Rocky's phone and it was disconnected. Rocky's sudden disappearance brought on suspicion. It angered Omega that he didn't see the signs. He had trusted Rocky and felt betrayed by him and Jazmin.

Omega had awoken early to find Jazmin gone. She took everything and actually left him. Jazmin had taken all she could carry and left in a cab before dawn. Omega was dumbfounded. He had gotten the news of Biscuit's arrest. His other lieutenants were being picked up by the police. Omega knew he could be next.

Before the feds came crashing through his doorway with warrants, Omega removed half a million dollars from his safe, important documents, papers and guns. He stuffed the contents into a duffle bag and tossed everything into the trunk of his car. Omega pulled out of his driveway at four in the morning and drove into Newark to meet with someone of importance.

Five in the morning, the FBI rushed into Omega's estate with warrants, but was unaware that they had missed their mark by an hour. Omega was miles away in Newark. And by mid afternoon, he was planning to be out the state.

Omega met up with a high price contractor on the rooftop of a parking garage. The well dressed man pulled up next to Omega in a gleaming white Cadillac. His gray suit, and patch over his left eye, spoke volumes about his character.

He was an international contract killer. The mysterious man was very well known in the underground, and went by the name, Edge. His service was very costly. The mafia, Triads of Mexico, and the CIA were the only ones who could afford his services.

The two men locked eyes. Edge stood near his car while Omega popped his trunk then handed him a hundred thousand cash in a bag.

"I want his family dead! Every last one of them muthafuckas," Omega instructed.

Omega passed documents taken from Demetrius accountant's office, and gave it to the contractor. It contained a trail for his hunt of Demetrius and his associates in Tivoli Gardens, Jamaica.

Edge quickly inspected the bag and nodded. Omega was convinced that if he was about to fall, he wouldn't be alone. His last breath would be spent trying to end Demetrius and his crew.

"It will be done," Edge said in a low, raspy tone.

The exchange was made and both men got back into their cars. They exited the parking garage and Omega now planned on hitting the road west, travel to Las Vegas, and maybe run to Canada. He was on the run. The record company had buckled. Federal agents raided his home, his downtown office, and seized everything. His bank account was frozen. He had four hundred thousand dollars to his name and speculated that it was enough for now.

He was reduced to a fugitive who didn't have many places to run. Omega drove his Benz toward interstate 80W with large sums of money and guns stashed in the trunk. He filled his tank, and made a quick phone call. Then he threw away his phone.

A couple miles from the highway, he came to a stop at a red light at a quiet intersection. It was a beautiful morning and Omega had his windows down and was listening to music from one of his artist. He was packed and ready to disappear for a long time.

Before the light could change green, a dark brown van pulled up beside the Benz. Omega stared at the van and his nerves tingled on alert. Reaching for his gun, he was ready for anything. Immediately the side doors of the van flew open. Omega was viciously greeted with automatic gunfire from two rifles. Ducking down, he scrambled to the passenger side. Glass was shattering in the Benz as armor-piercing rounds tore through his door, hitting him in the side. Omega dove out the passenger door, returning fire, hitting one of the assassins in the face. Stumbling down the street, holding his bloody side Omega was chased by two masked men. His gun was no match for their heavy automatic weapons. Taking cover behind a dumpster, Omega had a few shots left. He tried to breathe easily, but the pain in his side wouldn't let him.

The masked men were getting closer. Omega fired at them and was soon out of ammo. A sitting duck, he was defenseless against the masked men. Pointing the empty gun, Omega smiled. He was going to die like a gangsta.

"Fuck you!"

The two men opened fired. Then the van raced off leaving Omega's bullet-riddled body slumped against the dumpster.

26
Omar vs. Soul

Foster's funeral home on Linden Blvd was the last stop for Omega in Queens. There was hardly anyone in attendance. Gazing at his body lying in the casket, I thought the mortician did a good job. Despite being shot several times, he looked good. I wasn't surprised to hear about his death, he had reaped what he had sowed. His fate finally caught up with him. Unfortunately, Omega was killed the same day that his brother, Rahmel was finally released from prison.

Alone in the room with Omega, it was early afternoon and I was suddenly overwhelmed by sadness. Too many deaths were draining me. America was gone, now Omega. New York wasn't the place for me anymore. It was time to take my son and leave the city. I wanted to go south. My family lived in Greenville, South Carolina and a cousin was able to help me get a job. I couldn't raise my son in Queens. There were too many memories, good and bad.

I felt that some justice was done when I received the news that Biscuit was sentenced to life without parole for the murder of America and others. He copped out and took a plea bargain in order to escape the death penalty. There was front page news about police corruption, officers' moonlighting for Omega, committing murders, extortions and some were even addicted to meth. Most of Omega's crew was arrested and disbanded. The streets of Queens weren't any better. Many young teens were hooked on brown-brown.

Even though the killings weren't as high, the youths were still violent, and murders still happening. Sometimes I felt that it was a no-win situation trying to take back the streets.

Standing over Omega's casket, I said a quick prayer for him and America's soul. Someone entered the room. I turned and saw Rahmel approaching with an uneasy gaze. He stood next to me, with his eyes fixed on his brother. His beard was thick and dark. He stood silent in his white and gray tracksuit, Rahmel stood tall. I let him mourn his brother in peace for a moment.

"I come home after doing eighteen years in jail, only to see my baby brother in a casket. This game done took away so much from me, Soul," he somberly said. "I came home too late and couldn't save Omega."

"I tried, Rahmel. I was talking to him, but you know how he is," I said.

"I know, Soul. I know he was stubborn as hell."

"Indeed, I heard he had made a lot of enemies. I mean the hit could've been from any of them. The Jamaicans, the Mexicans, the Columbians... Or the crooked cops who was on his payroll. Somebody didn't want him around anymore. They didn't want him turning them in for a deal."

"Yeah, I hear that, Soul."

"He still ain't had to go out like that..."

"Soul, you know the last time I saw my baby brother alive was when he was twelve. Our aunt brought him upstate on a visit. He was smart and had the potential to do something else with his life, until I corrupted him with foolishness. I got him caught up with the drug game."

Rahmel never took his teary eyes off his brother while talking to me. His eyes stayed fixated on Omega. Moving closer to the casket, he slowly kissed his brother's forehead.

"I love you little brother. May God forgive you so you can rest in peace," Rahmel said.

He took a deep breath, and stepped back from the casket. Finally looking at me, he said, "I heard you're leaving to go down south."

"Yeah... It's time for me to move on."

"When are you leaving?"

"In a week, I'm going to take my son and start over somewhere else."

"Do that man. I'll take over what you started at the Center. I'll deal with the kids. I'll mentor them and tell them about my life, and my lengthy sentence. I will do my best with these troubled teens, Soul."

"I know you will," I smiled. "You still have one brother left."

Convinced that Rahmel had my back at the Community Center, we hugged each other for a long time. I walked out leaving Rahmel staring down at his younger brother's body in the casket.

"I know," I heard him saying as I was walking away.

Epilogue

Six months later…

The headline across the *Weekend Star* and *Daily Gleaner*, two Jamaican newspapers read like this, *Drug Kingpin Dies In Shootout With Police*.

It was big news throughout the island. The small community was in uproar about his death.

Demetrius Allen, a drug kingpin and gun smuggler from Tivoli Gardens was killed early evening as police raided his home with an arrest warrant in West Kingston. There was heavy gunfire. Demetrius, 36, was known throughout the community as a Jamaican Robin Hood. He had exercised his power over the most notorious slums in Kingston and other slums with brute force and murder.

Demetrius was facing certain extradition to the U.S for his crimes and the threat of extradition sparked several days of violence against police officials. U.S. authorities, who began investigating Allen's role in cocaine, gun and marijuana shipments to New York, Baltimore, D.C and Florida in early 2001, alleged that he gave out cash and weapons to solidify his power amongst gangs in Kingston and beyond.

Allen managed to elude police capture for months with the help from a network of supporters in his region. Many believed that Allen was killed to keep him from implicating others in the drug trade. He became the head of the Shotta/Shower Posse, a name that some accounts came from the gang's carrying out of "showering" its enemies with bullets.

But an investigation in Allen's death is underway, as residents suspect foul play. His mother, Gloria Evans and other family members close to Demetrius Allen had been found executed.

The pursuit and death of Allen is believed to be a turning point in Jamaica's struggle with gangs and violence, which has increased since the political and supporting factions and parties armed criminals in the 1980's to help rally votes. The killings struck a hard blow against the existence of dons and other gang members on the island. Before it all happened, Allen was believed to be the last of the untouchables.

The End

EXPRESS

If I were to express myself, how would I describe myself, *even wonder if I could trust myself, love myself. The things I've done sometimes make me wonder about myself in the many years I've live with myself. I'm Queens' born, with king's love, been through war, tried to feel love, but there been times where it felt I just didn't belong. Outcast like Tom Hanks, distanced like a shining star— always had a story to tell, wanted to express it like FedEx it. So I made my chain swing long and my rings bling like dawn, I wanted to be that superstar on the scene, have the ladies say my name and niggas praise my game. There was a time that I wanted to stand tall and make it rain on it all—spread that richness like a forming thunderstorm. Show the world that I was willing to die hard, go out like a cause, so I done picked up the mic, and picked up the pen, even picked up a chromed nine and was willing to go in…*

So if I were to express myself, how would I find myself, *how would the ladies rate a nigga like me? Would they see me as the one, a diamond in the rough or just another scrub, being clowned to be laughed at? Wonder would they give me love or give a brother the cold shrug? Yeah, I'm six feet tall, 200 plus, brown skin and all, but still insecure about a few flaws, sometimes willing to pay to play. Portray the image of a real street thug, designers jeans, having nice things, sporting timbs, wearing bling and winter leathers' I'm in it all, just another roughneck brother getting caught up like the others. So I pour out Hennessey for my departed brothers, light up a blunt for my lost brothers, representing my dogs cause that's who I'm all for. Love em all. Living in a world with an unknown cause, a war within walls—its dog eat dog. Living in a ghetto is like being in a Vietnam War, trigger-happy* *soldiers ready to smoke y'all if he sees y'all cause its props if he just bleeds y'all... For real thinking who needs y'all! My mind is just a careless thought, sometimes corrupt, sometimes destruct, sometimes I wonder do I just give a fuck? I look at myself and ask—who the fuck is that lookin' back?*

So if I was to express myself? How would I define myself..? *How much do I really know about myself? I grew up grew up in South Jamaica Queens, where every corner nigga gotta story for wax, where the streets used to be hardcore and mean, back in the days when Fat Cat, Supreme team and the 7 crown ran the scene. When everyday niggas was seeing riches like kings, in which it gave em greed and felt the end was far from near—smoking weed and pushing the streets', living to what was a true thug's life. And for a nigga to come up in the game it was to make the second man bleed, "taking the next man out." Cuz it was on like that, from Baisley to Rockaway that's how it got down like that. When back then you knew true niggas really had your back, cuz they showed no slack. And slip of a tongue it was reaction on a cat.*

So if I was to express myself? Who do I see within myself? *Do I see trouble within' myself? Am I just a lie to myself? Do I really give a fuck about myself? They say that sometimes I'm a quiet nigga, nice guy with a likable smile, kinda shy about it but really I can be raunchy like a porn-star, push me hard enough and you get to see a live nigga transform, deep down in I'm just that boisterous warrior, quick to tell muthafuckas to step away from me wit' that nonsense... never a bitch-ass that go half-ass, but always go all-out for the ones I love. Hate beef cause I feel that I may have to wild out on niggas—keeping my inner hatred conceal, like a desert eagle after a kill. My seething thoughts may cause distraught, especially when they took my friend from me, it was a long night after the shots, sittin' in the precinct asking why, after I beat one wit' that deadly tool, I wanted to kill that fool. I looked around and wanted to toss shit up. But as the world turns, niggas minds burns...my inner self lost within itself..killing fools with this ridiculous style. I know I wanna shine like one of biggies rhyme, spread my lyrics like syphilis and thnkin' how should I end this show? So I look at myself with inquiring eyes and once again, ask...who the fuck is I? That nigga who found redemption*

America's
Soul

with a dream and a smile, or still lost, trying to break myself outta a damn lie …but I'm gonna keep expressing myself, until that one day when I truly find myself…

Erick S. Gray…

Our titles interlace action, crime, and the urban lifestyle depicting the harsh realities of life on the streets. Call it street literature, urban drama, we call it hip-hop literature. This exciting genre features fast-paced action, gritty ghetto realism, and social messages about the high price of the street life style.

▲
DEAD AND STINKIN'
STEPHEN HEWETT

▲
A GOOD DAY TO DIE
JAMES HENDRICKS

▲
WHEN LOVE TURNS TO HATE
SHARRON DOYLE

▲
IF IT AIN'T ONE THING
IT'S ANOTHER
SHARRON DOYLE

▲
WOMAN'S CRY
VANESSA MARTIR

▲
BLACKOUT
JERRY LaMOTHE
ANTHONY WHYTE

▲
HUSTLE HARD
BLAINE MARTIN

▲
A BOOGIE DOWN STORY
KEISHA SEIGNIOUS

▲
CRAVE ALL LOSE ALL
ERICK S GRAY

▲
LOVE AND A GANGSTA
ERICK S GRAY

▲
AMERICA'S SOUL
ERICK S GRAY

▲
LIES OF A REAL HOUSEWIFE
ANGELA STANTON

Mail us a List of the titles you would like include $14.95 per Title + shipping charges $3.95 for one book & $1.00 for each additional book. Make all checks payable to: Augustus Publishing 33 Indian Rd. NY, NY 10034